TALES

FROM THE

RED ROOSTER
CAFE

SHAD OLSON

For my beautiful Duchess and muse. For filling my life with all the dreams worth writing about.

CONTENTS

CONTENTS (continued)

TALES FROM THE RED ROOSTER CAFE

Shad Olson

THE WAITING ROOM

James Grandy awoke to find himself surrounded by a blinding envelope of white nothing. His eyes fluttered for a second and then snapped shut again, awash in a sudden freshet of tears that stung his eyes and wet his cheeks. Where was he? What was this place? In the brief instant of vision, James had the peculiar sensation of what it must be like to be suspended on the inside of an electrified florescent tube. His teeth and lips quivered with a strange resonance of unfamiliar conductive warmth. Where was this place?

"Welcome, Mr. Grandy." The booming voice seemed to come from nowhere and everywhere at the same time. Rather than emanating from a single amplified source, it seemed to vibrate and issue from the very cells of his body. His eyes and skin and ears and hair tingled with the buzzing sensation. It would take some getting used to. Perhaps, he never would.

"Hello?"

"Where am I?"

"What is this place?"

As he formed the words, James realized that his own voice was carried with the same buzzing transcendence as the magnificent internal intercom from above. He heard the sounds in a muffled echoing blast from inside his head. It was like blowing the words outward underwater in the bubbling, swimming pool games of childhood.

Just like an underwater tea party at Cody Park Municipal Swimming Pool.

How strange it all felt! So very different from the vivid-real connection to the physical world of life on earth. For this wasn't earth anymore, or was it? James wasn't sure of anything, anymore, but he knew that much, at least. He was no longer on earth. Something had happened.

Don't be silly, Mr. Grandy. You've never been to Cody Park Municipal Swimming Pool.

What? Who had said that? The words came from inside his head, again, but this time, James jolted with a start as he noticed a newly arrived figure emerging from the milky stillness of one of the florescent walls, if this place had walls. He felt a certainty that the approaching entity had spoken the words, or was at least responsible for having them enter his mind. Was this the telepathy that people talked about, from time to time? *Aliens communicate that way, they do. Put the words directly inside your brain. Saves time and effort. It's efficient, that way.*

On earth, he had been a businessman of some distinction, in charge of financial strategies that made money for his investors and a comfortable living for his family; his wife, Susan and their three children, Tom, Molly and Sarah. Tom and Molly were away at college already and doing fine. Sarah was a high school junior, enjoying the absence of her older siblings and luxuriating in her newfound status as the lone recipient of her parents' attentions. The baby of the family, Sarah was smart, headstrong and independent, just like her mother, and pretty, besides. She had her mother's golden locks and the same set of dramatically arching cheekbones and pearly-perfect teeth. She was a handful of sass that was at once, gray-hair inducing, and undeniably, exuberantly invigorating to be around. She radiated the joy of life and celebrated every moment to the fullest.

Just like her mother. Just like her beautiful, unmatchable mother. My wife! My beautiful wife!

Suddenly, James Grandy collapsed to his knees, his eyes awash in tears and his chest constricted by the choking arrival of memory and grief. He missed his wife and his family. It was as if a portion of his most tender flesh had been rendered from his body and tossed away. His soul ached at the emptiness and at the hollow longing for reunion. Would he ever see them again? What had happened? Why had he been taken to this place?

"Don't be alarmed, Mr. Grandy. The memories will soften. They will fade with time, and once they've lost their jagged edges, you'll come to prize them as the greatest treasure of all. They will not remain as painful as you find them to be at the moment."

Grandy looked up from his kneeling collapse to see the figure that had approached from out of the milky stillness, beyond. It was a young boy of maybe seven or eight. He had sandy blond hair, cut pageboy style, framing a face that was to Grandy, both angelic and oddly familiar. His eyes, though blue and clear, seemed impossibly ancient and wise. They belonged in the face of someone much older, who had seen a life filled with both tragedy and redemption. Grandy found them instantly comforting and worthy of trust and respect. He was glad the boy had arrived. Despite his obvious disadvantage in stature, the boy had no trouble helping Grandy to his feet. Words entered Grandy's mind exactly as if they'd been spoken by a human mouth and resonated on human eardrums, but Grandy noticed, the boy's lips never moved. Not at all.

"Come with me, Mr. Grandy. Let me show you around, a little. There are some things I think you need to see."

"But, where am I?" James asked. "What is this place? Am I in Heaven?" James had the feeling he was capable of the same thought-speak that the boy was using to communicate, but he spoke the words in the normal fashion anyway. It was an earthly habit he wasn't ready to relinquish. Not yet.

"All in good time, Mr. Grandy," the boy said, without speaking. *"Let us walk for a while, and talk. It will give you a chance to relax and settle in. It's something that everyone experiences when they make their reawakening."*

With that the boy took Grandy's hand and began leading him gently forward, farther into the whiteness that seemed a formless void without wall, floor, or ceiling. Walking itself was a strange sensation to Grandy. Despite lacking any discernible surface, or distinguishing separation between up, down, or sideways, there was firmness beneath his feet that supported their progress. They were moving, to be sure, step-by-step, but direction and destination were impossible to determine. For the moment at least, it was utterly beyond Grandy's understanding. It was a predicament the boy seemed instantly to recognize and understand.

"Just walk with me, Mr. Grandy. Your eyes will adjust, as will your feet and your balance. You'll soon discover there's more definition to this place than you realize but with absolutely no danger of falling down, or up, or in any direction, for that matter."

Grandy was thankful for the stabilizing addition of the boy's hand in his own, and realized that like his attachment of familiarity to actually using his mouth to speak, his stepping feet were equally unnecessary. The boy was allowing him to walk to ease his adjustment to a state of being that was unsettling in every way. This place would take some getting used to. Again, the boy understood.

"What you're discovering, and about to discover, Mr. Grandy, are things that even the wondrous complexities of the human mind are completely incapable of fully containing. There simply isn't room for all of it, all at once. It would be like attaching a water balloon to a fire hose. There's no sense in overwhelming the system."

A water balloon and a fire hose. The mere mention of earthly connections sent Grandy into another memory rush containing a kaleidoscope of images from his earthly life. He saw himself in the backyard of the Grandy family summer cabin, the air filled with the shrieks and laughter of three children engaged in all-out combat. Armed with squirt guns and water balloon grenades, they were chasing each other this way and that, shouting threats of watery revenge before taking careful aim or ducking for safety.

Susan was watching them with smiling eyes, her thick hair pulled back in a rubber band. She was wearing a brightly colored, two-piece swimsuit and one of his button down dress shirts as a cover-up. She looked amazing, as always, sun-kissed and mischievous in that playful way that he loved, and could never resist. In one hand, she held a sweating glass of sun-brewed iced tea. Peppermint and Lemon zest. Her favorite. James saw himself, busy over a sizzling barbecue of hamburgers and hot dogs and foil-wrapped corn on the cob. It smelled delicious, and it had tasted even better.

Later that night, after the grill had cooled with the approach of evening, and the meal scraps had been cleared away, all five of them had relaxed on the sloping grass to watch fireworks burst and explode, high above the lake. As the reds and blues and showers of gold trailed down to leave their blurred reflections on the stillness of the water, his oldest daughter had laid a tired head against his shoulder. With his firm wife on one side, and his children snuggled around, his daughter Molly had wrapped her ten-year old hand around his finger as she watched the explosions overhead. It was their special game, he remembered. A reminder of the day she was born when he'd held her for the first time in the hospital operating room and she'd done exactly the same thing, grasping his finger tightly in one hand as her tiny lungs gulped in their first breaths in the bright and newly discovered world. He'd told her the story over and over as she'd grown up, turning that single moment into dozens more, when father and daughter would share again the joyful recollection of her blinking arrival into the world and into their family. It was one of Grandy's favorite snapshots of a life he'd loved, and would never live again.

I love you, daddy.

With those words echoing in his head, James Grandy realized he was weeping again, torn back to this empty place of never ending white where he was walking an unseen floor, toward an unseen, unknowable destination of light. The hand holding his finger belonged not to his beloved daughter but to his tow-headed companion, who was still leading him forward, deeper into the milky stillness of a dream.

"It's ok, Mr. Grandy. The memories will pass. They're painful, for all of us, I know."

James was puzzled at that, and more than a bit out of sorts. What could this boy know of losing a family? What could he possibly understand about having a life ripped away in an instant, never to be reclaimed, with so many unfinished moments and possibilities that would never be realized?

All of us? What did that mean? What did any of it mean? Why was he here? Where was he being taken?

"Be patient, Mr. Grandy. The answers to all of your questions are here. They are all here. But it isn't time yet, and there's just enough time for a nice walk to help with it all. You'll be glad for the walk, when it's all said and done."

James Grandy noticed that the boy never looked up at him when he spoke, and never made a move to draw closer, even when he'd been in the midst of his latest bout of memory and sadness. They never stopped walking, as if the destination mattered far more than anything James was experiencing along the way. The boy's wise and ancient eyes stared straight ahead in a fixed gaze, as if he was seeing something miles, maybe years away, behind a curtain that James could not yet see beyond. Still, there was something oddly familiar about the boy, and familiar too about the grasp of his small hand around James' fingers. Oddly familiar. James scanned the boy's smooth face for any sign that his thought had caused trouble, or reason for explanation, and saw none. For James himself, his own thoughts were proving troublesome enough. Why was he here? From where had he come? Swirling images of memory danced inside his mind, tumbling this way and that with smoky shreds of detail, here and gone again. Memories of journeys and rest, of love and of sadness, precious moments of simple pleasures, captured and floating like dandelion seeds, blown away in a spring breeze.

Dandelion fuzz. Another memory.

With a handful of words, James was gone again, back to the world of sunshine and clouds, and color, where three children frolicked and played in an open field. The girls in their summer dresses, and Tom in his overalls, they ran and raced and jumped in a green meadow, filled one end to the other with the downy cotton of dandelions, gone to seed. The floating mirage of liberated peach fuzz curled and undulated in exploding clouds, wherever the children's feet would touch. It trailed out behind them like the gauzy tail of a comet, marking their path. They were lost in the moment. From a soft picnic blanket, James and his wife watched their children's happy, dashing adventure before leaping to their feet to give chase. James tugged on his wife's hand to lead the charge as they ran whooping and laughing across the cottony meadow for a game of tag. One by one, they took turns running after each other and dodging, before collapsing in a giggling pile of sweat and exhaustion, ready for a glass of lemonade and a patch of well-earned shade. It was another wonderful day. A day he would always remember. A day among thousands that had made him the happiest of men, content and alive in the family-rich details of daily life. From the dandelion patch and the game of tag, James indulged himself with a series of clippings from his memory basket, smaller notions of this thought, or that, pausing only to absorb the simple emotions that acted as bookmarks in the vast filing system of his life. At times, a single object, sound, or smell that would carry him instantly to the places of emotion where he stored his favorite bits of a life well-lived.

> *The basketball hoop in the driveway.*
> *White flowers on his wedding day.*
> *A baby bassinet.*
> *Molly's favorite blanky.*
> *A tricycle.*
> *Fishing poles and cross-country skis.*
> *The family Christmas tree, trimmed in cranberries and popcorn.*
> *Susan under the mistletoe.*
> *His beautiful Susan.*

How he missed his wife! How he missed his family, his children, his life! Why had this happened? How had it happened? He was dead now, obviously. His life over in an instant to be replaced by this sterile waiting room outside of heaven, if that's where he was. There was so much he didn't understand and so many questions without answers.

"*No, James. Not dead. Not killed.*"

Still walking with his young escort in this place of blinding light, James was brought back to the endless trail of his feet on a path he could still not see. He was getting tired of this walking game. Of what use is walking in Heaven? What was it for? Where was he going? Couldn't luminous beings of spirit and light move about as they pleased, without the crude conventions of walking? Of course they could. James remembered a conversation with his childhood pastor from long ago, a man who had noticed James' abilities for deeper thinking and who had used that fascination to draw James' deeper into his faith. *Einstein got it wrong, my boy,* his pastor had said. *The most overpowering velocity in the universe is not the speed of light. It is the speed of a thought! The speed of thought is God's ultimate speedometer. It's the speed the brought the universe into being and flung the stars into space with a single word. It's the only speed that really matters.* The speed of thought, or the speed of a memory. James longed to wing away to this land of remembrance, and be gone forever, lost amid the stacks of his favorite earthly images. It was a tempting alternative to a journey he could still not understand or comprehend. Why did he have to die? What would happen to Susan and the children? Who would provide for them? What about their educations? Tuition? Books? Food? Mortgage?

A myriad of detail rushed through James's troubled mind as he struggled to piece it all together. Once again, the boy understood perfectly what the man was thinking and why. With a single sentence, he caught James' attention and held it, instantly drawing the man's eyes to his own, with a gaze that seemed finally ready to unveil the secret knowledge that had puzzled and perplexed the man for what seemed like eons, since his arrival. As the boy began to speak, James was suddenly aware that they were now surrounded, as far as he could see in every direction, by children dressed in white. They were similar in age to the boy who had led him there, and standing very still, as if they each knew what was about to be said.

"James. You never died. You haven't been killed."

A pause.

"You never died, because you were never born."

The words hit their mark. James staggered where he stood, collapsing again, downward amidst the outstretched tiny arms and hands of the multitude of linen-clad children who instantly pressed in to support him. Their knowing faces were filled with the light of recognition and sorrowed wisdom. James thought he finally understood.

"My mother. It was my mother, wasn't it? Did she......? Did they...before I was born....?"

The unfinished question, choked in his throat, was precisely the one the boy seemed to have expected, they had all expected.

"No, James. It was not your mother. That would have been impossible. You never had a mother, either."

For the first time in several moments, the young boy turned and lifted his face to allow James to look upon him in a way he'd prevented since they began their walk of memory, what seemed like forever ago, centuries ago, perhaps. The boy's clear blue eyes were brimming with tears that spilled onto his smooth skin, untarnished by earthly elements. The features were still familiar to James in the way that had at once comforted and puzzled him when he'd first arrived. Suddenly, he knew why. It was a face from his memories, but much younger than the way it was contained in snippets and shreds of what James had always believed were the earthly recollections of his life, past. The boy was his father.

"James, your mother did nothing to you, because she never existed." The boy spoke the words the old fashioned way, actually moving his lips for the first time since James had heard him speak. The movements of the mouth and the formation of the syllables removed all doubt as to the boy's identity, and instantly explained why he had chosen telepathy in the early going. The true depth of knowledge would have been far more than James could have handled. Even now, the implications of what he was saying were too much.

Never existed?

Never born?

Never lived?

But, you're my father! I remember you! I loved you! You hugged me and held my hand a thousand times, just as surely as I held the hands of my daughters, and hugged them and kissed the lips of my wife, and held my newborn children in my arms! I lived! I breathed! I watched all of it happen! I know it happened! It all happened! I lived it all! Every bit of it!

James screamed the words inside himself with a voice that was a crushing wave of bitter anguish and realization. Fragments of floating memory swam before him, seeming to lose their shape somehow, stretched and distorted like the overgrown soap bubbles he'd watched his children play with on the winds of a thousand, joyous summer days.

But I never had children? I never played with them? Never knew them? Never loved them? Never, really? It was all a dream? A dream I never lived?

"*A dream in the mind of God,*" the boy-father said.

From the depths of his soul, James Grandy was weeping now, but not alone. They were all weeping. As far as his tear-flooded eyes could see, James saw he was afloat in an ocean of lost and crying children, just like himself. From horizon to horizon, forgotten children, dressed in white, swaying together in a mass choir of shared sadness and the longing of memories they had never lived. They knew his pain, and he knew theirs. They shared it, together. It washed over them and across the far reaches of this whitening place like a torrential chorus of pleading voices lifted to heaven.

We lived!
We loved!
We remember!
We remember!
We lived!
We lived!
We lived!
WE LIVED!
WE WANTED TO LIVE!
WE WANTED TO LIVE!

Over and over, their shared shout of lost lives echoed and tumbled. James and his unborn father lifted their voices in unified longing, cleansing and capturing the sadness of new arrival and awareness in a way that began

13

to soothe and quiet the ragged edges of pain too deep to measure. And then, from somewhere amidst the stilling crowd of forgotten mourning, it happened. A tiny hand, much smaller and more delicate than the boy's, reached up to grasp a finger of James's right hand. The encircling warmth of a familiar grip caused James to look down into an upraised face that had filled so many of his sweetest memories. It was the face of his oldest daughter, smiling the familiar smile that would never be seen, or enjoyed by eyes of flesh and blood and heartbeat. It was Molly. And beside her, a younger boy and girl, their faces and hair so soaked with tears it seemed they had come fresh from a water fight in the backyard of a summer home they would never truly know.

> *I lived too, Daddy.*
> *And I.*
> *And I.*
> *And I remember you, Daddy. We all do.*
> *And we love you.*
> *We love you, still.*
> *We've always loved you.*
> *And we always will!*

The words brought James Grandy to his knees, for good, dissolved in hugs and kisses and the ocean of tears that would never end. Generations of souls, set to flight in the Creator's mind, yet never allowed to spread their wings on earth. The weeping chorus of reunion and regret began anew, and continued, until the oldest soul of the Grandy clan spoke again.

You see, James, my son, our destinies exist, and ultimately, whether we are born or not, have their only existence, inside the mind of God. For Him, there is no past and no present, no future, and no end, no distinction between His purpose for us, and what ultimately happens in a sinful, fallen world before our birth. There is only the, "Eternal Now," as we've come to call it. And the sadness of a Father-Creator who has watched generations of His children snuffed out before they lived to see the physical destinies of His creation. An ocean of souls He has breathed to life, never allowed actual breath down below.

For James Grandy, the words were only the start of a journey that would require dozens more connections before his understanding would be complete. Hadn't he still a thousand-thousand memories of life on earth, containing even the most minute details of physical experience? The sweet taste of a juicy watermelon on a summer day. The musky stir of an autumn breeze as it rattled through piles of crispy fallen leaves. The creamy-cool goodness of a vanilla ice cream cone. The gentle brush of his wife's sugar-sweet kiss on his lips. What of those? Where had they come from? How could he be so certain of a life he was never allowed to live?

The answer is simple, my son. What you feel and taste and touch and "remember," as you might say it, about your life and the memories of it, are the dimensional tracings of what your life would have been, but that exist now, only in the mind of God, Himself. You are conscious of them, because He allows you to be, in the same way He allows all of us to see the goodness and beauty of our lives as we soak in His presence and His infinite love. I've come to understand that it's a gift that He gives each of us as a sort of compensation for what we never experienced in fullness. A final confirmation of the good and perfect gifts He intended for us to enjoy on earth, but that were never allowed manifestation in the physical realm.

With that, James Grandy, his unborn father and unborn children and all the million voices of lost and misplaced generations turned as one to make their way toward the source of the brightness taking shape beyond the veil between fading memory and pain. *HE* was waiting for them there, as He always was when new arrivals had been suitably welcomed and settled in. It was time for reunion, and peace and healing; the kind that only their Papa-Yahweh could provide. A precious embrace reserved only for those forgotten, eternal souls destined to spend their forever's forever, remembered only as the snowy-white wisps of a dandelion dream, breathed to life inside the mind of God.

⌦⋆ ⋆⌫

"Before I formed you in the womb, I knew you..."
Jeremiah 1:5

JACOB'S LADDER

Jacob Wilmer was building a ladder to the sky. The work made him tired and cross, for he had only just begun when the townspeople and their questions began to press in and suffocate his ramshackle world on the edge of the tiny desert town.

"Why would you build a thing like that?"

"What is the good of doing it?"

"Where are you planning to go to?"

"You'll never manage at anything, besides mucking up the skyline and killing yourself."

He had long stopped paying attention to their queries, but had failed in his quest for total ignorance of their generously volunteered thoughts on his endeavor. The lost productivity and the general clutter of the mind produced by their obtuse reasoning left him grinding his teeth and muttering to himself. For the crowds that sometimes gathered to watch, this only added to the already irresistible spectacle of an aging man with graying hair, working himself silly with blowtorch and scrap alloy, erecting a seemingly endless patchwork of tubes and rungs and struts, a thousand feet and rising. He admitted to himself that it was an auspicious beginning, but quickly extinguished whatever satisfaction the realization offered so as not to compromise his stern and implacable resolve.

Every day, his routine was the same. He would wake just before dawn, eat a pauper's breakfast of canned frog legs and dust crackers and step out of his rusting, sheet metal shack to begin the search. His first hours were spent finding and procuring suitable material for his ladder. Old scaffolding, bed frames, exercise devices, discarded plumbing, fence supplies, lampposts. All were carted back to his home where each was meticulously inspected, altered, reinforced, stripped of unneeded varnish (in some cases) and otherwise prepared for assimilation into his grand design. The hardest work of all, of course, was the climbing. When he had first begun, it had required only a handful of steps to reach the summit, if it could have been called summit, in those days. Barely ten feet off the ground, he would climb down, select the next piece for fitting, place his pocket auto-welder between his teeth and head back up the steps.

Progress had been rapid, allowing him to add twenty or thirty feet a day in the beginning, but as the ladder extended higher, simply reaching the top could take as much as a quarter of an hour, and all of that to grow his creation by a half-dozen feet, or less. Up and up and up he would climb, a chosen length of re-purposed metal lashed around his waist by a tether, sweaty hands swimming in leather gloves that threatened to squirt off and away, and send him plunging and screaming to a clattering, impaling death below.

Once on top, his work was simple. His younger life as a pipe fitter and general machinist in the Galactic Navy had honed his skills with a torch to a fine edge. Three explosions of brilliant blue light and it was done. *Zuuzzzzzzattt! ZZzzzzaaatt! ZZZzzaaamattt!* Then he would carefully wind up and stow his tow-tether (so as to avoid becoming tangled and losing his footing) and begin the long climb to earth to for the next length. It was satisfying work that would have done much to sustain his happiness in what he knew were the waning days of his life, if it weren't for the townspeople. He couldn't make them understand his ladder and so they did everything they could to find statute or legality to put a swift end to his ambitions.

In years gone by, antiquated laws regulating the flight of aeroplanes and the skies they crisscrossed would have prevented Jacob from even beginning the notion. But as everyone knew, rockets and hover ships had relegated other forms of terra-travel to rusting obsolescence, and the rules against tall towers had been discarded alongside the rotting machines they had protected. Still, his fiercest opponents persisted in their schemes and even as his ladder grew and grew, he knew they were scouring laws and archives and municipal code, searching for any obscure twist in the bowels of whatever long dormant statute might bring the humbling of Jacob Wilmer and his silly metal needle in the sky. At a town assembly, called uniquely in the interest of addressing the "strange little man" and his "troublesome undertaking," people he counted as neighbors and friends stood up and demanded his death, or at the very least, they said, the destruction of his ladder, and immediate, irrevocable banishment from the city.

"Wasn't he always a bit of a strange duck?"

"He must've gotten the idea from unnatural spirits!"

"It's a lightning hazard!"

"Perhaps it will just fall down!"

"Hope he's up top when it does!"

"Good riddance!"

In the end, the town's esteemed legal counsel had prevailed on city leaders that there could be found no justification for causing the forced abandonment of the property or the spire springing from it, and most certainly, no objective reason for killing the man who owned it. At five after midnight, the meeting had disbanded with angry grumblings about the sorry impotence of local government these days, and threats of vigilante vandalism or even murder. Thankfully, from Jacob's view, an immediate and stern warning from the town Sheriff had held such threats in check, at least thus far. That's not to say that there hadn't been a tickling or two of mischief, now and then. Jacob had been startled awake in the wee hours one morning to find the base of his tower painted an inch thick with a stomach wrenching mixture of axle grease, pig excrement and #8 lead shot. A groping inspection in the dark left his hands a sticky, squishing mess that required ten minutes worth of turpentine to reconcile.

By daylight, Jacob could take heart only that there had been no significant structural damage. It was a thought he called upon frequently as he spent the next two days ridding the lower rungs of the mess. He supposed he could have, and perhaps should have, reported the incident to authorities, but decided not to mistake the

Sheriff's lynch mob warning at the meeting for anything beyond a fiduciary obligation to his duties under the law. Sympathy could not be counted on, and beyond that, the accompanying attention for one round of daring-do might only encourage others with similar ambitions but weaker resolve.

And so, Jacob had said nothing, and had simply returned to the repetitive shelter of his routine. Scavenge, climb, weld, descend. Repeat. Repeat. Repeat. The rhythm of days and nights quickened and comforted the old man. He found new strength and life in his movements. His hands roughened and his muscles hardened in the working sun, pulling skin loosened by age newly taut and firm over a framework that seemed to grow and change to mirror the rising wire from the earth. And still, up and up he climbed, higher and higher until he could rest between welds and look down to see birds and clouds flying beneath, gilded and burning with the shared flame of sunset. Far, far below, he saw the miniature world of tiny houses and airlocks and the slow motion scurrying of the people who wanted so badly for him to teeter and fall to his doom. Part of him knew that was the sole reason they came to watch. It wasn't the grandeur of his ladder, or the pure curiosity and pleasure of witnessing an undertaking so strange and genuinely pursued. It was him. They were there every morning like clockwork, just in case the little man with the lithely hands and feet had an off second of inattention and came hurtling back into sight at a speed that would singe the clothes from his body before he made like a human meteorite detonating on the oven-cake sand.

They want to be here when I die. They want to see me flame out, reach terminal velocity, buy the farm. Might even take more than a few of them with me depending on where they stand for the day. Would serve a few of them right, it would.

But there would be no such sideshow. Not now. Jacob's hands and feet never faltered, and with every step, it seemed, his grip on the rungs grew more certain and his sheer delight at his craft deepened and sang.

"But what keeps the damned thing from falling down?"

"There aren't any wires! No braces, No supports!"

"It just hangs there, straight as an arrow with no help at all!"

The questions and gossip never bothered him now, but he knew what people were saying. His tower had grown far beyond a nuisance or mere parlor chatter, into the realm of observable explainable physics. He knew people simply could not bend their minds around what they were seeing. A simple, two beam ladder, without warp or wiggle, that went straight up into the vapors like a laser beam coated in steel and Lumivox. No guywires. No stanchions, or struts of any kind, and yet it didn't bend or sway in the wind. Never creaked or vibrated or shook or even hummed. Even as its queer little builder monkeyed and raced to the top of his perch, it stood firm and still. They had to know why. In their uneasy twilight beds they tossed and argued, aching to understand whatever magic or madness it was that propelled the mystery of what they could see and touch and still not believe. *And they never will. Ever.* If his neighbors and friends were unsettled and driven to violence by the simple notion of building a giant ladder, Jacob knew the reason for it's stoic and unshakable constitution would incite mass hysteria. It was a dilemma he had puzzled over long before he had actually sunk the first poles into the sand. He knew it would be only a matter of time until the dimensions and characteristics of his ladder would so unnatural as to cause panic. It was happening now. He could feel it. He was running out of time. *But there is still so much work to do! So much farther to climb! To build! To dream!*

⊂═⋄ ⋄═⊃

With fevered hands they attacked the wiry deity, tearing first at the earth around its base and wheeling away with heaving clumps and clots. Like a convulsing mass of soldier ants enveloping and devouring a felled carcass, they dug and rooted, snorted and spat. Across the front lines of the onslaught, skirmishes broke out among the defilers themselves, gouging flesh and eyes and crusty discs of broken clay with equal ferocity. And then they were upon it, and, at once, silent. There in the depths of the wallowing pit was the naked embodiment of all their questions and fears. And somehow, they knew. With unified and bone wrenching certainty, they understood. Slowly, a single figure broke free from the zombie collective and advanced to the object. Fingers clumsy with communal rage only a moment before were now dexterous as a surgeon's as they caressed away the final scatterings of dirt and dust to reveal what human eyes would now behold for only the second time in all of universal history.

Placed directly below and in direct contact with the seminal posts of the monster-ladder was a black-onyx oval approximately a foot across. Its surface was as black and shiny as a pooling of crude oil or molasses, and it seemed to hover within itself, as if trapped in the flexing membrane

23

of an impenetrable soap bubble. Over time, Jacob Wilmer had come to call it, (or at least think of it, as he never spoke of it to anyone) as a gravitational stabilizing orb. But on his third commission to Jupiter's largest moon, he had at first spent several minutes wondering how, and more importantly, if, he should touch the strange and wonderful rock, hovering inches above the dust of the satellite surface. For the grunting rabble standing in the crater at the base of Wilmer's life's work on earth, there was no such restraint. Three large men were already hard at the task, wiggling and leveraging, tugging and tilting, until they dislodged it from beneath the ladder as if yanking a badger from his den. One man held it aloft like a hard won trophy, turning it this way and that to satisfy the coliseum of eager spectators waiting to gaze on the alien thing. Their rabid eyes swelled wide to explore the swirling petroleum window flung open before them.

And for some, it would be the very last thing they would ever see, for at that instant, the sky became a rocketing thunderburst of metal tubing, a hurtling barrage of precision welding turned to a million tons of Tinker-Toys, fifty-thousand feet above. The fusillade of shrapnel and smoke lasted for seven minutes, pulverizing everyone and everything within two blocks of Jacob Wilmer's home. In the days and hours of excavation that followed, ten dozen bodies were counted and cataloged, matched to weeping families with a lift of a sheet and a knowing nod of confirmation, but Jacob Wilmer was not among them. No matter how they scratched and searched, or where, they could find no trace of the man they had hated and misunderstood and wanted to destroy. Except this. On a wrinkled flat of white-enameled tin scrap found in the mushroomed remains of his now subterranean shack, there were words.

We flattened the mountains to make room for cities. We filled in the canyons and the oceans to make more convenient living space for the sprouting trillions and their broods. And when we were done, we had rendered our Earth billiard flat from one pole to the other. We smoothed the nicks and grooves and rough spots of our planet until it became just another marble in the heavens.

My grandfather used to read me books and tell me stories about faraway places where men scaled tall rocks and even the world's tallest peaks, if only to prove that it could be done. Just to Prove! Courage! Tenacity! Adventure! I just wanted something to measure myself against. How can a man learn the depths of himself, with nothing tall, or deep or wide, to challenge him? How can he learn his limits if he is the highest and deepest and hardest thing he ever meets?

I know that you hate me. I know that you wish me gone, and my devil's ladder melted to ruins as a warning against anyone who might dare to listen to different dreams. And so I am going away. For Good.

Jacob.

METAL MAKER'S DAUGHTER

"Would you love me if I were not so beautiful?" Richly bronzed and smooth of skin, the two lovers lay entwined in the island moonlight, their bodies pressed together in the peaceful retreat of passion. The rush of small waves on the beach and the rustle of palm leaves overhead had concealed all but the most ardent cries of their lovemaking, and now they lay spent. Tarita, the daughter of the village metal maker asked the question again.

"Would you still love me if I were not beautiful?"

As she spoke, she trailed her delicate fingers through the tangled hair of the man she hoped would soon be her husband. His name was Silvas, and his thickly muscled form and wavy black hair were the cause of frequent female whispers in the small fishing village where he lived.

He too hoped for marriage with Tarita, but her frequent questioning often made him cross.

"Why again with a fool's unction such as this," Silvas replied after a moment.

"You might as well inquire of the sun whether it would still shine were the earth made only of tube worms and jellyfish. Perhaps I will ask you whether your love for me would fly away if I were not so clever with my boat and sail on the water, and if my nets did not overflow with the fine fat fish that fill the bellies of half the village."

"Of course not, my love."

As she listened to Silvas' words, Tarita's fingers had stopped their playful wandering across his broad fisherman's chest. She seemed to contemplate for a moment before speaking again.

"It is good to know that our children will always have plenty to eat and that your catch can be traded for anything else we might need," Tarita said, her fingers again caressing her lover's skin.

"But it is not your talent with a boat and net that captured my heart, husband-to-be, nor even the high esteem those skills have earned you with the old men of our village."

Tarita's hands had found their way farther down now until she grasped something that made the fisherman's breath catch in his throat. With another kiss, the two were lost again in the rhythm of the rushing waves.

⚬━◆ ◆━⚬

Some days later, Silvas was hard at work on a secluded stretch of beach not far from the place where he and Tarita shared their kisses. He was building their wedding house in secret and had taken a day from fishing to do it. Several times in the past month he had followed the same ritual. Tarita and her mother would see him stretching his nets and rigging his boat as on any other day. They would smile and wave and wish him good fortune as he pushed and strained his skiff into the foaming surf. He would wave in return and set his sail for deeper water before changing course and tacking around to the familiar spot.

In his heart, he hoped the sentimentality of the location and the quality of his craftsmanship would show Tarita how much he loved her. He imagined their children running and laughing along the shoreline and climbing the coconut and banyan trees that grew around the building spot in an almost perfect alternating circle. Through the tree line only a few dozen steps was the gentle stream that serenaded their nights of love beneath the moon. Now, that sound would be with them every night after and would offer a short and easy walk for Tarita to bring fresh water into their house. Silvas knew they would make a happy life here, and the knowledge made his heart full and strong for the work of building.

First he had collected and stripped several straight and strong serrated trunks from the trees. He had scraped them smooth and cured them with oil squeezed from drying shark flesh before pounding them deep into the island sand. To these he fastened a crisscrossing array of rails of split palm wood, bent and shaped to form the curving walls. He tied them in place with strands of twine twisted from dried palm leaves, just the way his grandfather had taught him when he was a boy. Now, the frame and roof were finished and all that remained was to weave the latticework walls and pack and smooth the floor. Today, Silvas was holding two heavy stones on his shoulders as he stamped his feet forcefully into the sand. Around and around he walked inside the frame walls, until his feet burned and his legs ached and his shoulders began to cry out with the burden. Sweat glistened on his strong body, dripping into the sand to join the seawater he had sprinkled to help tighten and form the floor. When he began to tire from the work, he turned his mind to his beloved Tarita and his strength and vigor would return. He imagined her swaying body firm and upright as she carried her water jug on her head. The thought of her curving form and lovely round face made him smile a face of white strong teeth. Soon their hut would be complete and then they would love and live every day near the singing stream.

⊂══◄· ·►══⊃

On the days he worked on the wedding hut, Silvas would watch closely the sun's progress through the sky. When the painted hues of blue and white began to turn yellow and orange, he would stop his labor and make for his boat on the shoreline. Quickly he would sail for a place he had found where the fish swam thick and fast. It was a spot none of the other fisherman had yet discovered and Silvas hoped they wouldn't just yet. If he fished there for a full day, his boat would certainly founder with the haul, and both of his secrets would be ruined. As it was, he could toss his net three times before returning home and catch enough fish to maintain the appearance of an average fisherman's day on the water. Those days would do nothing to deepen his reputation with the villagers, but there were plenty ahead to make up for the loss. Tarita's happiness with their home would more than repay a few bad days with the net. What could replace a happy bride? What could recompense for an unhappy one?

Silvas stroked his paddle strongly through the water and remembered Tarita's question from nights before. It wasn't the first time she had asked him to reaffirm his devotion to her. He supposed that such misgivings were a common thing for women who are afraid of losing the men they love. Still, her preoccupation made trouble in his mind. Did she curse her own beauty? Surely the most comely maiden in the village would not wish to deprive herself the favors that status employed. What woman would? Silvas hoped she could see that he found her gentle heart as inviting a destination as her waiting arms and lips. It was true after all. He had always felt that the magical reflection in her eyes was, in truth, the magnified contents of her soul laid bare. While other girls had boasted and strutted for his attentions, Tarita had allowed him to come to her. Her peaceful way put his own heart at ease from the start and only deepened the maddening pulse of passion she stirred in him. As he tossed his net into the water, Silvas made a wish in his deepest heart that she would not ask the question again.

⊙═◄· ·►═⊙

The lattice walls were now complete. He had woven them himself, a single strand at a time, making sure to push the fibers tightly together to leave no space for wind or rain to get through. So thorough was his attention that standing inside the wedding hut at midday, not even a pinprick of light could be seen between the weavings. The roof and walls meshed solidly so that heat from the fire pit would find no escape on cool rainy nights. Silvas knew the same could not be said of any hut on the island. What a fine home for his young bride! What happy times it would hold. He imagined the day of their wedding and envisioned her smiles of joy when she would finally see what he had made and they would go inside together. She would embrace him softly with her tender skin and thank him with tears and whispers. They would partake of love for the first time as husband and wife, and then drift to sleep as the singing stream ran its course beside their fine new hut. Everything would be right and good. She would stop asking him the question.

⊜⬩⬩ ⬩⬩⊜

Again they lay on the empty beach. Silvas could feel Tarita's retreating passion quiver through her as they embraced and lay still together and silent. The time had come to talk to her father about taking her in marriage. He would do it tomorrow. Silvas had been contemplating what to say since he had first held the metal maker's daughter in his arms months ago. Now, the seriousness of the oath and the pride of his trade must be put to good use. The metal maker was a serious man, after all. Like Silvas, he was a strong and physical figure who spent his days bending and shaping hot metal into knives and spoons and fishhooks. Even before their children were old enough to fall in love, Silvas's father had spoken reverently of the metal maker's skill. They used his straight needles to sew their sails and nets, his sharp knives to carve paddles for their boats, wooden spools for line and to gut the fish they kept for their family. Silvas liked the way the quick blades of the metal maker's craft could swift and steer through fish flesh, separating meat from bone and head from tail.

Whenever his father needed a new blade, or a fresh set of hooks, young Silvas had skipped eagerly along to the metal maker's shack. He loved to watch as the glowing coals shared their orange fire with shards of black iron. He loved the *clank-clankum* of the hammer as it flattened and purified the metal. He always listened closely for the churtling hiss the metal made as it hit the water barrel to cool. Many times, the metal maker would let him be the first to hold a new hook or fish knife after it had come to life on the anvil. His father and the metal maker would chat happily about fishing and women and hard metal and which could be counted on most often. Metal, then fishing, then women, in that order. Young Silvas had first seen young Tarita when he was six years old. She was half hidden in her mother's wraparound skirt, toting a colorful feather from some tropical bird in one hand as her mother spoke to her father about a trip to the market. In those days, Silvas had found Tarita an intriguing creature, but was still more interested in the glowing creations her father made with strong hands. It was something time had fully changed.

"Would you still love me if I were not so beautiful?"

She had asked it again. Silvas felt the air and the life go out of him in a long and wearied sigh. He pulled Tarita's soft form tightly to him and put his lips to her ear to whisper.

"You are my dove, little one," Silvas began. "I cannot imagine life before or without loving you, nor do I hope to."

Tarita's eyes were half-lidded and directed down toward her feet as she lay in the crook of the fisherman's arm. She seemed unaffected by his response, and so he went on.

"Truthfully, I know that if I were to spend the last night of my life in your arms, that taste of heaven would transcend all that might follow in the paradise beyond. Your eyes fill my dreams and your kisses calm my fears. You are my dove."

He sealed this last declaration with a gentle kiss and relaxed his embrace before speaking again.

"You must no longer worry yourself silly about things that can never fully be understood, little one. There is no service in it. Only trouble and discontent. I must ask you to never again make this question to me, or I fear that my patience for fishing might be extinguished, leaving us to starve,"

Silvas accented this with a playful chortle, gently ruffling Tarita's sweat-damp hair.

"I love you," he continued. "I love you, and you are beautiful, and neither of those things can be changed. You will always be beautiful to me. And I will always love you. That is that."

Silvas seemed satisfied with his oratory and nestled back with his arms over his head, waiting for her response.

"I know that you love me, Silvas," Tarita answered finally. "I know that you are as decent and strong and handsome a husband any woman could ever want, my love. But my heart wants to be sure that what you desire in me goes deeper than feminine charms."

Lying on her side, Tarita pulled herself up on one elbow, allowing her soft and ample round breasts to spill together and press outward against the sand. She spoke again.

"Our passion is great, my love, but my heart wants to know that you love my very soul, and that you always would, no matter if I suddenly were as cold and homely as a monk fish."

Silvas laughed at this, and the two lovers embraced again, even more deeply than before, holding on to one another as the first light of dawn began to twinkle on the morning waves.

⚬⟞ ⟝⚬

With the wedding hut complete, Silvas turned his attention back to his boat and catching fish. Out on the water the next day he spooled out half a league of line and attached a barbed hook to one end. Using a sharp knife from the metal maker's shop, he carved off a piece of chunk bait from a stale grunion and mounted it on the hook. There would be no net fishing today. Early this morning he had stopped by the house of another fisherman and finding him already out on the water for the day's work, had bartered with his wife for some bait. Silvas supposed it was silly for a fisherman to be buying fish, but he knew Wapte had sailed to the western shoals earlier in the week and had brought home a nice passel of grunion. Grunion was the perfect enticement for today's task and he had paid Wapte's wife handsomely for the chance. He hoped to send his bait hook deep into the sea and pull back a giant sailfish or marlin. He would yank the line hard to set the hook and pull the mighty fish into his boat as a dowry gift to Tarita's father. The metal maker would be impressed. With any luck he would have the fish in his boat by noon and a father's blessing by evening. It would be a very good day. He imagined his mother's happiness at his coming marriage to Tarita. He could see his father's head held high and straight above his broad chest, watching and smiling as the tribal elders made the ceremony. Silvas had always tried to make his parents proud. It was important to him that they understood he was a good and decent man who wanted them to be prosperous and happy in their older years. His skill as a fisherman and accompanying popularity in the village were a good start, but Silvas knew that for aging parents, these were no match for a good daughter-in-law and strong, healthy grandchildren. A happy marriage to Tarita would provide both. The family line would continue. Silvas tossed his line into the water and waited for the monster to bite. It would be a very good day.

⇾ ⇾

Tarita had been carrying her water vessel to the village cistern when she looked up and saw the horror. At first, she had questioned what her own eyes had seen. Had it really been Silvas leaving the strange woman's hut so early in the morning? And with a breakfast of small fish under one arm? She tried for a time to blink the image from her mind, but in the end could not assuage the truth. She would have known her beloved's masculine shape from a mile distant in a typhoon, much less on a clear morning only a footrace away. The rest of the path to the cistern and back again, her fevered mind had puzzled over what to do or say. Part of her had wanted to run at the strange woman and crash the clay water vessel down on her again and again. She imagined the shards of broken pottery littering the woman's hut and mingling with pools of dying blood. Then she would take one of the shards and carve the woman's skin from her face. Anger and vengeance boiled inside her like a tempest. Sullen doubt that had festered slowly even in the warm glow of their passion now burst to full flame. She had been a fool to believe that a man as vigorous and sought after as her Silvas would limit his affections to a single woman. Perhaps indulging his passions in the arms of Wapte's wife was his way of finally answering her question. She remembered how cross he had become on the night when she first raised it. She had felt his muscles clench and tighten under her fingertips and his breath swell in his chest. For a moment she had feared that he might become very angry and push her out of his arms. Instead, he had responded to her with kindness and playful jostling, embracing her tightly and speaking lovely words into her ear. She had loved those words, and their sweetness had become a waiting confection whenever she asked the question. It was a sure way to hear his devotion repeated to her satisfaction. But that was long before this hated business with Wapte.

Such deception! Professing his love for me and all the while yearning for another man's wife! Tarita's rage quickened and roiled. Her thoughts filled unstoppably with dreamlike shadows of Silvas and Wapte together in their secret places. The vivid imagery of forbidden passion brought Tarita to her knees on the path. *And to discover the truth only now, with so little time before they were to be wed!* Tarita raised her hands to her face and wept streams of hot and angry tears. Cascading salty streams turned to grimy rivulets along her sand-caked cheeks. After long moments, her sobbing slowly abated to silent shivers of halted breath and she returned to her feet. Her once sparkling eyes now seemed to dull and deepen in their sockets. She stared straight ahead as she realigned her dainty feet to a new destination. She was going to her father's workshop.

Silvas' broad paddle dug deeply into the foaming waves as he turned his boat for shore. In the gunnels of his speeding skiff lay the largest line-fish he had ever snared. With gasping gills and fixed eyes, it rocked and shifted limply in the wet bottom of the fisherman's boat, spent from the fight and resolved to its fate. Silvas' himself bore the signs of the struggle, but his wide smile left no doubt as to the victor. The strong line had cut into his hands as he strained and lifted against the captive's run for deep water. The two masters of different worlds had used all their wiles and strength against one another, trading advantage and loss for more than an hour until hook, line and muscled arms finished the score. Silvas' rippled shoulders had stretched mightily as he hauled the bested beast into his skiff. Now, those same muscles were groaning anew as each stroke of the mighty paddle brought the fisherman and his catch closer to shore. Silvas' smile grew wider at the thought of his arrival at the village and the hero's welcome to come. His monster-fish would be the largest ever brought to market. The old men who could remember the truth would hail his prize and there would be the shouts and laughter of celebration and excited talk. And when they had marked their memories and given their due, Tarita's father would laugh and smile most of all. The giant creature from the deep would serve on land as a fitting dowry for the most beautiful bride in the village and secure a father's blessing for Silvas. The metal maker's daughter would be his wife.

From inside the metal maker's shanty, the first cries of discovery turned to shrieking wails of anguish and loss. They found her as she lay, surrounded by spreading scarlet estuaries of her life's essence and a circling array of her father's sharpest blades. Her father was not there. He had taken a day at the family home to bury daikon bulbs and till the garden plot for a new planting of taro root and sweet potatoes. Now he gathered with half the village to see his only daughter's fate and to weep.

Tarita's mother cradled the girl in her arms, rocking and shaking on the workshop floor. Metal filings and her daughter's pooling blood clung to the hem of her dress. With a shaking hand, she had covered her daughter's face with the brightly colored kerchief that normally secured her black hair in a tight round coil. Her dark eyes were tightly clenched and soaked with tears. With the newest arrivals of neighbors and friends and customers now pressed in, close and silent all around the shop, Tarita's mother lifted the scarlet-stained veil from the most beautiful face in the village. A gasp went through the crowd.

As his fisherman's skiff cut into the island shallows, Silvas could hear the whoops and shouts of the villagers. Were they gathered at the shoreline? Perhaps they anticipated the grandeur of his latest catch? Had the welcome party already begun? In the distance he thought he could make out the silhouettes of his parents and several of the village elders in their mustard robes. He would be there soon. *How happy they would be!* Silvas and his monster fish would make a joyous night for the entire village. It would be a dowry celebration as had never been seen before. Silvas and his beautiful Tarita would smile and laugh and feast on their dowry fish that would give everyone their fill. They would dance and sing and give thanks to well-wishers young and old. And as the fading sun sank beneath the evening waves, he knew they would find loving solace in the island shadows as they always did. The gentle darkness would hide their escape and the softness of her passion would fill the fisherman with joy as great as the waves that filled his boat with fish.

⊂═◦ ◦═⊃

In the quiet of the wedding hut, a gray-haired fisherman with broad shoulders sat at a small wooden table and sipped warm maté from a burnished coconut bowl. On the other side, a gray-haired woman watched her husband with twinkling eyes. She reached her hand across to his and gently caressed the large strong fingers that had loved her for so long.

"My darling, Silvas," the woman said.

A single, glistening tear spilled from one dark and perfect eye before tracing a zig-zag path down a beautiful and now wrinkled face, covered with fading scars.

THE LAST PREFECT

Lord Zucker emerged from the still steaming transport chamber and stepped into his brilliant-white office suite looking smugly refreshed. Instead of virtual golfing with United Global Overlord Ojamba for the 2,411th time, he'd just spent his regular Friday afternoon quatrain in a chat room orgy of "Hot Girls Twerk Island," an especially rambunctious social reality construct in the LifeSpace network of his own fabulous and fabulously wealthy creation. He was famished and dehydrated and half-deaf, but smiling a smile stolen from Alfred E. Newman at birth and kept out of stubbornness for his sixty-four, life-enhanced years. Age was as irrelevant in the construct as fitness regimen and dietary habit and dental perfection. Everyone was hot, handsome, sexy and fit online. And well-endowed. Male and female alike, he had created them and recreated them and now, recreated with them, in his perfect Boolean garden of earthly delights. And he looked and saw that it was very, very good. The deity-Zucker in the digital Eden of his creation.

"Forever and ever, Amen," Zucker punctuated.

"Welcome back, Lord Zucker," the sing-song unison of the Strawberry Twins. Another of his virtual reality creations that habitually followed, welcomed, praised and lavished him over the course of their scripted, animatronic lives. If given ten spare minutes, Zucker realized that he would gladly reprogram them for silence, or at the very least, something less cloyingly annoying than the cotton candy and bubble gum that they perpetually lofted, even with their clothes on. Years ago as an emotionally stunted nerd with a rejection complex and an unfortunate face, he'd required and designed their praise as deliberate antidote for his own insecurities, and lacking self-esteem. But no longer. Since transitioning his global network of collected human profiles from a glorified social yearbook with email to a full-fledged, virtual reality construct and space conservation alternative, Zucker now had his pick of the women of the world.

And pick he did. Blondes, redheads, brunettes and baldies, top and bottom. Asians, Africans, Danes and Profanes. Every woman of every race, size, curvature, endowment and cultural technique could now be accessed at the touch of a motivating switch or the spoken word of the voice activating console. Men, too. As Zucker's vertebrae, knees and ears could attest, today's selection had been a dizzying and impossibly acrobatic romp with two Swedes and a double-jointed Icelandic brunette whose only verbal ability it seemed was to cackle like a McCaw and screech like a Howler Monkey when aroused. And screech she had. For two solid hours. Zucker wondered if the humming between his temples would never cease, before his appointment that is. Today was the day.

"If a guy is going to suffer tinnitus, I would guess there are far worse ways, eh, my Strawberry shortcakes," Zucker said, mostly to himself, but in the direction of his two mussy tufted concubines, each garnished with a ridiculous shock of what looked more like shredded licorice ropes than bright red hair. The carpet matched the drapes.

"Of course, Lord Zucker. Hehehehehehe."

Their laughter had the sound of a Mariah Carey whistle-solo on a scratched and skipping track of one of the compact discs of his youth. An outmoded laser-coded invention that had gone the forgotten way of 8-tracks and vinyl albums and cassette tapes, but still came to mind as descriptive analogy, the way memories often do. A reprogram of the twin's voice modulator was definitely in order. If only it mattered now. He knew that it didn't. Nothing did.

"Make a note of it, LifeScript," Zucker spoke anyway, to the always listening, interactive walls of the Lifespace Helper, a global integration SMART system that had become required fixture in every human living space on the planet. Zucker's system was identical to those of the average undercitizen in all respects, save one. It wasn't attached to the global network, unless he wanted it to be. And he never had.

Pouring a cocktail of white wine and Bull Roar, an energy concoction rumored to contain the vital essence of an intact bull, Zucker sank into a white velveteen lounge chair for some much earned recuperation from his legendary session. As was his luxury, Lord Zucker never disclosed actual details of his carnal exploits to anyone, despite his own ability to simultaneously watch, monitor, record, consume and eventually visit the virtual lives of his beloved universe of fully uploaded and supplicating humans. The watcher of them all is never watched. Privacy was now and had long been the sacramental caviar and Dom Perignon of the selected ruling class and he enjoyed his own for the spiteful, ironic jab that it was. There was sanguine deliciousness in being the very man that had conned the masses into willingly surrendering any expectation of a private life and volunteering any and all of their personal details and eventually, even their physical bodies and lives to the whims of cyberspace, while still having the reserved ability to conceal his own activities and those of the ruling supers from watchful eyes that had rewarded him for his dutiful service. Assimilation complete. A job well done. Forty-billion people served, uploaded to the server in twenty years time.

Zucker glanced to the far wall above his desk for tangible proof of his contribution. A framed and preserved duplication of the Ojamba Medal of Meritorious Valor, one of seventeen similar duplicates that Zucker had commissioned and deployed throughout his various environs to ensure they were always within sight. Even onboard his six private jets. Some things were worth savoring and remembering, Zucker told himself. Though they'd had their differences, especially of late, his long friendship with Global Overlord Ojamba predated the virtual realm and was a source of great pride and validation for Zucker, who had grown to adulthood still wondering if anything he ever did or said would ever matter to anyone at all.

Being the architect of what had become the preferred, and eventually mandatory, virtual living space of the planet was more than he'd ever hoped for or dreamed. He had solved the propagandized scam-problems of overcrowding and global climate and had made every human's richest and most gloriously tantalizing physical fantasies come to life at the same time. Seventeen medals wasn't nearly enough, he smiled to himself. And the women of the world would certainly have agreed. After all, what do you give the man who singlehandedly makes diet and exercise and diet and venereal disease and diet and bouts of boring sex with boring men with boring bodies and disappointing appendages, altogether obsolete? The miracle worker who makes it possible to enjoy both unlimited chocolate and indefinite sexual attractiveness and release without ever worrying about one interfering with the other? What gift can possibly repay?

"You give him yourselves, over and over and over and over again, my young pretties." Zucker toasted the ceiling with omnipotent madness, thrusting his glass in a ridiculously overstated gesture that slopped Bull Roar and wine onto his Spotted Owl and baby sealskin ottoman. Another sacramental double standard. Just like his indefinite pollution exemption and carbon nullification status and his second favorite immunity of all, his virtual murder punch card, good for 130-dozen, flesh and blood virtual homicides without arrest or prosecution. He still had four dozen left and was saving them for boredom or necessity of purpose, whichever came first.

One vice led to the next and the next and the next, sometimes. Life and death without limits and without walls, as the supers so frequently said. So unlike the undercitizens of the construct, who even in the digital confines of the virtual realm, could earn access to the pleasures and necessities of life and even life itself, only through their absolute obedience and ideological conformity to the supers. Even after their enforced upload into the digital construct and the destruction of their mortal shells, pleasure credits and virtual lifespan tokens were awarded based on ideological purity of their political thoughts and the demonstrated depravity of their lustful thoughts, which were juxtaposed into a composite social compatibility score that determined the quality of their virtual lives. Controlling through both subjugation and pleasurable distraction was seen as an evolutionary imperative, to incorporate characteristics into the virtual construct that it was felt would make a more stable and easily managed society. And the hornier the better. Human companionship, existence and qualification reduced to a single number. And for Lord Zucker-Creator, who had maintained dual citizenship inside the virtual construct, while still retaining his organic, physical shell on good old Terra Firma, only the highest-scoring virtual missies needed apply.

"What could be finer than an eight or a niner?" Zucker exclaimed, repeating one of the pieces of information warfare that had been used to wear down public resistance to what had been a primary opposition to the final transition to the virtual construct. People were concerned that the unfettered and libertine dimensions of the fully artificial realm would have very real and very obvious implications regarding certain activities and proclivities. Sex with children would be possible, probable and unstoppable. Zucker himself didn't go in for that sort of thing and had suggested a programming nuance that would age every assimilated human to the age of adult sexual consent. Eighteen. What followed was a protracted and insouciant outcry and outrage from the supers, who as a population Zucker realized were disproportionately represented among the ranks of those who prefer pedophilia and the debauchery of destroyed innocence to vanilla sex between consenting adults. Grand Overlord Hilda Klarton and her lecherous husband and creepy campaign manager had privately been among the most vocal opponents to the automatic maturity feature. They wouldn't hear of it, they said. What was the point of having a virtual construct, if their beloved "Pizza Parties," and "Special Toppings" and trips to Pedophile Island weren't at least approximated in the rendering of that virtual world? Life would be dull and unfulfilled, ever after, they said. And thousands of the supers agreed. Having the ability to track, catalog and peruse the online tendencies of any human being that became ensnared in his social networking webwork, none of their deviances or individual peccadilloes came as a surprise. But it was the boldness of it. The shameless and dauntless boldness of their need of that sort of vampirism of the soul that had been a true elucidative moment for Zucker. But what then do you say to the woman willing to kill, dismember and bury dozens of living, breathing people and indeed, lay waste to the democratic will of an entire nation in her unstoppable pursuit of the Presidency of the United States?

"The last President and Empress of Atlantia, Miss Hilda Klarton, may Lucifer rest her ugly soul," Zucker said, becoming drunker with each solitary toast in the now darkening surrounds of his suite. Hilda had been there and had been the driving force all those years ago, as the last real threat to their hegemony of plan and purpose had been turned aside, just a few years before global consolidation under Overlord Ojamba. A man by the name of Trumpkin had waged a populist campaign in the last free election in Zucker's own former and very unruly United States, winning that historic and improbable election against then-Lady Klarton, who was, even then, a perpetually miserable battle axe of a candidate who suffered from innumerable physical ills and was a mental incompetent and sexual deviant besides, with a penchant for embarrassingly awkward attempts at secrecy and intrigue that invariably blew up in her haggard face. As Zucker remembered and had bravely assisted, every advantage had been borrowed and stolen for Hilda's demanded run for office and still it had not been enough.

In the crude beginnings of his LifeSpace platform, Zucker had hidden and censored and buried negative press reports about Klarton all of which were true, while placing every shred of sensationalized Trumpkin scandal and falsified character dross front and center for every user. On the television, controlled networks did same, blasting anti-Trumpkin thought messages and Hilda-approved news scripts from every outlet in a psychological deluge it was believed would greatly minimize the need for election fraud that the leftist supers always employed to ensure victory.

Thanks to mountains of false polling data showing that she had an insurmountable lead, she would only have to steal a few million votes to gain election, it was said. But none of it had been enough for the miserable old crone. The unbearable witch had still managed to lose the campaign outright, forcing the supers to convene an especially extraordinary effort of stealing the election result by way of the antiquated Electoral College, unseating President-elect Trumpkin just a few days before he had opportunity to take office and begin revealing and dismantling the full extent of their global plan. In that same year, a conspicuous wave of celebrity deaths and suicides and disappearances threatened to disclose the Final Objective before it was even perfected and unveiled to the public. A disproportionate number of voluntary preemptive uploads by rock stars and movie stars and famed authors left their publicists and the blessed illuminati minions scrambling to cover their tracks with stories of illnesses and heart attacks and plane crashes as has-been members of A-list royalty decided it preferable to live eternally in the digitally preserved and reconstructed era of their cultural zenith, rather than fading gracefully into whatever awaited them beyond the uncertainty and moderation of middle age.

The odd confluence in celebrity demise reached a ridiculous apex when a diminutive purple rock legend, an Oklahoma rockabilly genius and an androgynous British glam-rocker self-uploaded within days of one another, leaving behind a talent void that was so noticeable that it overtook conversations on LifeSpace and spurred conspiratorial questions that blossomed into full-blown investigations by members of the uncontrolled media. A journalist from Nebraska and a radio host and blogger from Texas had to be snuffed out just to keep the true nature of the project from coming to light a full decade ahead of schedule.

The year 2016 was at once, the greatest triumph and the great crisis moment of the antihuman movement, Zucker recalled. Lords Brzezinskow and Kissinler and Gorbachez and Ladies Ope-Ra and Pelosski had called Zucker in succession, treating him to ranting tirades of blame and ignominy, asking why he had allowed unsanctioned outlets of journalism to dig so deeply into the plans of the construct and even more glaringly, to trumpet the shortcomings and political reality of Hilda Klarton across the LifeSpace, as if any of it could have stayed hidden from anyone. Zucker had endured their unpleasantness as best as might be expected of the richest man in the world and had promptly complied, allowing an old woman and her cat to become chief arbiters of what was approved and true thought and what should be termed, "Fake News," and censored out of existence.

"Good old Mrs. Snoppies," Zucker toasted again, remembering what had become one of the most unlikely and ridiculous examples of manufactured credibility and self-appointed authority in political history.

"An old cat lady, the designated and blessed oracle of truth and deception for all of the virtual construct. Ridiculous and ridiculously effective."

Just then, the LifeScript narration module in Zucker's suite crackled to life with the dulcet tones of his chosen female narration bot.

"Lord Zucker. One hour until final upload. One hour until final upload."

The audio link switched off, leaving Zucker again in the silent solitude of his highly priced executive flat. He'd been given triple the normal 500 square feet of livable space as further evidencing of his preeminence and importance to the cleansing and salvation of the planet from the human scourge. One last hour to recount the memories of his earthly distinction and to ponder at the final goodbye that he'd always known would come. Holding his third or fourth wine and Bull Roar spritzer in a sweating right hand, Zucker rose from his repose and walked to the sliding glass door on the 483rd floor of the LifeSpace executive monolith. He looked out over the barren moonscape of a collapsed desert waste that had once been Cupertino, California. He could see the abandoned freeways with their cracked pavement and vegetative overgrowth, like the clogging arteries of an aging body, now devoid of blood. There were no cars and no people and in the final gathering twilight of the day, empty buildings and empty windows, without a single light. A metropolis of human innovation and consumption and excess that had served as the infant cradle for the advent of artificial intelligence, now abandoned, empty and quiet as a museum to the death of human knowledge and the species of men.

As a young man, Zucker remembered the vitality and rushed euphoria of their brilliance and hubris. Intoxicated in the silicon moments of discovery that enabled first baby steps and then running leaps of the digital experience, until finally, all the nuance and personalized sensation of any human life could be contained in a few hundred terabytes of digital code on a single diamond chip. The Master Chip, they had called it. The formula for final assimilation had been simple and inescapably direct. Under Hilda Klarton's famous Directive 21 and at the behest of Supreme Overlord Ojamba, all undercitizens whose carbon footprint exceeded their annual income were slated for the first wave of immediate transferal to the virtual construct. Subsequent waves were of thought dissidents and the mentally and physically infirm, against their consent.

And finally, the general population, suitably sold on the genius of the solution to all of mankind's imperfections and unhappiness and scarcity of resource. With the persistence of bombarded sleep messaging over smart phones and pocket computer devices already in saturation, convincing humans to trade their carbon-based earth bodies for the perfection of their virtual selves had been shockingly simple. After years of convincing both men and women that their bodies were flawed and ugly and in need of constant alteration, repair, surgical enhancement, supplementation and genetic revision, convincing them to forego the endless hassles of maintaining a carbon shell was nothing more than the logical last step of an image-obsessed human culture. Suicides halted altogether as the overweight and underdeveloped and unattractive and lonely became the first of the desperate and voluntary customers.

Final patches of the organic resistance were found among Christian believers and those of other faiths who believed such an act to be a desecration of the divine body given to them by the Creator. With the hedonists and nymphomaniacs and addicts of every substance or experience of humanity already easily convinced and cataloged, overcoming the objections of these most devout practitioners of faith became a task given to megachurches and televangelists, who painstakingly convinced the universalist cloud of witnesses that according to their interpretation of prophetic scripture, the virtual construct was indeed, New Heaven, Shangri La, Nirvana, Paradise, or whatever name of corresponding afterlife silliness was suitably needed. Followers of Mohammedan Islam were told that every Muslim believer would be uploaded to a construct containing not seventy-two, but 72,000 virgins of their choosing. Followers of Shinto Buddhism and Confucianism were shown virtual clips of their waving ancestors and deceased loved ones, beckoning them from inside the construct. Christians were shown a cerebral brainwave of a gold-paved and ethereal palace of splendid white clouds and angelic chorus, with bearded figures of saints and martyrs and loved ones welcoming them onward and upward to their mansions in gloryland. Heaven it must be and so, heaven it became.

Even the nature of the newest programming technology lent itself perfectly to the grand deception of the age. Diamond microchips, artificially composed of the steam-compressed carbon ashes of the dearly departed and cremated were used to house the personality, memories and consciousness of each new upload, carefully inserted into waiting notches in the master mainframe, the solar-fusion powered monstrosity occupying two-hundred and thirty stories of space directly beneath Lord Zucker's palatial abode.

"Become a forever diamond." The marketing slogan had implored, with help from Zales, Jared's, DeBeers and the dozen or so best known marketers of precious stones that had gone nearly bankrupt as the increasingly outmoded practices of monogamy and marriage took their toll.

"Find your shining place in the starry sky of A.I." Those old-fashioned couples who clung bitterly to the primitive notion of mating for life, used the occasion of a double upload to cement their partnership for all time and eternity, ensuring they would indeed inhabit the same plane of the virtual construct for uninterrupted eons, without death to even part them. Romantic rubbish to be sure, but it had worked like a charm. With seven wives and seven divorces to his credit, including three of the five most expensive in history, Zucker found that particular prospect one of the more terrifying to be contemplated. Being incarcerated, digitally or otherwise, with any of his ex-wives would have left him looking for some backdoor hacker's trick to remove his own microchip from the motherboard and blink out of existence voluntarily. Goodbye, cruel, cruel construct. Or maybe, something better. Maybe a death befitting the creator, himself.

"Lord Zucker. Ten minutes to final upload. Ten minutes to final upload."

The LifeSpace anointed talky again, filling his ears with the imperative and impending approach of his own assimilation, diamond crematory microchip and all. The last of all the last and final goodbyes in a now completed singularity of an erased humanity. All of the rushing millennia of creation and ascension put to rest in the past twenty years. And now, just time for one last cocktail. The Google-Uber enforcer-bots would be here soon enough to escort him to the upload portal. He hoped he could make the journey with dignity. His mind still floating with the flotsam of the timeline that bore his inexorable John Hancock right across the bottom line, Zucker walked to his liquor cabinet. He removed a few small bottles of clear liquor from the bottom row and then almost as afterthought, a smaller grayish vial filled with some unidentifiable silver-gray goo. In a crystalline tumbler, Lord Zucker, encoder and swallower of a human race, emptied two minibar bottles of vodka before opening and adding the gray metallic liquid to his glass. He stirred the mercurial globs absently with two cubes of nitro-genic ice and his fingers before draining the thermometer-tinsel-slurry down his gullet. It tasted of old pennies and carried the faint electrical tingle of touching one's tongue to the terminals of a small battery. Within a minute, his spastic and trembling body gave way as he careened to the floor of his executive suite, in haphazard, twitching repose.

"Ohmigosssh, Lord Zucker!!"

"What happened, Lord Zucker?"

"What happened, Lord Zucker?"

"Are you alright, Lord Zucker?"

"Can we help you, Lord Zucker?"

"Do you require assistance, Lord Zucker?"

But there would be no reply, not even for the singsong Strawberry twins left only to amuse and console themselves with their fully articulating limbs and symmetrical perfection.

⚬══⚬ ⚬══⚬

At precisely 9:14 P.M. Global Pacific Time, 21 June, Year 2046, exactly seven minutes after Lord Zucker's still cooling diamond chip was robotically delivered to the blinking and endless menagerie of the LifeSpace server facility. And exactly three minutes after said chip was snapped deftly into the waiting and designated port of the LifeSpace server unit. And exactly 27-picoseconds after powered chip gave living birth to a roiling, teeming litter of the newly minted and nano-sized masters of the planet, any human eye yet remaining at suitably safe distance would have glimpsed on the horizon a joining of earth and sea to sky in a blinding column of orange and then dimming light. Seconds later, like a poppy flower bursting forth generations and fields of new life, the silver-gray spores and seeds of the nanobot-Zuckerites danced and wafted in the traveling metallic breezes of a new earth, scattered and settled and planted in the fading and final sunset of a swiftly passing age.

WOODEN HEART

Her name was Adelaide Almirante, and from the first moment he beheld her, soaring high above circus crowd inside the musty big top pitched nightly at whistle-stop towns along the main rail line, his heart was her willing slave. But for Simon Alexander, whose only dance partner was the stinking muck broom he used to sweep the fresh dung of the performing animals, she was an impossible ephemeral dream and source of continual longing and interminable desperation. With lithesome grace the envy of angels and an assemblage of curves and aphrodisiac glory that would make a vixen blush, Adelaide's list of male admirers and aspiring gentleman attendees was the stuff of gossip and legend and whispered envious women and jealous wives in every town where the circus train and ballooning tent came to rest.

She was perfect vision of feminine delights, aromatic and delectable and overpowering in all the ways that

Simon was stained and sullied and stinking and pitiable, cast down as he was to a task every bit as deplorable as the filthy dungarees and crusted shoes that he wore to complete it. For what at all can be politely said of a man whose practiced familiarity and informed preferences for the kinds of animal excrement a circus produces allows him to expertly identify the distinct dietary predilections of primates and equines and elephants, lions, tigers and giraffes? The sideways avoidance and held noses of silent strangers was answer enough, leaving Simon only to return their silence with his own, becoming shrunken, skulking and unseen, invisible and unheard, speaking so rarely and in such hushed mumbles that for several months after joining the troupe, people had believed him a deaf mute or a simpleton or a hunched moron, incapable of conversation or of anything besides the rhythmic thrusts of his advancing broom against the mounds of filth.

In the humble shame of his avocation, Simon himself knew better than the folly of his frequent gazes heavenward toward the celestial form of the trapeze artist in the glittering costume, but his eyes and his longing heart could not be denied. Every afternoon and evening, he watched from side stage shadow as she transfixed hushed audience with a whirling vision of miraculous beauty that made steady gaze as intolerable and tearful as the noonday sun. And still, he could not look away, any more than he could halt the pulsing gallop of his heart whenever she was within sight. She was Ambrosia on two willow branches of long and callipygian leg.

"Laaaay-ddeeees and Gentil-menn, Adelaide Almirante, the mistress of the air."

The ringmaster's stretched and mellifluous baritone gave dramatic entrance to the surpassingly dramatic spectacle that was Adelaide's transcendent beauty in motion. Swinging, swinging, flying, leaping, floating and swirling from catch to catch and bar to bar with gravitational defiance so breathtaking and impossibly contrived as to leave spectators as overwhelmed by her mastery as they were overcome by the rapturous divinity of her physical form, the full milieu of which was frequently too much for men to behold without spontaneous expressions of overeager applause and catcall and often lewd and lurid suggestion.

For Simon, hearing the open and often obscene adulation of coarsened tongues directed at the object of his purest affections was an agony too deep to endure. The whistles and words and cackling lasciviousness pierced his soul and bloodied his heart and sometimes, in the bunked darkness of the crowded sleep wagon, wet his cheeks with the sullen barbarism of those leering and ugly jackals who wanted nothing more than to defile and consume for themselves what he so desperately wished to enshrine and protect for all time.

In private moments of splendid dream and daydream, he imagined himself as Adelaide's suitor, or husband, or beau, escorting her regally to her nightly spotlight and then away again, after her triumphant spell had once more been cast like sorcerer's magic on the window of the waiting world. He imagined the warmth of her graceful arm encircling his own and her delectable bosom heaving with breathless exhaustion and delight as she waved farewell to admiring supplicants and grotesque leering miscreants alike, retreating to backstage solace and perhaps a grateful goodnight smile for her adoring and faithful liege. A bolder, more heeled man doubtless would have indulged imagination for a kiss or even more, but Simon's adoration was so sublime and pure he would never allow such transgression or imposition of common lust. In Adelaide's honor, his mind became separated from natural hungers like a curtained stage, beyond which he dared not look, unless and until his heart was granted entrance, lest he suffer blindness of soul and calloused hands. He knew it an impossible dream and still he could not relent nor retreat. And so there came a plan. An improbable plan that began as a block of wood and a Sunday dessert of Key Lime pie.

He'd stumbled upon it at a stop at a roadside diner in a dusty town called Wilsonville. Among all the hundreds of towns in half a dozen years, Simon remembered it precisely because of a giant red rooster atop the restaurant where he and the backstage help had been relegated for a midday meal. After a Reuben sandwich and french fries and two bottles of Nesbitt's strawberry soda, Simon had emptied his pockets at the register and ignored the indignant sniffs and stares and grumbles from those unaccustomed to his grungy attire.

His hands and face were always clean at mealtime and his dark and wavy hair neatly slicked and combed, a fastidious affectation that he supposed was futile compensation for the knowledge of shoes so hideous that every restaurant on the tour gladly made exception to policy and allowed him to dine barefoot, or in his cleanest pair of wrinkled socks that he tried to scrunch and conceal under tables. It was embarrassment he'd learned to ignore, even as he'd learned to eat his meals quickly inside, or even outside, if disapproving patrons with wrinkled noses proved too persistent for management to afford. It had happened just that way on a Sunday in June at the Red Rooster Cafe in Wilsonville, forcing Simon to return to the dusty parking lot to kick rocks and stare at the giant red chicken that was taller than a circus giraffe. A jostling fat woman in a robin's egg dress several tables away had made severe spectacle of Simon's appearance, leaving a polite and pretty waitress named Mabel no choice but to direct Simon outside with apologies and extra napkins and a second bottle of strawberry soda for his troubles. Kind soul that she was, Mabel had even thrown in a slice of Key Lime pie for dessert, paid for by her own tips and a winking smile, after catching Simon staring intently through her at the whirling lighted display case that was the talk of four counties.

He'd scarfed his meal with practiced speed, savored his pie in eleven bites and was enjoying a few wasted moments without a broom in his hands when he'd spotted it just off the edge of the road: A twisted chunk of solid butternut wood twice as big as his fist. It gleamed in the June sun with a deep and flowing grain that seemed to catch flame without burning, partially hidden by a patch of wild oats but still alive and resonant with a reddish blaze of Jehovah's fire. The moment he saw it, Simon had retrieved a patch of waxed paper that had contained his french fries and with trembling hands had wrapped the chunk of wood in it, both to add some oil to the grain to protect it from moisture and to spare it from absorbing the smell of his trousers as it traveled concealed in his grungy front pocket. He'd learned to whittle as a boy on his grandfather's knee and knew varieties of wood on sight, both for their visual appeal and for ease of workmanship. He knew butternut was softer than cottonwood and more forgiving even than basswood for fashioning shapes and meticulous lines and detail. When carved and finished and hand-rubbed with a cloth of linseed or even mineral oil, it had the look of pink gold, suited perfectly to the only shape that Simon had envisioned when he first glimpsed the now secreted treasure in his dung-laden trousers.

⊷ ⊶

It had taken Simon seven weeks of skipped lunches to pilfer away enough of his meager wage to buy a penknife befitting the task. Seven weeks of swept piles of stinking manure and sodden clothes and invisible stares and loathing of ticket holders and children with hands sticky with cotton candy or yellow with popcorn grease. Seven weeks of attending the cages and rolling prisons for the animals people paid their Sunday tithe to see, up close. On most days, Simon's monotonous hours were spent cleaning and spraying the empty railcars while the four-legged performers were earning their flea-bitten keep inside the billowing red and yellow and orange circus tent. As he crouched and hunched his angular frame to enter the dripping cages, Simon grew to understand the misery and imprisonment of sad beasts, once wild and free, now impressed to servitude in the carnival spectacle of performance and punishment and rotten meat. It was a nightly task for animal trainers and stagehands to visit a nearby market or restaurant and scour garbage cans and refuse piles for discarded scraps and stinking cutlets of hog and chicken and cow and to carry their bleeding carrion back to the rasping leviathan of the circus train preparing for departure.

Nine cars of the jostling calliope of red and yellow and blue freighters contained the animals with one of three from the end where Simon's attention was most frequently drawn. It belonged to an aging but still ferocious specimen of an African lion, tattered in places but still drawn of remarkable musculature and velvet coat and an assortment of huge and blinding white teeth as deadly as the day they sprouted in its humid and ever ravenous mouth. Churning rattles of deep bassoon emanated from the lion's vibrating jowls when it growled. To Simon, they sounded like the plaintiff but still defiant protests of his own stifled mumble. A captive kingly beast of foundering spirit still daring to reach and touch the air in squelched mourning for lost freedom, lost love, or lost dominion and reign. Watching the trainers jab and goad the mighty beast while it was chained and dragged to nightly ovation made Simon wish to pull the pinion from the gate clasp and let it run free and wild into the beckoning darkness.

With even greater temptation and delight, he imagined the regal machine of tooth and claw set loose against the constant mob of lecherous leering fools who sullied his flying Adelaide on every occasion with their taunts and brazen gazes of lust and rapacious, drooling dross. He could see the animal charging and leaping and covering their hideousness with its bulk, tearing and chewing and scratching and silencing their throats with slashings of blood and swallowed agonizing gurgles of surrendered life. At times the vision was so strong and so rich in his mind's eye that he believed it to be real. Watching Adelaide's hip-tilting and tantalizing walk and climb to and from her appointed perch, the pelted obscenities of the male gallery filled him with a boiling rage that wrapped the vision with fantastic wishings for giant jungle cat and tenderfooted buffoon to make frantic and deadly acquaintance of fang and flesh. How he wished for it to be! How he longed to see their smug and impertinent faces torn apart and buried in the darkness of his obstinate and jealous and languishing heart. Still, he could not bring his hand to cause the deed.

And so, both stinking wretch of a man and ferocious jungle cat remained resigned and entombed in their mutual rolling prison of circus life. Seeing the lion and the other carnivorous beasts pacing torment and emaciating frames, Simon had the feeling of watching his own starving diminution along the same iron road of endless stops, eating his pay down to the nub and watching his own sagging dungarees give way to threads in his daily wrestle with varieties of foulness so ripe and pungent as to make an undertaker wretch.

Over days and weeks and months, the two pleasures of his life aside from eating were contained in the twice daily performances of his darling Adelaide. He timed his completion of scouring the animal cars perfectly each day to allow furtive entrance to the main tent just in time for the ringmaster's familiar drumroll and call and trumpet blast, heralding her angelic arrival from high above the ring. For a handful of moments he was a visitor to Shangri La, marveling at her natural ease and grace on the swinging bar and her defiance of gravity as she took to the air and flew like a free and beautiful bird of the most elegant plumage his eyes and heart would ever know. And in the evenings before settling in to the jostling bunks of the sleeper car, Simon would unwrap his hidden treasure, and keeping Adelaide's perfect aerial vision alive and ablaze in his mind, like a dancing spot of lingering glare from staring too long at the sun, his work would begin.

As his worn and weary hands attended to penknife and butternut, Simon let the blazing sunspot of her beauty envelop his visage of the wood pressed carefully and warmly between practiced fingers. With cautious slowness of a man holding dynamite, he carved and chiseled, removing smooth strands of curling grain from the soft piece, working it down and down and around, bending it to the vision in his mind of the artful angel of the trapeze and emerging curvature of the place she firmly resided within his very being. Steadily, the rounding hips and corners of a pink Valentine's heart took shape, with symmetrical precision matching the hiplines and deeply clefted backside and tapered waistline of his resplendent Adelaide. At points, the similarities and righteous femininity of the splendid roundness in his hands caused Simon to blush and smile, piercing through the prurient veil in his mind that had prevented any imaginings of her in *that* way. With each passing stroke of the knife, the smoothness and tactile nuance of his craftsmanship became loving repast and a workman's caressing adoration of his muse. The heart in his hands was his. But made real in her molten image of carnal fire. It was them, joined together in the curvature and matchless splendor of her soaring, immaculate form. And soon she would hold it in her own hands, wrapped within his.

And she would know.

⊙═⊷ ⊶═⊙

Simon finished the butternut heart on a September Thursday, carving A.A. and A.S. in scrolled letters across its center and lovingly burnishing the brandished jewel to a high sheen with borrowed linseed oil and a can of discarded lane varnish from the back alley of a bowling hall they had passed on one of their stops. When it had been dried and rubbed and buffed to gleaming completion, he wrapped the gift in a swatch of muslin cloth that was used to polish the brass fixtures of handles and hardware that festooned the show's center ring. Two weeks later after three failed attempts of lost nerve, he decided on an approaching Friday night after late performance to either make his crusade, or that very night, to throw himself and the perfect rendering of his affections headlong from the speeding trundle of the sleeper car into the awaiting banishment of darkness and death. On contemplation, he found either eventuality a welcome relief to the daily tonnage of endless stench and slime and the pelting torment of his silent longing for Adelaide to know the contents both of his pocket and of his swollen and suffering heart.

When the day arrived, with quickened and trembling hands he made his way through the filth of his work, shortening rapid broom strokes and rushing madly through the cleansing ritual from cage to cage. The afternoon sweat of his effort mingled with that of his hammering nerves which sent him frequently to a patch of outdoor latrine to calm his overactive kidneys and bladder. Each time, scurrying back to complete his chores in compressed time allowing for what he hoped would be an early finish and a chance to clean and polish himself to a presentable state prior to Adelaide's final performance of the night. And finish he did, removing the final specks and flecks of waste from the last car of the day with fully an hour to spare and then traipsing from car to car to car at the conclusion of the night's animal performance to help deliver each captive occupant to their confinement.

In a final flurry, Simon performed the ritual with the hackneyed ballet of rote detail. Gates clanked and closed. Latches latched. And checked. And away he ran. Already tugging buttons and belt from his stiffly soiled work clothes, he flew on springing feet back to the bunk car and a waiting washbasin with soap and comb. Reaching under his Spartan bunk, Simon retrieved a blanketed bundle that had for two months concealed the purchase of his wages for an entire summer, now past. Unrolling the woolen sheaf revealed a brand new pair of black shoes, mirrored and shining with matching belt, a crisp white shirt with pearl buttons and sharply pointed collar. And marvel of unsoiled marvels, an unworn pair of vivid-blue denim jeans, still smelling of the indigo dye of Levi Strauss and Company and still smartly creased from a Woolworth's shelf.

Like a demon of remedial hygiene, Simon stripped and scrubbed and scrubbed and rinsed. He combed his hair with a touch of fixative wax, imparting a curling wave to the fine blackness of it. Finally, after stepping into his new costume of cleanliness and pristine cloth, he pulled the familiar muslin bundle from his work pants and plunged it into the right front pocket of his new denim where it bulged and waited. After a deep breath of realized preparation, Simon could hear the distant call of the big top master of ceremonies beginning his baritone windup for Adelaide's announcement and always stunning entrance. Simon strained himself against a nervous shaking of the moment and took brittle steps out of the train car and into the evening air.

He had entered the blasting cacophony of the big top world just in time to see Adelaide's ascent into the heavens. Flexing barefoot and climbing the impossible slenderness of the cable ladder high into the rigging, her pointed toes and dramatic flourishes of hand and arm drew inhalations of awe and wonderment from Simon and from the entire crowd of transfixed audience. Her golden sequins and black lace barely constrained the uncharted miracles of her feminine flesh, visibly threatening to burst forth from the straining architecture of costume with her every movement and devouring the expectant and upturned eyes of attentive dreamers in the seats below and beyond.

With incessant perfection of practiced routine, Adelaide completed her sequenced mastery with usual flawless aplomb, gathering the thunderous ovation of her worshipping public both from the small parapet of platform high in the air and again and as she bowed and bowed and bowed after descending from heaven to earth with pert derriere and elegant leg marking every bouncing step before a scorching and nimble retreat from the ensconced glare of the spotlight that was followed by every eye in the house. With predetermined timing of restraint, Simon watched her go and waited and waited for what seemed like seconds turned to stone, knowing the exact distance to her predestined dressing car at the end of the train and the necessary margin needed to encounter her just as she reached it but before she climbed the steps and disappeared into her private sanctuary, a place for a brief but still polite moment that his gentleman's mind had scripted and retraced and reenacted a thousand-thousand times before tonight. As the eclipsed seconds transpired and went, Simon began his walking pursuit, his right hand tracing the bulging outline in his jeans pocket. The place where his telltale heart pulsed and pounded and throbbed with every step.

⊂═►◄═⊃

Simon had only barely breached the tent flap exit when he heard the yells and curdling female screams from the back of the train.

> *The lion is loose!!*
> *THE LION IS LOOSE!!*
> *For the love of Gawddd!!*
> *Somebody help!!*
> *Helllp!! HELLP!!*

In an instant he broke into a desperate sprint, weaving through streams of panicked faces running in the opposite direction across the field and away from the snarling horror, already somehow knowing exactly what his eyes would encounter when he arrived to the pooling dimness of window light from inside the dressing car that was the only illumination to be found along the rails where the screeching and deadly struggle was in full contest. Surrounded by a handful of stagehands and two lunging and retreating trainers with their whip-poles extended in futile and jerking desperation, stood the lion, free at last and with a mouthful of meat. For there, clasped within its horrible jaws was the unmistakable and delicate golden form of sweet Adelaide, her languid body a dampening rag doll morsel of pitiful helplessness, caught firmly as she was by upper left thigh and right arm as the cornered cat looked to and fro for an escape to enjoy the freshest and sweetest quarry of its captive life.

On massive padded feet, the big cat circled and whirled in a cornered death dance of vengeance, with tiny Adelaide still shrieking and flailing like a plaything in the lion's clenching and razoring jaws. Circles of crimson now spread and stood out against her tender ivory flesh, easily visible even in the encroaching dimness of the night. And still no one moved. Not daring to approach the same deadly fate that now seemed assured for the miraculous trapeze artist of circus renown and unsurpassed beauty. As his desperate dash brought him into and through a secondary circle of brave onlookers upon his arrival to the grisly scene, Simon could hear the muttered questions and shocked incredulity of their gasping dismay.

>*But how did it.....?*
>*Who let it out?? How could it possibly be???*
>*Someone get a rifle!!!*
>*Had someone forgotten to lock the cage.....?*

But Simon knew there would be no time for guns. The rifles were at the head of the train, in a car directly behind the engine and tender where they were kept locked away for safekeeping.

>*Had someone forgotten to....*

The last question from the crowd had only barely entered his burning mind when, with suicidal deliberation, Simon broke from the ranks of gobsmacked rubbernecks and hesitating circus hands and ran at the savage beast, abandoning all sanity or care for his own safety, until he was within arm's reach of the animal and the whimpering prey clamped hideously in its merciless mouth. After searching madly and finding nothing to suffice, Simon considered for an instant before deciding upon the only thing time would allow.

Reaching into front jeans pocket, he retrieved and unwrapped the butternut heart and with unmitigated strength and grievous fury, drove darting fist and rounded object like a burnished wedge, jamming it firmly between the crushing teeth at the very hinge of the lion's gnashing and gaping jaw. And there it stuck for a moment and scraped and splintered behind massive grinding teeth before holding fast and finally halting the animal's deathly vice of blood and foaming spit.

With Adelaide's shattered and crimson-stained limbs and hands finally dragged away and free from the beast's killing grip, trainers looped their strangling cable snares around the lion's neck and drove the beast with desperate might and levered poles, up the side ramp and into the cage where they slammed and at last, fastened the forgotten door. Through the bars, Simon's swiveling gaze ripped between the broken flying angel on the bloody ground being rushed away in desperate rescue and the seething demon cat that had torn her so deeply and to the brink of death. As he watched, Simon realized only at the moment it happened, even as his precious Adealaide was scooped up and torn away, from inside the prison bars came a final splitting snap and a dislodged swallow, the lion's gulping confiscation of the splintered butternut heart and the work of human hands, now deep within the churning entrails of the damnable beast.

And so, in the weeks and months that came, with splintered mind and heart, he set about perfecting his love for her, even in her grieving absence of miracle convalescence, as if carving a brand new wooden heart that she might never see, nor touch, nor hold, but no matter. For he would know again of the smoothness of it and the hours of painstaking strokes and splinters that his hands endured and the sweat and strain of eyes and fingers, if only to make of himself a thing she could finally hold in her own crumpled and bandaged hands without being further scratched or cut or torn. How he hoped and dreamed and earnestly prayed for it to be true, just as it was true that more of anything or anyone other than her would forever be less of everything. And that would mean the end of his world. But even if she never knew of it, or ever again took his heart and warmed it unto herself, he would know what had been given and what was contained in the roundness and smoothness of the work. And that knowing would be his final and perfect gift in tribute to a great love offered and spent, once given and swallowed and turned away. A round and perfect wooden heart to hold unto himself, until such day as he felt his own heart of flesh and fire, alive and beating again in his chest, awaiting the blessed warmth and hope of Adelaide's return.

WHEN TOM CAME HOME

M aisie Adams bent up from her daffodil bed at the
sound of crunching steps at the end of the long
gravel drive and rubbed her eyes. *Could it be? Was it him?
Was it really him? But I thought... But it is! He is! He's here!*
In a rush of crinoline and honey curls, Maisie scrambled
to her feet and ran to him, her dainty booted steps leaving
a Morse code of miniature dust clouds behind. After three
years away at war, her husband Tom swept his young wife
into his arms in a laughing, joyous pirouette.

"Oh, Tom! Oh, OH!! Tom! Tom!" Over and over and
over she said his name as they kissed. The name she had
barely allowed herself to breathe since his departure for
the front, and had barely allowed herself to think since his
letters, once so faithfully delivered to the rusting country
mailbox had stopped, almost a year ago.

"Oh, Tom! Let me look at you! You look so handsome in
your uniform! Even nicer than in your picture! And you're

here! You're home! Home at last!" Maisie stroked and preened at the soft blue felt and fidgeted with the gleaming brass buttons, sparkling with starfire. Hot streaks of tears were drying now on her fresh beaming face, still smudged with dirt from her gardening. Her husband pulled her firm, slim form tightly to him again and spoke wonderful words in her ear.

"And you, Maisie, my darling! You are more beautiful than in my dreams."

Like all wives in time of war, the specter of separation and loss, and the fitful nightmares of death had visited her in the empty farmhouse, pulling at her mind like a thread from a raveling sweater. In her sleep and in the noonday sun, she saw her husband's face on the bodies of a thousand dead and dying men. Reports on the telescreen showed the uprising had gained an early advantage, sending thousands of Central Militia soldiers back to their families in the shining metal tubes reserved for heroes of the cause. *But no one around here. Not since poor Esther Beasley,* Maisie had thought. Joseph Beasley had been the first man from the plains sector to be killed and the only one from the small town nearest the Adams' farm.

Since the early days of the fighting, Maisie could not recall a single woman made to weep the bitter unspeakable tears of a husband's death, and there were plenty in line. Chastity Parker. Mildred McLuen. Tess Hunt. Mary Franzen. Hilary Stampe. Five friends from Maisie's quilting guild with men off at war. Five husbands that had returned, one by one, safe and sound. *The tide had certainly turned quickly. And thank Jehoshaphat, for that! The uprising is finished! The uprising is finished!*

Maisie had heard the exultant news on the telescreen some weeks earlier, met with a cacophony of shouts and praise for the Central Militia and for the leader, himself. The war was over, they said, and the rousers of the uprising captured, and now her beloved Tom had returned, even after the long months of wondering when his letters dwindled and ran out, making her fear the very worst.

"Tom, your letters," Maisie began, still clinging to Tom's side as the walked together up the dusty gravel drive to their home.

"Why didn't you keep on with your writing? You made me worry deep in my bones when they stopped. I thought I had lost you."

Tom did not look at her. He chuckled a light flutter of air and tightened his hold across her shoulders as they walked.

"There was no need to worry, Maisie," Tom replied.

"There was no way you could lose me. Honest truth."

She was weeping again. The happy-sad tears of relief, still unable to believe that she and her handsome, strong husband were together again, to live and breathe and love in all the ways that filled their hearts with wonder and light.

"War or no war, there was no way I was ever going to let something get between us, my love," Tom said. "Not no way, not no how!"

And with that, the pair had reached the neatly painted plank steps of their front porch. Tom swept up his reclaimed bride and mustering his strength, covered the six board steps in two strides, flung open the screen door and the pair disappeared into the cool waiting darkness.

The coming days were a whirlwind of remembered delights, of moments both large and small when Maisie would find herself overcome by the sheer wonderment of having the only man she had ever loved with her again. He had arrived just as planting season was underway, and busied himself in their clean, bare fields, turning earth with tractor and plow, and scattering seed. The barn needed painting and the fences mending, too, but besides the urgent work in the fields, Tom's every spare moment was spent with his bride. They talked into the early hours before sunrise. They ate their lunch on a crisp checkered cloth beside the mumbling brook that cut their farmstead in two. After their evening meal, Tom would take down his forgotten harmonica and send lonesome mellow tones into the night air as the two sat close and warm in the front screen-porch of the farmhouse.

Life was life again, and Maisie's heart was full from familiar, predictable rhythm of it all. She often talked and marveled at her good fortune to friends and neighbors still curious about Tom's return. Grocery days in town she would bump into this friend or that, and relate her newest astonishment and happiness while filling her cart with Tom's favorite foods for the week to come. Last time it had been Mary Franzen alongside, with news that three more husbands from the quilting guild had arrived home without a scratch. *Wasn't it wonderful! How blessed we all are!*

Mary's own husband, Frank had been home now for almost a year, and was doing splendidly well. He seemed to have adjusted perfectly to his return to civilian life, Mary said, and had never once complained about the experiences of war, or the terror that flashed on their telescreen every night for months after his return. *In fact, he seems happier and more at peace than he was before he left. Isn't that marvelous?* Mary's face was smiling then, but Maisie would think afterward there had been a hint of something unspoken in the eyes that never met her own.

The war had ended now, and with it the bombastic imagery of the Central Militia in their glorious defeat of the uprising, leaving little reason to discuss the carnage, or the reasons for it, or whatever regret or disturbance her own husband may have carried. If he were troubled in some way, Maisie had never heard Tom speak a single word about it. Most likely, she thought, he was simply shielding her from the realities of a subject good wives were better off remaining ignorant about. *And wasn't he happy now, too? Perhaps even more contented with our life than before?* Tom had always been an amiable soul, but even in the nearly perfect timbre of their early union, there had been moments when one or both had been cross or surly. Simple, tiny moments between man and wife when an angry or selfish word or a difference in plan would, for a moment, cloud and complicate an otherwise flawless day. They had never amounted to much, Maisie remembered, but they happened, just the same.

But now they never do.

The realization was there and gone in an instant, leaving her to spend the days and hours since then with an increasingly uneasy mind. Had Tom raised his voice, or scolded her, or even said a single word of displeasure about anything, in the six months since he came home? Maisie knew the answer was no. *Imagine a wife finding imperfection in the fact that she never quarrels with her husband. Imagine that!*

At first, she had believed their tranquility could be simply explained by their undeniable joy at being reunited after a long period of loneliness, uncertainty and fear. Hadn't they both spent a thousand nights, wondering if each would ever see the other again? Hadn't he told her as much as they lay together, exhausted in the moonlight on the first evening after his return? She was being silly, she knew, but still found herself unable to discard the gnawing of tiny mice that gathered now at the tattering ropes of her mind. Always before, the model of wifely efficiency and industry, she now spent more and more of her time doing nothing at all. Sitting in the screen porch, watching the distant tractor growling across the ripening fields beyond she would lament the odd peacefulness of their existence, and relive the most vexing moments since her husband's return.

She remembered that day at the Red Rooster Café in town when the busy Sunday crowd had exhausted the dessert case of every variety of pie, save for two: rhubarb and the Rooster specialty, key lime. Tom hated rhubarb pie. Always had, always would. But when the waitress informed him of his choice, Tom had happily requested the rhubarb and had devoured the last remaining slice with obvious relish. It had seemed nothing more than an anomaly at the time, quickly forgotten and overshadowed by the horrific storm that had blown in that same day, toppling the café's giant rooster mascot from on top of the building. It had been the talk of the town for weeks after, and her own husband had been among the men who set to work putting the Red Rooster and his café back to right. *It's no wonder you forgot about the pie until now, what with that huge thing crushing the old Butterworth woman, dead in the street, and all.* Maisie was working hard to give herself the benefit of the doubt, but in light of her growing concerns, the rhubarb event took on beastly proportions. *What is wrong with him? Hadn't he remembered how much he dislikes Rhubarb Pie? Can a man just up and forget a thing like that?*

Two weeks after her talk with Mary Franzen, it began. Small things to start, like leaving the butter out of the icebox to spoil, or purposefully burning his toast black and putting it on his plate next to two eggs cooked over, hard. She knew he liked his eggs sunny side up. He had told her as much on more than one occasion when they were first married, and once, had walked out the door and into the fields without any eggs at all, rather than eat a set that had ridden the skillet perhaps a minute too long. The new Tom had come down to breakfast and cleared the entire plate without so much as a sigh. He had even slathered his pitch-black toast with the rancid butter she had purposely left uncovered on the counter for buzzing flies and heat to destroy. *He ate every bite, and smiled, besides, didn't he. And gave you a happy kiss on his way out the door.*

He certainly had, and after his departure for the day's labors, Maisie had sat herself on the floor, covered her face with her apron and wept. *Not a word. Not a single blasted complaint!*

That night, filthy and tired from chores, Tom sat down to a dinner of soured liver and raw potatoes. A week later, the feet and feathers from a freshly plucked chicken. A week later still, a slice of fuzzy cheese and a boiled onion.

The week after that, two eggs in their shells, fresh from being lost a month under the wall of the chicken coop, and a loaf of moldy bread, all washed down with lumping milk, stored with care in the sweltering sunlight of the garden walk.

And not a word. Every morning, noon and night, Tom Adams would sit at their table and devour whatever Maisie saw fit to set before him. Without hesitation or protest, the hideous concoctions that sometimes required hours of planning and preparation would disappear, and always, the grateful kiss and a smile, after. And it was that kiss Maisie had come to loathe, most of all. That faithful, punctual gesture bestowed with the same warmth and affection as if she had just fed him a dinner of roast lamb and mint jelly.

Maisie had stopped bathing, now, and had stopped brushing her golden hair. She dressed each morning in an empty flour sack tied with bailing twine and wore orange peels and squash rinds for shoes. The tidy farmhouse, once sparkling and serene, now reeked of filth from stem to stern. Maisie rustled and bustled during the days, swabbing the floor with pig's grease and wiping the windows with chimney soot and bird droppings. She carefully washed the dishes after each reprehensible meal, and then dipped each sparkling plate, cup and fork in a lovingly prepared potion of frog's blood and vinegar. Clouds of gnats and flies, once dispatched with aplomb by Maisie's quickness and grace with a swatter, now ruled the house in great, whining clouds. They buzzed and dived at all hours, adding their crunching presence to her recipes, swarming this way and that over piles of food and waste, and plugging the moaning air holes of Tom's nightly harmonica. On and on, he would play, the muffled notes punctuated by the halting start and stop of sounds held silent and then released by buzzing wings and carapace. Still smiling. Still, smiling.

⊂══⋅⋅ ⋅⋅══⊃

In the thirteenth month after the end of the war, they took them all away; waif-like creatures with haunted eyes, dressed in rags and scraps and mumbling as they were carried on gurneys and in straight-jackets, to far away places for the infirm of mind. From putrid farmhouses, and reeking city bungalows. From country cottages and third-story apartment buildings lined with filth, they emerged, never to be seen again. And in each mailbox, long omitted from evolving routines that left no longer left room for the conventionalities of the daily mail, was found a single letter, sealed or unsealed, read or unread, with the same terrible words.

Dear, Mrs._____.

It is with heavy heart that the Central Militia informs you of your husband's death. He served honorably and with great courage, till the end. We must also inform you that his sacrifice has been in what can only be described as a losing effort. The uprising has succeeded and has been declared victorious in assuming power over the nation.

In their benevolence, the uprising has taken an unprecedented action to soothe the grieving widows of a nation. Each wife who has lost a

80

spouse will in short fashion, take delivery of a state-of-the-art automaton that will look, feel and function in precisely the same way as her husband. With utmost care afforded to capturing the programming essence of your husband's personality and mannerisms, it is hoped that given a break-in period of the past several months, each woman will find the replacement a more than adequate compensation for her loss.

Sincerely,

JM & R Robotics C/O Central Militia Benefit & Life

THE NEPHILIM

I mbued with only middling common sense even when not imbibed, Seth Manly had a mouth four times larger than his brain but only a quarter the size of his ten gallon ego. On a Friday evening passing through the dusty barrens of the scrub country, he was obliged to find repast and refreshment at some abandoned patch of nowhere in a ramshackle bar down the street from a restaurant with a giant chicken of some sorts on the roof. He'd passed it on the way into town and let out a backslapper of a chortle. Seth Manly was not impressed. Never was.

"I says, what in the gawdsakes kind of cowtown is it when you perch a galldarn red chicken on top of a beefsteak restaurant," Seth said.

"Beats all I ever seen, bunch of bumpkin-morons." The stools at the bar resembled a mouth full of gapped and missing teeth, with every odd seat filled with a local so-and-so who came to drink their amber mash or malt in silence and trade glances and grunts every few years over hunched shoulders and under low-tipped hats they hadn't bothered to remove. A few were glancing sideways at the miserable stranger with the big mouth who had taken exactly half a minute to level insult against the tumbleweed town's most famous and prized landmark. They were sly to strangers as a rule and liked this homely and noxious visitor even less. Not one bit. His cavernous gob was in motion, again. His voice was a gargling drawl that was more laziness and unfinished syllable than geographic affection.

"I says in a decent patch uh ranch country like these parts you bunch of ninnies could at least have made it a steer or a bull or even a 'Hungry Hungry Heifer,' up top of that roof," Seth said. "Made a whole licking lot more sense than that idiot contraption of a cock-a-doo you went with. Beats all, that's what." With that, Manly lifted his beer mug to snakeskin lips still slimy with wind-parched miles without a drop of anything except his own spittle. He sucked noisily at the foam and drank to the dregs. Glances came more quickly now as darting hat brims tipped first to see the clock on the wall above the saloon door and back in the direction of the unpleasant two-legged donkey braying away over his beer in seat number four. Jake Gully the bartender polished a highball glass down the bar with deliberate slowness, willing to let the drama unfold. After all, entertainment of any kind was always in short supply and he knew better than to get in the way of a good spectacle. So long as nobody smashed anything over anyone else's head there was no harm in letting the stranger stir the pot. And he'd certainly brought a good-sized spoon. Boy howdy. Besides, on a Friday night, everybody knew it was closing in on time to clear out. Or else. And not a minute late. *He* would be here within the hour.

"Tomcat got y'all's tongues or just your brains, boys? Maybe your balls, too?" Manly again, causing the drinking birds in their bobbing hat brims to pivot like pinball flappers in his direction. Dick Longmire, the local shadetree mechanic finally broke their longsuffering repose.

"Mister, you've got time for about one more beer. I'd oblige to buy it for you if you close that mouth of yerzz and leave us to finish up in peace and quiet. Time's gettin' short, tonight."

Manly scanned the room of peering eyes, satisfied that the dozen or so local boys had elected Longmire their spokesman. The rest seemed more than content to keep their silence. They looked like men about to face a march into the ocean.

"I says what I wants to say, mister," Manly replied.

"It's still a free country and all, last time I looked and I'll done clear out of here when I decide I'm good and ready to go if it's all the same to you. But you've got a deal on that beer."

Bartender Gully and Dick Longmire exchanged a glance and a nod before Gully pulled tap and dispensed the foaming delectable at Manly's direction. While he waited for the mug to fill, Manly reached under the wrinkled pocket flap of his grungy seersucker shirt and produced a rolled foil pouch of Red Man. Wintergreen. He pinched a wad large enough to fill a shot glass and used thumb and forefinger to lodge the bulging owl pellet in his lower lip. He looked like a man trying to swallow a rusty clump of steel wool.

Orphaned strands of the Carolina coleslaw still clung to his sticky lips like coconut sprinkles. Even in the dusky-dim interior of Gully's Gulp, he was a sight, alright. And not for sore eyes.

"Y'all keep any lady company round these here parts, or do you gents not go in for the gentler sex?" Manly asked with a sarcastic cackle, breaking the contracted silence for his charity suds before he'd taken his third swallow. It was as deliberate as the bristled hair protruding from his crusted nostrils.

"I tole you to keep to yourself, stranger," Longmire said, his ignored benevolence only adding to his rising annoyance with the unwelcome slug of a man.

"The womenfolk around here don't come out on Friday nights anymore," he continued.

"They gots their reasons and that's just the way it is. Reasons you don't want to learn about for sure. Now finish up your beer and clear on out before things get testy. Tyeiime's a wasting."

Longmire's words motivated a unison glance at the wall clock which now read twenty-five to nine. Time was a wasting, indeed. Noting the fading minutes, the passel of locals lifted libation in ritual unison to consume their penultimate sips. It was almost time to settle up and get a move on. Or else. Bartender Gully added backup to his friend Longmire's entreaty.

"You're getting righteous good advice right there, stranger, not that you'd ever know it," Gully said. As bartenders go, he was accustomed to dealing with the odd vagrant or sketchy interloper from time to time, but this current occupier was a scale-tipper at the head of the class. And on a Friday night, to boot. And only a few more minutes, at that. Gully reinforced the urgency of the approaching hour and gave standard Friday warning to the room.

"Just about time to finish up, settle up and saddle up, boys," Gully said.

"Give yourselves plenty of time for the door and for safe passage out of town. We all know we don't need the whys and what fors. Not anymore."

Acknowledged nods and mutters came from the locals, who looked to a man like a football team of pallbearers ready for an Irish wake. A few cracked their last peanuts and crunched the bits. Others lifted glasses and toasted their last toasts with grim faces and sallow eyes. A three man poker game in the corner booth folded their final hands and scraped up the till, counting up winnings and losses in silence. Depositing nickels, quarters and dimes in waiting change purse and repurposed chaw can. Manly surveyed their reticence with quizzical eyes, not quite sure what to make of what he was watching or why. *8:40 on a Friday night and they're already packing it in? What kind of hickory-nutted fruitcakes were these folk, anyway? Hadn't the front window sign listed midnight as closing time every day but Sundays? What in the blazes?*

At the very least, he'd kept his perpetually impertinent thoughts to himself, overcome by the curious observance of what a smarter man might have indubitably recognized as time-honored ritual and forethought with an apparently justifiable and still hidden cause. Something was brewing that had brewed before. Seth Manly had the sudden awareness that he knew exactly what that something was and that he'd seen it happen more than once. He knew himself as a corker of a man who'd lived enough life to realize his own capacity and perspicacity for clearing a room before closing time. But this here was different. This was conspiracy, conveyed cleverly and quietly by a group of men who were running a practiced fireman's drill to get Seth Manly to hit the exit early so they could have their country bar and their blessed silence and their damn chicken-topped restaurant of a town to themselves. They were trying to scare him out, plain and simple and he wasn't about to overlook their steaming pile of sniffed-out treachery, bygawd. Not by a long shot. Seth Manly was nobody's huckleberry. No sir.

"Alright you bunch of mud-sucking sand rats," Manly bellowed, in a volume of voice that might have been appropriate to call a dog back to a front porch at sundown.

"I'm on to you, you gutter tripe. I knows a hatched plan when I sees one and I'm not falling for it, yuh hear?"

The stirring locals now paused frozen, staring at the miscreant in their midst without so much as a peep or a twitch. Manly had squared to the room and was just warming up. They were going to get the full load, whether they swallowed or not. He was calling their bluff.

"Y'all think that you can scare me into leaving and making out for other parts just cuz I'm not your cousin or your uncle or your Tom, Dick or Harry, well think again! I'm not falling for any of it, you hear?!!" Manly was shouting, now, leaning into his sermon with indignant gusto, venting his offended spleen with relish.

"Sign on yonder door says midnight closing time. Sign in window says the same," Manly said.

"I'm sittin' reich here and finish me another four beers and maybe a shot a whiskeee or three. And and there ain't no Good—God—Dammm, any of you country busters are going to say or do 'bout it, you get me? That's THAT. And that's WHAT. Hooo-aaaawww!" Manly punctuated with pursed grotesque lips and expelled a long slobbering giblet of mahogany slime in the direction of the floor spittoon, missing short with intention allowing the pungent gunk to crawl down the side of the brass receptacle like the creeping trail of a monsoon-engorged slug.

He scanned the room for effect, to see what this slithering nest of trickster-snakes thought about being found out and called out in full. Boy howdy. Five seconds. Ten seconds. A minute, was it? But he waited and watched in vain. They were all staring at the clock. Oblivious to his rage. As the ticking circle extended long hand to a quarter of nine, the motion began. First Frank Lawson, the barber and Jake Gunthman, the gas station hand. Then spindly Henry Butterworth, the lone mail clerk and Tom Bunting, the ranch hand and furrier. John Brown, butcher and Doyle McQueen, boot and saddle maker. One by one they rose from creaking bench, booth and stool and made a line at the register. In reciprocal fashion, Jake Gully pressed the keys and rang the chime with aplomb, cashing each man's tab and giving change with practiced ease. The line jostled and dwindled with patience and efficiency, until George Lantern, local undertaker, was the last man to pay up, save Seth Manly, the perplexed and intolerable grifter who could only watch, mouth fetidly agape, catching flies, eyes wider. *What in the good goddam?*

George Lantern opened his palm for his change and then slid two silver dollars back across the polished bar in the direction of Jake Gully.

"Consider it hazard pay for a night well played," Lantern said. "If not cleanup costs and defrayment of disinfection for your broom and floor scrub for your mop, Godspeed and good luck."

"Goodnight, George," Jake Gully said, pocketing the two silver moons with a grateful half-smile. Cleanup costs and floor scrub? Godspeed? This last bit struck Seth Manly as an odd farewell in any sense, much less at the end of such an inhospitable evening in a bar that hadn't seen so much as a nosebleed, a fistfight or a slopped drink for an abbreviated night. Why the display? A tinkling bell at the front door signaled George Lantern's clipped departure, leaving only the gobsmacked Seth Manly and the patient bartender to consider ticking clock in the stillness of the empty joint. Four minutes to nine. Jake Gully polished highball glasses with a virgin cloth, his eyes never leaving the numbered dial, blinking back each passing second in the deepening gloom of the shrinking room. Manly watched him, unable to move or speak.

"Your turn, mister, while you still can," Gully said, eyes still fixed on the second hand's halting voyage round the earth. To the end of the world and back again, if either man were lucky.

"You'll want to take the backdoor now, and quiet, quiet like a mouse," Gully continued, hushing his own measured tone and placing a final piece of polished glassware on the mirrored shelf behind the bar. Manly still didn't move, but watched as Gully walked stealthily down the rail, swiping ceremonially at a last few misplaced bits of detritus and moisture on the bar top, making way as he swirled and wiped to an out of place and heretofore, unnoticed, corner cabinet against the farthest wall at bar's end. It looked to have come from some faraway kingdom of antiquity and was ornately carved of what looked to be ebony or some similarly blackened hardwood.

Likenesses of snakes and leering dragon faces and scorpions meticulously coiled and slithered and intertwined across a ribbed and horrible expanse of thorny bramble and forest inlay on the cabinet's surface. A skilled artisan might have finished the piece in a year or four, assuming he somehow survived the curse of the awfulness of his own beholden handiwork. Gully was there now, poised with cloth in hand to turn the cast iron clasp at the double door. He reached as if reaching into an orange-smoldering campfire to retrieve his mortal soul. And turning the handle with tremulous fingers and shaking arm, wrenched open the impossibly ancient door to reveal a dark velvet interior the color of old limes. Peering futilely in the dimness, Manly could just make out the fleeting silver glint of goblet and drinking set that seemed every bit in keeping with the meticulous and grotesque exterior of the time capsule cabinet that now seemed lit from within with some carnivorous thrumming of approaching splendiferous doom and damnation. One minute to nine. Gully's hands now moved with hesitating surgical delicacy, grasping goblet and decanter of same strange, rainbow metallurgical sorcery and placing the pieces on the bar's central station.

"Go. NOW, you FOOL's-FOOOOLL!!" Gully fairly squealed the command with imploring desperation in Manly's direction. But it was too late. The clock read an angled J. Nine o'clock, sharp. From the weathered outside front of the establishment came the skittered dragging of rapid-fire footsteps that sounded the hideous approach of the appointed patron. Whatever IT was crossed the front of the building in two ticks of the clock, not that Manly heard either of them. He was catatonic now, a frozen statuary relic subject to the captive hideousness of an overstayed unwelcome, hearing only the pounding throb at his own ears and temples and the clasping thickness at the center of heaving, concave chest. The walls and high ceiling of the dingy saloon now seemed to dance and undulate with the onslaught of some yet uncategorized malevolence that human eyes and ears were worthless to contain or describe or even endure. And then, the door opened. Untouched.

At that moment, Seth Manly, cantankerous bane and improbable blight of humanity, emptier of rooms and annoyance of annoyances composed his life's masterpiece of malignant, unmitigating folly. He was laughing. Not chuckles or peeled giggles or choking chortles, mind you. Not even the random raucous backslappers previously reserved for the diminution and derision of giant barnyard chicken-freaks perched atop hapless restaurants in silly towns where men of Manly's incorrigibility might seldom stop, but never stay. He was bowing and standing repeatedly with nearly silent involuntary churnings of spastic laughter that controlled him from hair to heel. Bowing. Heaving. Pointing obscenely in the gesticulated direction of the doorway, incontinently overcome by the revealed visage of a what looked to be an impish boy of six or eight, standing stalwart in the tiny boots, chaps, vest and duster of a miniaturized Chisholm Trail cowhand, a century and a half out of place. He was a spaghetti western cliché shrunk to ridiculous dimensions, now stamping tiny booted feet, dragging costumed chap and spur across the dusty floor, ambling comically toward the waiting bar. And still, Manly laughed. And pointed. And laughed. And snorted. And laughed again. He turned bleary-teary eyes and ruddy-flush of punch drunk face to Jake Gully, who never so much as returned Manly's grotesque gaze, but stood firmly at attention and in silent vigil, eyes dead ahead, staring unswervingly, unflinchingly at the far wall opposite the fastidiously placed ancient drinking service atop his proprietary bar. Hands clasped. Chin bowed, ever slightly.

Four seats down from Manly's begrudged outpost came the jingle of oversized spurs as the central casting, mutton busting buckaroo pulled itself into appointed stool and settled in with folded child's hands in supplicating repose, waiting to be served. Manly had halted his display to an interspersion of gasps and odd heckles that faded entirely as Jake Gully sprang to motion, pulling the stopper from waiting decanter and dispensing a greenish, syrup-crystalline liqueur into matching goblet. His task complete, Gully moved sprightly on padded steps to return mated service to waiting lair and fasten the cabinet's doors before returning to the designated spot and resuming reverent vigil.

Manly was equally silent now, as the childlike hands extended from oversized sleeves of oiled duster to raise the goblet to lips that belonged to a cherubic and innocent face. With the neatness of an oft-scolded and conscientious youngster, the boy emptied the goblet and placed it back on the counter. A waif's arm wiped glistening mouth in the familiar way any child might wipe away a milk mustache after a long, cool drink. Still, Gully didn't move and barely breathed.

"So, was it green applejack Ripple, or absinthe, short stuff? Looked mighty tasty, I might say."

What would be Manly's brazen epitaph exited his slimy lips, propelled by what would be retold and recorded celestially as his final words and breath on the earthly sphere. The resulting sequence of events bent the laws of the known universe inward and down, inhabiting mere fractions of a second and spanning all eternity at once, stretching back through experienced and discarded lifetimes of ancient wrath and back again to the moldering domain of an abandoned bar in a forgotten town on the nowhere edge of the world.

In a flash of molten brilliance and unsheathed hideousness of revelation, the impish cowpoke stretched, transformed and disappeared with blinding gargoyle detonation to reveal an awfulness and evil from beyond the ages that radiated and pulsed beneath scaled skin and leathered wing of a creature that now stood eleven feet tall and filled all time and space inside the roadside bar that churned and bubbled and ballooned like the interior of a Uranium sphere given unholy impetus by Oppenheimer's triggered disintegration. The paper beings that had been

Seth Manly and Jake Gully, still rocking and swaying in the onslaught, now melted in the conflagration of windows and craters and vented expulsions of displaced molecular life as cell and membrane and nucleus raced apart at the elemental bidding of the towering Archinot of Atlantis, Goliath of Gath, Gargantuan of Gaul, Behemoth of Baphomet, the hallucinated terror of battlefields and epidemic conflicts from Rome and Runnymede to Hastings and Da Nang and Hiroshima. From the banks of the Volga and the red-stained snow banks of the Black Forest to the pink foaming beaches at Normandy and the carcass-littered sands of Kabul and bone pit jungle paddies of My Lai and Kampuchea. The demonic worm-Lord of Gehenna, destroyer of worlds and devourer of souls.

THE SHOPGIRL AND THE
APPRENTICE

"I shall marry rich, or not at all." Doris Apple produced the words with the flourish of a Broadway actress addressing the very last row of the theater. Instead, she was helping her friend Bessie as the two store-mice arranged the display of yellow's and pinks and blues and violets. An Easter offering of women's dress hats on the third floor of Bigelow's department store on Fourth Avenue. She had worked there for over a year, but had still not advanced upon her true and singular objective: to find a willing and wealthy young man to help her tender her resignation from the ranks of the working single. Truth was, his age was not of much concern so long as his qualifications in the former category were sufficiently advanced. Doris knew she would enjoy the life of leisure and luxury afforded only to those so fortunate as to stumble across the right wallet attached to a man. Today, she was providing a similar education to Bessie, her colleague of only a month.

"Love is nice, dear, but the delights of the heart may as well happen with a man of means as with a working stiff," Doris intoned. "There is no reason at all for a woman of even middling intelligence and beauty to ever settle herself into the struggling routines of the masses. Poverty is a life sentence, and love carries no guarantees. Choose well, and both your parents and your children will thank you, ever after."

Bessie seemed to weigh the words of her superior like a wiggling fish pulled from the pond, before tossing them back for being too small. "Is it really as simple as all that?" she began, "I mean, love is a precious thing, and one never knows when or where, or with whom it might blossom and grow. I would prefer to be sure of love and love alone and then hope for fate's blessing to help my husband and I secure our life's fortunes."

Doris gave a look as if the notion had never found its way inside her skull. She was fidgeting with a pale green pillbox on its stand, the last of the shipment to be put out for the day. Like the teaming columns of twenty-something women with similar ambitions in the city, her choice of employment was a calculation of proximity and opportunity. A simple arrangement that made here visible and available to the privileged men of the stock market who shopped for neckties and new suits one floor above her head. They had to take the stairs, didn't they? And on their way to their dapper attire, they would see

Doris Apple, and that would be that. No more ham and beans.

"Excuse me, miss."

Intent on their hats and with their backs to the counter, neither Doris, nor Bessie had noticed the young man standing there. "I wonder if either of you could show me a hat for my mother," the young man continued. His plain attire and soft, humble speech told Bessie he had no business in a store like Bigelow's, much less inquiring about the most exclusive women's hat collection in all the city. She was not in the mood to be troubled.

"Now, why would I want to do that, mister?" Doris said.

"We both know these are more than a little rich for the likes of you. You'd have much better luck down the street at Billingsley's or Bosley's, or even Crowder and Mather's, for goodness sake."

Doris had turned to face the man only long enough to make her rough appraisal of his bank account and had now busied herself again with the very hats he had inquired about. She believed it part of every shopgirl's duty to put the riff-raff in its place. How else could a store like Bigelow's maintain its mannered and well-bred clientele? Undeterred, the young man stood his ground as if the words had never been spoken, or as if they were exactly the words he had expected. He twirled a battered bowler of his own in his right hand and rested his arm on the counter before speaking again.

"I'm sure, you're quite right miss. Those are truly first rate hats. Much nicer than any I've ever paid for, but I'd like a particular one I've noticed as a surprise for my mother when I return to Boston."

Doris was still making busy with the hat rack and becoming more than a little perturbed by the man who simply didn't know when he'd been tossed away.

"I believe dear gentleman, that I've adequately addressed the subject of your mother's hat by directing you to a number of stores more befitting a man of your station and means. Now hurry off before those establishments close their doors for the evening, leaving you without anything to show for your unfortunate errand." Bessie, who had watched all of this in silence was clearly dubious about the exchange, but was allowing her underling status to keep her tongue. Doris quickened her movements, adjusting the rim of this hat and then tufting the feathers of another, before straightening the pearl band of still another, hoping that the muskrat in the shabby brown suit had taken her words as a souvenir for his journey down the stairs and out of the store. He had not.

"So sorry miss, but I'm very certain those stores you mention have wonderful hat displays, in their own right," the young man said calmly. He was studying the band on his own hat, measuring his words patiently, not daring to look at the fashionable and stubborn girl behind the counter.

"...but I've come to Bigelow's specifically for this very display. Its reputation is quite unparalleled in all of New England..."

Doris cut him off.

"Which is precisely the reason we cannot abide this type haranguing and buffoonery by customers without the common sense to realize they are out of their depth."

She turned to face him as she delivered what she hoped would be the final word. "Goodnight, sir." The young man seemed to resign himself that the cause was lost. He placed the battered bowler on his head and turned slowly from the counter, walking away with the solemn, somber steps of a man who has seen his best efforts decisively outmoded by a formidable opponent.

The following Friday, Doris Apple was out of a job. Attached to her final pay voucher was the triplicate rendering of a letter received by the store's owner, Mr. Thomas C. Bigelow. Doris had read it twice before lowering her eyes to the floor and pitter-pattering her discount heels out into the crisp, Manhattan evening. As she walked, the words burned a hole in her mind.

Dear Thomas,

I greatly enjoyed my stay in New York, as always, and appreciated my tour of your deservedly reputable establishment. As I was leaving however, I must confess to a very troubling and unpleasant encounter at your hat display. You must certainly understand my reasons for wanting to inspect that portion of your store! I asked an attractive young lady for assistance in procuring a hat as a gift for my mother's Easter outfit. No matter how I requested or cajoled, the young lady would not show me a single hat! Not one! Since you are the exclusive merchant of hats designed, sewn and marketed by my late father's company, I would greatly appreciate it if her services no longer be applied to the sales of our line. The old man would turn in his grave if he knew of such treatment! Perhaps the perfume counter would be more fitting remedy for her disposition.

Regards,

J. Quentin Rigglesworth III

P.S. I wonder if it would be too much for you to make an introduction for me on my next visit. There was a second girl arranging hats who seemed a very lovely and pleasant person, if only a bit reserved. I would very much like to meet her.

THE BOSON BOX

The doorbell rang on a Saturday morning at 9:37. Mrs. Juniper Augustine was a vision of slim frame and satin skin wrapped in apron and housework, scurrying this way and that with the hurried motions of a speed addict playing solitaire. The children were scampering for their televised cartoon ritual and Mr. Augustine was at the kitchen table reading newspaper with the help of Maxwell House and the family dog. Domestic tranquility evaded their regimen as it did every Saturday breakfast, but it was certainly routine. Perfunctory pantomime, even. Boring as shredded wheat but regular and incremental as a slide rule or a ticking clock.

"I'll get it," cooed Mrs. Augustine primly, heading for the front hallway and loosing her dust bonnet from her head as her sensible heels clickety-clacked on long and shapely legs across the shining tile floor of the entry chamber. Pressing a button, the Augustine front airlock door whisped open to reveal a medium sized gentleman in a shabby suit holding a briefcase in his left hand and waving enthusiastically with his right at the visibly crestfallen woman behind the airtight observation glass. Mr. Augustine had forgotten to reactivate the LED "No Solicitors" sign again. The switchable display feature had been a pricy add-on to the purchase of their airtight and ultra modern, stainless steel living module, but still required the diligence of a perpetually forgetful husband to turn it on at appropriate times. Mr. Augustine had failed the test. Again.

"May I help you?" Mrs. Augustine asked the man, clicking the intercom relay to allow conversation with visitors to the front stoop. Another pricy addition.

"Just a moment of your time, ma'am," the man replied, finally ceasing his exuberant waving and removing a battered fedora with a stained hatband from his balding pate. Fingerlings of misplaced and unkempt hair clung to his head in sweaty strands. The atmospheric particulate level was especially high this morning and the man's labored breathing added to a general picture of uneasiness and desperation. He was an uncomfortable sight.

"I have something to show you that I think you're going to want to see," the salesman said.

"Something new and improved and impossible to properly describe. It must be shown and felt, rather than talked about." He spoke with the clipped upspeak of a carnival barker or an infomercial pitchman. Rat-a-tat-tatting the sharply separated words like frozen peas spilling onto a kitchen floor.

"Sir, I believe we have everything we could possibly need," Mrs. Augustine replied, reaching behind her back to untie apron strings and tidy up and reflexively smoothing the bunching of her dress.

"We just purchased this housing module three years ago and spared no expense with the number of mechanical add-ons and doodads. Completely eliminated the need for any other sort of enhancement. I don't even shop for groceries anymore," Mrs. Augustine said.

"I can't possibly think of anything else we might need."

Her tone was resolute, but the salesman at her doorstep was undeterred. It was a speech he heard two dozen times a day on every street in the city. Since the invention of holographic manufacturing and three dimensional molecular printing, it had become virtually impossible to make a living as a door to door salesman of anything. New homes now came equipped with onboard ability to catalog, envision, select, manufacture and repair any household item that was needed and to replace such items repeatedly and indefinitely without even a dollar of added expense. New dishwashers and toasters and ovens hid inside walls. New lawnmowers and televisions and computer phones and garden hoses and spark plugs and curling irons and electric razors and dog leashes and frozen waffles and gallon jugs of chocolate milk sprang from the whirring entrails of living modules with no more inconvenience than pressing a touchscreen and speaking a creative word. Even household garbage was whisked away to be handled by the mechanized apparatus of the Amazonia home, reused as synthesis material for the endless wants and needs of the dweller. "Every home a factory. Every homeowner a god," as the famous Amazonia Homewares Division advertising slogan went. Trips to the store were as obsolete as the vehicles once used to get there. There were no stores and only a very few cars, kept mostly as stubborn relics and heirlooms of an antique time, driven sparingly if at all. For a stubborn moment in the aftermath of modern convenience, unfortunate men like Arthur Hoskins had made their living hand delivering groceries and hocking the small list of items that homes were unable to produce internally. It was frustratingly futile work from a forgotten time. How do you sell anything to someone who can create the universe with a spoken word? Housewives like Juniper Augustine were now the omnipotent potentates of their own shiny, steel solar systems of consumption.

"Ma'am, you obviously live the Amazonia life. I'm quite sure that your A.H.D. home provides everything you could possibly want or need, but what I've brought with me today is something you don't know yet if you want, because you've never seen or heard about it, until now."

As he spoke, Arthur Hoskins the salesman reached into his trousers pocket and retrieved a small black device no larger than an electronic phone or a television remote control. Mrs. Augustine watched intently, but with her right hand still poised at the airlock button, ready to snug the door on this sweaty salesman in an instant should he not succeed in gaining her attention. As he began manipulating the small keypad on the black device, Hoskins knew he was on borrowed time. Something more dramatic was always necessary if he was to be allowed inside an Amazonia home. His fingers still rapidly keying the device, he glanced at the woman's impatient face and spoke again. "You are Juniper Jean Augustine, age thirty-four, yes?" Hoskins asked.

"Yes, yes, that's right," she replied, hesitatingly.

"And how are husband Herbert and children, Meg and little Carter?"

At this, Mrs. Augustine's eyes widened. She leaned toward the door, seeming to press in to get a better look at the gentleman caller on her front step. His fingers were still working the tiny keys of the small device. A quiet thrumming whistle could be heard faintly through the glass door. She dropped her right hand away from the airlock switch.

"How do you know our names?" she asked, her elegant face a mixture of concern and curiosity about the nature of this visit and how an apparent stranger might be privy to such personal information. Had Amazonia given out their vital details again without so much as asking permission? It was the only logical possibility, aside from magic or fraud, as if there was any discernible difference between the two.

"Never mind all that for the moment," Hoskins said, his fingers still moving steadily at the device. He was fully concentrated on a small display screen above his darting thumbs, engrossed in some shred of yet undisclosed detail there. Mrs. Augustine was engrossed too, all thoughts of dispatching this uninvited man now discarded as she waited for whatever it was that he was in the business of providing.

"Mrs. Augustine," Hoskins continued. "I've been instructed to extend a warm greeting to you and a sincere hello from one Aleister Jones. He says to tell you that he misses you, dearly."

At this, Mrs. Augustine sucked in a sharp gasping whimper while raising delicate hand toward the perfect bow of her ruby lips. It gave the odd impression that she might accidentally inhale and swallow her fingers. Her eyes were suddenly luminously alive with the translucence of tears. Realizing her involuntary response, she gathered herself after a moment and glanced nervously back down the hallway toward the kitchen before stepping closer to the glass partition and speaking in hushed tones. She seemed at once pensive and offended, but still curious, like a woman who has had her pocket picked clean at a carnival but still wants to know the thief's secrets, even if her change purse is never returned.

"What sort of a tricks are you up to," she asked, her eyes narrowing slightly with a seriousness that did nothing to diminish the stunning beauty of the floridly feminine face Hoskins was absorbing at full effect for the first time. Her pert nose, finely-royal cheekbones and dramatic jawline framed a set of green eyes that were so intensely deep and beautiful that Hoskins felt guilty for the tears he had inflicted on them. The wetness of her dark lashes against the lustrous doeskin of her delicate face only heightened her magnetic power and appeal. She was visibly moved and troubled but not angry. He found her unnervingly, richly attractive.

"What could you possibly know of Aleister Jones or of me, or my family or of any of this?" Her question was equal parts fear and desire and Hoskins recognized fully that the device he held in his right hand had once again succeeded in honing in precisely on the most powerful source of emotion in the life of a woman he had only just met. What she couldn't have known was that Arthur Hoskins, traveling salesman, already knew everything there was to know about Aleister Jones and about Juniper Augustine and about their torrid university love affair more than a dozen years ago. The deep romance that remained in her heart the greatest she had ever known and that had also become her deepest scar after he had been killed in a jeep accident the summer she had agreed to marry him. Aleister Jones, gone in an instant, leaving her to settle quickly and irrevocably for the life now contained in the allergen-free living space enclosed in the steel box of Herbert Augustine's Amazonia housing module. A pretty bird in a sterile, gleaming cage. Smallish husband. Bored wife. Average children. Done, done and done.

"I hesitate to reveal too much too quickly, Mrs. Augustine," Hoskins said, pausing from manipulating the device for just a moment to look into her eyes and emphasize his attentiveness.

"I want you to know that I mean you no harm. I am here to share with you the latest advances in the secret knowledge of the multiverse and how that power can be used to give you a happier and more robustly enjoyable future."

Hoskins sped through the rehearsed and scripted line as a preamble to gauge the interest of the customer before him who now wore a look of helpless resignation. There was simply no escaping her need to understand why this stranger had arrived at her home and how the device in his hand gave him the ability to speak the name she had given herself only grudging permission to think about and hadn't spoken aloud in more than a decade. She needed to know.

"Undoubtedly, you've heard about the recent advances in Bosonic String Theory and our burgeoning understanding that the universe is actually composed of multiple dimensional streams of reality," Hoskins said, matter-of-factly, reciting elementary knowledge that was by now the stuff of grade school science books and children's rhymes.

"Yes, of course," Mrs. Augustine said, quickly. "Everyone knows of Dr. Boson's work in the field, long ago." She remembered her own grammar school lessons about the branching of the multiverse and the theoretical possibility of traveling between dimensions and even to other parts of the universe simply by harnessing the power of subatomic bombardment and reassimilation. The subject matter had given her a headache, but she was feeling far more inquisitive at the moment. Hoskins again busied himself at the keypad of the small device while continuing to the meat of his pitch.

"Very good, Mrs. Augustine. And you should also know that Dr. Boson's historic discovery has over time, helped us to understand and define the phenomenon of perceived reality more fully than we ever have. No more staggering in the dark believing that we humans are limited by our present perceptions. No more falling victim to the notion that our decisions and choices are impossible to change or remedy, or that consequences for mistakes or accidents or bad habits should be life sentences of permanent misery."

"All well and good, but I'm not sure what any of that has to do with anything," Mrs. Augustine said, her tone shifting slightly back toward bored skepticism. Hoskins moved quickly to expand the point.

"The complexity of the Bosonic universe now teaches us that each and every human choice causes a spontaneous branching of the fabric of space-time," Hoskins said.

"Literally every choice you make from the moment you awaken in the morning creates a cascade of created universal dimensions that are the direct result of your exercising your free will as a human being, with either happiness or unhappiness concealed in the fabric of those choices and decisions over time. For example, what did you have for breakfast this morning, white toast or wheat?" The burnt toast analogy. Hoskins used it frequently to teach clients about the finer points of interdimensional travel and the metaphysical power of human choice. It worked like a charm.

"Wheat toast. With cinnamon-sugar and apple butter," Mrs. Augustine replied. "Aaah, a fine selection, indeed. I can almost smell the cinnamon," Hoskins continued.

"Now, what if I told you that at the very moment you decided to have that wheat toast with apple butter this morning, at that very moment, you were also enjoying white toast with marmalade and rye toast with honey and sourdough toast with strawberry jam and croissant with buttered custard and pumpernickel with a smear of Vegemite?" Hoskins made a buttering motion with his free hand, pretending to spread something on the black device in his right hand. It looked ridiculous, but Mrs. Augustine wasn't about to have endured this much without getting to

the blessed culmination of the spiel. Aleister. Her beloved, handsome, robust Aleister. With those large hands and broad shoulders and mysterious, glinting eyes. And....
Hoskins was still speaking.

"And what if I also told you that in another dimension, you burned the toast black and ate it anyway, spread thickly with rancid butter and a few dead flies for good measure?"

Mrs. Augustine recognized *that* reference immediately. Who didn't? Hoskins was a good one for creating curiosity.

"Like one of those crazy war widows with the robotic husbands after the Great War," she murmured. Everyone knew the stories of grieving wives who welcomed home their dashing war-surviving husbands with miraculous joy, only to turn up weeks or months later in the psychotic wards of hospitals after realizing that their real husbands were dead and that the National Army had gifted them with identical automatons as some miscreant gesture at kindness and recompensed replacement. Her aunt and uncle had neighbored next to such a woman.

"Maisie Adams." Mrs. Augustine said the name absentmindedly, away in her own remembrance.

"Precisely, yes, ma'am," Hoskins said, his illustration still weaving together on the opposite side of the Augustine family airlock.

"A tragic incident, to be certain, but I can assure you, motivated only by the deepest caring and compassion for the suffering hearts of the aggrieved. A true humanitarian effort, albeit misguided."

"I thought it was plastic and cruel," Juniper Augustine said, remembering well the horrors of the Adams ordeal and the scene of a home that her next of kin had discovered after it all. A bloody mess.

"They should have known better than to think they could fool a husband or wife who knows things about their lover that they might not even know themselves," Juniper finished.

She had no intention of taking in the full implication of the things spoken by this sweaty, disheveled man, but the mere mention of Aleister's name was all the catnip she needed to remain his captive audience until he arrived more closely to the point. Soon, she hoped.

"A more than fair point, Mrs. Augustine. But back to that toast," Hoskins sallied onward.

"You see the truth is that for you to even wake up with a choice of which toast to have, every single option you might select, or purchase, or synthesize out of your Amazonia onboard fabricating module, must exist all at once in different branches of the multiverse. Otherwise, none would exist at all. And simply by exercising that choice, you, YOU, Mrs. Augustine are responsible for creating another universe. And another and another."

"Think of it like the tines on a fork or the bristles in a hairbrush," Hoskins continued. "All pointing in the same parallel direction. All running parallel lines of exactly parallel existence, but completely separate from one another and distinctly positioned."

"Yes, I suppose I have a general idea," Mrs. Augustine said. Hoskins was leaning farther forward now and had lowered his voice to a controlled, measured melodium, just above a whisper. His hands and fingers moved in hypnotic, illustrative arcs, emphasizing the importance of what he was about to say.

"Now, imagine being able to leap from bristle to bristle and stream to stream like a flea switching hairs in the fur on the back of a dog. The dog still moves in the same direction, see, as life still moves us along with the same energy and destination. But we choose the individual hair where we live. And that choosing makes all the difference," he said.

"I like to think of it, as your, 'hair of happiness.'" Hoskins used his hands and spread the words like a banner in the air as he said them.

"But why are you telling me any of this," Mrs. Augustine asked, ignoring the overdone oddity.

"And what does any of it matter? If all of us are here in our present lives, what does it matter if there are parallel universes where we're happier and more content? Knowing that would only seem to add to the misery. Being ignorant of a happier version of me in some far off place would seem the better option, frankly."

"But that's precisely the point, Mrs. Augustine," Hoskins shot back, too cheerfully to be normal.

"Think of how much of life energy is spent pursuing happiness. It's in the damned Constitution for God-sakes. The pursuit of happiness. And oh, brother, the price of admission. The time, the money, the excess, the emotional pain and the trauma of broken relationships and ruined lives. The swirling mass of humanity, yearning for things to change. To evolve. To be what we always wanted our lives to be, but missed by fractions that turn into miles because of circumstances, events and consequences that are eventually out of our control, or too inconvenient to ever experience again. Applying and refining those discoveries into a usable therapeutic device became the work of one of Dr. Boson's most talented assistants."

Mrs. Augustine found herself wishing that she had chosen an alternate string in the multiverse where she hadn't answered the door. Still, her thoughts of Aleister held her firm in the resolve to see where all of this blather was headed. Hoskins was at a dead run, now, lifting the black device in his right hand closer to the glass enclosure to give his prospective customer a closer look.

"It's ridiculous, really. Hate your life? Down a bottle of gin. Hate your spouse? Have an affair. Hate your wrinkling face? Stick yourself in the Amazonia surgical rejuvenator for a little nip and tuck. The time. The headache. The hassle of coping with life. When what we should always have done and can now do, through the power of Bosonic science, is to change reality back to what you and I want and need it to be. Simple. Automatic. Painless. And of no more moral consequence or failing than changing a channel on a video device or a television."

With a final flourish, Hoskins opened his palm holding the device with the reverence one might expect to reserve for a Dead Sea scroll or a very large diamond.

"May I present to you, the Boson Box," Hoskins annunciated with ridiculous prosaic.

"The world's first and only multidimensional rectifier."

Mrs. Augustine stepped closer until she was nearly nosing the glass, peering at the small black rectangle with keyboard in Hoskins' hand.

"Newest technology. And completely Bosonic-based, which we now know to be crucially important to safety," Hoskins said.

He knew that earlier versions of the device used Fermion particle waves instead of Bosons to execute the same dimensional travel and that the results had been tragic and hideous. Fractional integer spinning of the quarkian and Fermion particle streams resulted in only partial transmission rates. Hoskins continued.

"Quarks and leptons gave us two-thirds or one-half of a human being taken from one stream to the next. Hideous mutations and dissections resulted, nearly always fatal and even more grotesque when the subject survived. We could never predict which portion of their body would make the trip." Hoskins chuckled wanly as he described the grisly fallout of the development phase with no more upset than mentioning a burned meatloaf. Mrs. Augustine was clearly disturbed by it.

"Horrific and catastrophic in the testing phases, years and years and years ago. But all of that is behind us, now, I assure you, Mrs. Augustine. Forty-seven million launches and return trips without a single human loss and counting. Quite safe."

Mrs. Augustine glanced at the living room clock and then forlornly down the hall toward the kitchen, where even after nine minutes at the door with a strange man, her out-of-sight husband hadn't so much as budged or inquired who was on the porch, or why. The rustling pages of his rechargeable digital newspaper were the only indication he was still alive. She found herself wishing that she could walk down the hall and find handsome Aleister had invaded the assortment of molecules and empty space that were now occupied by her husband.

"But how does it know," Mrs. Augustine asked softly, as if worried of having her truest feelings betrayed by the question within earshot.

"How does it know which life I prefer and where I would be happy, or happiest?"

It was a familiar question. Hoskins gave a chuckle.

"Oh, ho, my dear, it doesn't know. But you do. And you'll do all the telling."

He retrieved a faded kerchief and wiped his gleaming forehead before stowing the fabric back to waiting pocket.

"What you should understand, Mrs. Augustine, is that the happiest and most joyful potential for your life always resonates at the highest frequencies. The energy of that radiating signature makes it a simple task to tune into your happiest life course and steer you gently back through the decisions and events that have made you lose touch with what your life could and should have been. With just the slightest adjustment in the attenuation of your Bosonic motivator, you can travel between realities and parallel dimensions with the same effortless ease as running a comb through your hair."

"Eternal happiness at the touch of a button."

Hoskins now stroked the Boson Box lovingly with a finger, as if bestowing somewhat creepy affection on a pet hamster.

"No more medications, no more drugs or alcohol or risky sensual behaviors to try and cope with the unhappiness of the moment. In the past we've always depended on these clumsy methodologies to make it possible for us to tolerate our static version of reality. Unhappiness is the greatest disease in the history of mankind, responsible for crimes of all size and description, murders, wars, theft and abuse. But unhappiness should never be viewed as a human frailty or shortcoming. Being unhappy is not your fault and it certainly can't be fixed through crude tinkering in the same broken dimension that has you trapped and unhappy. "

As he paused, Hoskins recognized instantly that he had no more convincing to do. A familiar expression now spread across the face of the pretty woman on the other side of the glass. She was thinking of her lost love and lost life and all the cornucopia of undisclosed delights and details that had slipped her grasp long ago. The imaginary life of perfection with which no real life could ever compete. For Juniper Augustine, it was the perfect and unfulfilled world of Aleister Jones, whose memory still succeeded in twitching her toes inward and causing a flush of extravagant memory that brightened her delectable skin three shades on the crimson color wheel. She was with him now in her mind, running and laughing on the sandy beach. Splashing in the cool, pristine water of a summer creek. Collapsing bank side in soaked underthings and streaks of mud and nothing else. Stealing pleasures in broad daylight, far away from the eyes of nosy onlookers or passersby. Rinsing clean and dressing in the sparkling sunshine of a last, youthful summer that had become Aleister's permanent home. It was a larger and longer drink of his emblazoned image than she had allowed herself in many, many years. It made her catch her breath. Hoskins set the decisive hook with the precision and mastery of an aging angler ready to land his prize fish.

"And what if I told you that at this very instant, you could transition directly into the dimensional stream where you and Aleister Jones are married and still deeply in love, living out the life that you always imagined and experiencing every happiness that you lost at his death, and that you could go there, right this moment?"

He knew full well he scarcely need ask the question. The answer was pooling even now, with implicit certainty in luminescence of Mrs. Augustine's hopeful and liquid-green eyes, mere inches from the glass enclosure which served as no impediment whatsoever for the powers of modern physics. Mr. Hoskins positioned the device at the ready and prepared for activation. It was a mere formality, now. She was his. Or so he believed.

"Andrew, or Arthur or whatever your name is," Mrs. Augustine said after a pause and a bit of a start. Her expression was now one of resignation and remorse in a losing battle with resolve. She glanced again in the direction of her waiting kitchen and children and husband and life.

"I'm afraid, sir, I need to forego your offer and get back to my morning chores. Even an Amazonia house doesn't clean itself without a little help. And besides, my family lives in this dimension and they need me here." She seemed regretful, but more than concrete in her declaration.

"No Boson Box for me, I'm afraid."

With a smiling look of knowing acquiescence, Mr. Arthur Hoskins took her words with chivalrous grace and temerity. He had taken his best shot.

"Very good, Mrs. Augustine. I bid you, good day." Hoskins lifted his tattered hat in farewell and watched the steel airlock liner whisper closed abruptly before his eyes. Opening his waiting salesman's case, he took out a marking pen and a swatch of tape, carefully applying it to the back of the black device that Mrs. Augustine had so politely declined and began making letters. As he wrote out the client's name for the completed delivery, he counted out the familiar handful of seconds that had by now become a trademark of the Bosonic Technologies Corporation. One second per letter.

A-L-E-I-S-T....

From across the internal electronic void of the forgotten, still-activated and very expensive Amazonia Homewares intercom came a joyful female shriek of surprise. And another and another and another and another and another.

A Rescue Denied

"I am sorry, constable. I don't believe I can save him." In the rain-soaked alleyway, the youthful but eminently talented doctor Peter Strauss rubbed bloody hands on sodden trousers and rose to his feet. With halting resignation, he returned the fruitless scalpel to the contents of his medical bag and folded closed the leather cover. The policeman put a comforting hand on the surgeon's wet shoulder and spoke.

"You did the best you could, Doc. Just like always. He wouldn't have fared any better in the best emergency room in town. It was just his time to go."

Slumped roughly on the pooling cobbled filth of the alley pavement at his feet was the rapidly cooling body of his colleague and friend, Dr. Ian Malcolm. Malcolm was a specialist in the digestive ailments, a man highly cherished by the ranks of the aristocracy, whose discriminating and sophisticated habits of plate and palette often disagreed with their insultingly pragmatic and decidedly less pretentious intestinal canals. Strauss imagined Malcolm's death would leave empty spaces in the medicine chests of some of the most well to do neighborhoods in the city. The man's potions, if not his dispensary arrogance, would be missed.

"So, you say the two of you stopped off for a few drinks here, Malcolm headed for the john, and then you heard the shot?"

The police sergeant was holding a mushy notebook in one hand and the gnawed nub of a pencil in the other.

"Yes," Strauss replied after a moment.

"Ian left to use the restroom in the back of the bar, and didn't come back for quite a while. After a bit, I became worried, so I followed him back here to see what was wrong. I didn't find him in the men's room, and as I turned to walk back into the hallway, I heard a single shot."

Strauss looked down at his fallen friend. A burgundy stain draped across a white shirt highlighted a ragged puncture at the center of the dead man's chest. The gunman had hit his mark, all right. A killing wound in a single round. Strauss turned and took a few steps back toward the rear exit of his familiar evening hangout, seemingly reliving the terrible drama from moments before.

"I heard the shot, and I…I looked back and noticed the back door at the end of the hall was open."

Strauss continued his pantomimed recreation of the grisly discovery; raindrops streaming like tears down his nose and cheeks.

"When I pushed the door open, I saw Ian lying there, bleeding."

Bleeding indeed. The bullet had deprived the victim of one lung before lodging so close to the younger doctor's heart that even a gifted surgeon less than a dozen steps away couldn't sufficiently intervene. Retrieving a handkerchief from his front pocket, Strauss futilely wiped the pelting onslaught from his forehead before blowing his nose. He went on.

"I rushed to him of course, and seeing the wound and the blood, immediately began trying to trace the bullet's path. I always carry my compact valise for occasions of public emergency and I used my scalpel to make an exculpatory incision."

Strauss's eyes contained a faraway mixture of grief and helpless resignation. "I realized immediately that the wound was too grave," Strauss continued.

"Ian took his final breath before I even located the slug."

The police sergeant was nodding at this, faithfully recording the doctor's observations. He appeared ready to close the case.

"Just one more thing, doctor," the Sergeant inquired.

"Did you look around for the guy what did this? I mean, somebody shoots my best friend in the breadbasket, you better believe, I'm hunting the scumbag down for some pay-backs, capiche?"

Strauss seemed amused by the policeman's folksy expression of valor and friendly loyalty. He smiled inwardly and massaged his jawbone in contemplation before speaking again.

"I believe I already told you that I scanned the alleyway both right and left before rushing to my friend's aid," Strauss replied.

"I didn't see anyone in either direction, and at that moment, my chief concern became the medical welfare of my wounded colleague. I would have expected no less from him, had our fortunes been reversed."

"I'm sure not," the sergeant responded, closing his notebook and sliding the stunted pencil behind his right ear.

"It's just a shame we can't give some kind of description to headquarters so they can be on the lookout for this creep. With his wallet emptied and his pocket-watch missing, it looks like a simple muggin' but you never know when some guy decides he likes the blood better than the cash and goes on a tear."

"Yes," Strauss agreed, "you never know."

With that, three men loaded the body of Ian Malcolm on an ambulance gurney and pulled a white sheet up over his head. A police photographer and another officer made a final sweep of the crime scene before packing into a black squad car at the end of the alley. The sergeant reached out his hand.

"I am sorry about your friend, Dr. Strauss. If there's anything more we can, do, or if you think of something you forgot, give us a ring, you hear?"

Strauss nodded, silently staring at the smudgy remains of a chalk outline on the pavement that was quickly being erased by the falling rain. He shook the sergeant's hand.

"Almost forgot, Doc," the policeman said suddenly.

Reaching into the marginally dry interior of his canvas trench, the earnest cop produced an envelope that had suffered an obvious soaking before being evacuated to the dry pocket of a constable's waterproof coat.

"We found this on him," the sergeant recalled.

"It has his name on it, but it was so wet, we couldn't tell if he'd had a chance to open it and read it before he died. Any idea what it is?"

"Oh, it's probably nothing, officer," Strauss said, taking the moldering envelope from the cop's hand.

"Probably a thank you note from some wealthy socialite who was the recipient of a famous Malcolm stomach cure and developed an infatuation. It's been known to happen."

Strauss tucked the letter inside his own overcoat and refastened the buttons.

"Old Ian was never considered handsome, but he could be deceptively effective with the ladies," smiled Strauss. It seemed an impromptu homage to the deceased doctor brought on by the spontaneous memory of a skilled friend who had tried vainly to save him.

"One summer a few years ago, there was a batch of spoiled oysters at a debutante soiree out on the island," Strauss continued, "damned if 'Malcolm the stomach wizard' didn't fill a year's worth of Saturday nights in one fell swoop."

Strauss was in full smiling remembrance now, recalling the exploits of the brilliant Ian Malcolm. Friend. Confidante. Competitor.

"After that, he was flush with these simperingly grateful female patients convinced that his potion was the singular reason that their seafood-ridden gullets hadn't fallen out.

Never let any of us forget it, either. All because someone let the ice melt at a party buffet."

The police sergeant took in the story with all the enthusiasm of an undertaker, but his tone was comforting and warm.

"Must have been quite a guy and a good friend, doc. Sorry again for your troubles tonight."

With a final squeeze to the doctor's shoulder, the officer walked to a waiting patrol car, straightening his stop sign shaped hat with one hand and flicking away a cigarette. He gave Strauss a final wave as the car pulled away into the night.

After a few moments, Dr. Peter Strauss decided it was time. Reaching into his coat, he retrieved the last letter ever written to Dr. Ian Malcolm, and still walking, began to read.

Dearest Ian,

I've made up my mind, and I wanted to tell you as soon as I could.

For the longest time, I haven't known which way my heart would lead me, and until I was completely sure, I didn't want to say anything, but I'm ready now.

I love you, Ian, and I want to love you forever. That part is simple, my love, but the identity of the other man in my heart makes things more complicated than you could have ever imagined. It's Peter Strauss. As a nurse who worked for, and with, both of you, I know you are friends, and that neither one of you had any clue about my faithless indiscretion, or my inability to decide between you. Please understand it was a secret too deep and dark to reveal until I had made my choice. I hope we can all remain friends, even if you're the one who took me from Peter's arms. There is no shortage of young women eager to take my place in Peter's life. The same can be said of you, if you decide your friendship is of more value than my love. I know that the two of you are too close to let something like this be the end. We can make it work out for all of us. I know your heart wants that too.

Love,

Sally

For a second time that rainy night, Dr. Peter Strauss refolded the letter and put it back in the envelope addressed to his faithful friend. As he walked along the waterfront fence, far from the downtown bar and the bloody alleyway behind, he retrieved his black surgeon's valise from his other pocket and opened it up. From inside, he took out the blood-covered scalpel, and too quickly to be seen, a small, pearl handled derringer that smelled of fresh gunpowder, and a gold pocket watch, torn from its chain. The pieces of hard metal glinted in the moonlight like bits of cheap jewelry in a pawnshop window. On the other side of the fence, three muffled splashes and a shower of torn up stationary fouled the polished surface of the harbor calm, and Dr. Peter Strauss started the long walk home.

FRAGAMUMP

He'd seen it again. Playing in the backyard sandbox, the boy had spotted the creature at the edge of the woods behind his home for the third time in a week. In the birdsong sunshine of morning, with splotches of shadows and forest sunlight dancing across orange and green and purple skin and with three giant eyes in a sideways, oblong head. With three arms and four legs and two noses. If they were noses. And were those wings on its rounded, hairy shoulders? The boy had been frightened at first and rushed inside to tell his mother, who had at once dismissed the matter as nothing more than the imaginary babblings of her ever excitable and ever inquisitive six-year-old. Another imaginary friend for her precocious and perspicacious son.

"Three times? That's very nice, dear," she said.

"Why don't you take it an apple and share it?"

"But how do I know it likes apples?" Billy had asked, scrubbing a sneakered foot nervously against the kitchen floor with hands in pockets and tipping his chin to his chest.

"You like apples, don't you?" his mother asked. "And anything you like, I'm sure your brand new friend enjoys as well."

She never looked up from her copy of *Popular Science*. She was engrossed in an article on recombinant DNA research and the newest theories about protein sequencing as the Rosetta stone of genetic variability. Billy knew better than to expect her attention.

"Anything I like, it will like too," Billy repeated hollowly but hopefully. "Of course, dear. Now run along and quit being such a fraidy-Fred."

And mommy had been right as rain. After leaving the apple in a patch of sunshine at the edge of the woods, Billy had watched in wonder as the creature, no larger than a plump house cat, had stood upright on two lower legs and munched the apple in three swift bites before retreating again to the cover of bushes and brush. And those weren't noses after all, but two pieces of a strange little mouth that worked together to dismantle and swallow the apple with an efficiency that a cynical observer might have found disconcerting in anything but a vegetarian.

Billy, on the assurances of his mother and in his determination not to be thought a fraidy-Fred, put his normally itchy mind to rest. From behind the bobbing leaves of an especially lush and softly verdant patch of shrubbery, Billy could make out the creature's large and blinking trio of eyes. They were the size of golf balls in triangular arrangement and looked vaguely human, except for the brilliant golden prisms of crystalline striation that seemed to float within each dazzling oversized iris. As boy and strange visitor stared at one another, Billy noticed the creature's equally large pupils gaped and closed and gaped and closed in interdependent sequence. It was only after several silent moments that he realized the rhythmic and ratcheting contractions were in perfect unison with the syncopated pounding in his own chest. Somehow, the creature was monitoring his heartbeat and timing his pupillary dilation to match.

"My name's Billy, what's yours?" the boy ventured, not truly expecting any kind of response. To his surprise, a series of clicking gleeks and blurps and whirs came from behind the dancing leaves. The creature shifted foot to foot on its tiny lowest legs, dancing like R2-D2 in need of an oil change. Billy laughed.

"Did you like the apple?" the boy asked, all traces of previous apprehension completely gone. "My mommy said you would."

More cleeks and cheeps and whirps. The leaves of the bush rustled and stirred as the creature seemed to dance in some thus far indefinable response to the boy's speech. They were trading gestures like baseball cards, though any observer would have surmised neither had ability to understand the other. It didn't matter. The boy was in full fascination now, craning and straining to peer deeper into the foliage and get a better look at his newfound friend. Mommy would be so proud. He wasn't a fraidy-Fred after all.

"For us to really, really be friends, I should know your name," the boy said. "Do you have a name, or can I give you one?"

More flerps and queeps and burr-gwinks. The sounds were unmistakable communiqué of some kind, but nothing that the boy could recognize or utilize or attempt in return. It simply wouldn't do.

"I will call you, Fergamump." the boy said, declaratively, before pausing and cocking his head in retraction. "No wait, Fragamump. Fragamump is better." And so, Fragamump it was.

For several days and a bag full of Jonathan apples, the boy and the strange creature played their game of walkie-talkie pantomime. While their schedule became staid and familiar routine, the Fragamump never ventured out of the concealment of the brush and never expanded its lexicon beyond the squelching, squeeching, greeping and boinking potty dance of their earliest meeting.

It was of no matter to Billy, who gave up any attempt at convincing solitary mother of the existence of his new friend and could barely sleep for excitement of what the next day's meeting might hold. On successive nights, his fitful dozing gave way to vivid dreams of the colored creature and the strange sequence of vocalizations that began to root their way into the malleable and miraculous elasticity of the childhood brain, filling him with an unraveling vocabulary that slowly but certainly unfolded imagery and repetitive familiarity in his mind like alphabet soup poured into a Coleman thermos. Blurps to vowels. Ker-gurps to consonants. Gleeks and Gadjoinks to words and phrases. Cleeks and whirps to sentences and paragraphs. And the creature was learning, too. Absorbing the boy's innocence and cherubic energy like a sponge and reflecting it back in ways that enhanced the familiarity between their disparate biologies and eased the discomfort caused by the creature's admittedly ghastly appearance and the natural fear and disdain the boy initially felt.

The Fragamump's gaping and squenching eyes softened and became more soothing and less refractive. It stopped timing the boy's pulse and respiration and learned to suppress the probing intensity of an intellect many multiples of a human mind to a level less off putting and it hoped, if hope was an emotion within the palette of a Fragamump's octave of expression, less detectable to a boy it recognized as intuitively and empathically attuned to such measures. It danced and blerped. It hopped and gleeped. It droned and bounded. And waited. And hid. On a few moments of desperate reaction, the Fragamump had sensed another set of human eyes staring into the small woods behind the boy's home from the kitchen window. It felt the gaze of the boy's mother by reading the natural impulses of her optic nerve like the braille imprint of a telepathic encephalograph. It could parse and peruse the transmitted contents of her conscious mind simply by retracing the energy of her stare and deducing the resonating digital transmission of rod and cone to determine whether she had seen it or not.

Fortunately, she hadn't. She was curious. She was distracted. She was mildly depressed. She was not motivated to further inspection. She knew her son was behaving differently and that his latest fixation with an imaginary being was taking him farther away from the predictability of his normally desperate demands for her attention. She felt guilt at the relief of those diminishing demands. She felt self-loathing for her lack of interest as a mother. She was not concerned for her son's safety. Not even a little bit. All of this and more the Fragamump absorbed with each fleeting glance from distant house. Her trips to the window to watch the boy crescendoed over a pair of days and then halted altogether, leaving her satisfied in the harmlessness of his preoccupation. Insouciant mother finally leaving precocious son and unseen being to continue their green-way communion at the forest's edge.

Eleven days in and they were nearly speaking. Or more rightly, nearly understanding one another's gestures and thoughts without the need for language. While general intentions and feelings were well within the Fragamump's ability to poach and absorb without knowledge or consent of the inspected life form, as with the mother, actually deciphering the boy's words remained beyond reach. The boy's dreams meantime, had ripened and deepened, bringing him closer to the ability to hear language in the odd collection of burbles and qwerr-pinks of the Fragamump's whirring dialect. It was only a matter of time now. With each day they spent, the boy became more attached to and more fond of his new companion. He laughed and laughed as the two sat with scattered assortment of brightly colored trucks and cars and digging machines, separated as they were by a few feet of spongy, mossy earth in the soft sweet grass at the edge of the wood. The Fragamump, still wary of detection by anyone but the boy began to understand his human counterpart as a brilliant mind. Rapaciously inquisitive. Irrepressibly smart. Analytical, methodical and with near limitless potential for critical analysis and innovative, creative expression. The very qualities that often left young Billy Jenner isolated and alone among his misunderstanding peers were exactly those of greatest interest to the orange and purple being with the strange, misshapen features and face.

At times when they were together, the boy was aware of a sort of peeling sensation that played at his temples and at the back of his head. It gave the feeling of warm water rising over the ears and tickling the sides of his face the way water did when he relaxed into a bathtub full of bubbles on Wednesday and Friday nights. Once or twice, the two beings had locked eyes at the exact moment of that warm water sensation and the Fragamump had been nearly certain that it had overreached into the delicate folds of the boy's remarkable and labyrinthine brain. But after brief moments of inquisitive gaze, the boy had returned to the benign ritual of playtime, constructing roadways and bridges and tunnels in the sandbox or collecting odd assortments of stubby twigs and chips of tree bark that he sorted into mounded piles of prospective cargo for his dump truck and bulldozer and backhoe. For his own part, the boy's mind hid more than it revealed and concealed a growing sense that his playtime companion wanted something from him and was searching for it with a determination that felt less friendly and more necessary and frantic.

On a couple of mornings, Billy had arrived at the trees feeling certain that the creature had visited him in his dreams the previous night. Not in a dream-dream, but a physical presence in his room that had left him barely able to finish breakfast before bolting out the backdoor to find what was what. On another occasion, not seeing the Fragamump at their usual meeting place, the boy had ventured back into the vegetation and hearing the familiar gleek-gleekum of the creature's odd elocution had watched and listened from a distance as the Fragamump spoke for several minutes in a tone of apparent urgency and distress the boy had never heard. To no one at all. When the string of rapid fire guttural gibberish had ended, the creature had emerged from beneath a thicker portion of vegetation with what a human might have recognized as a momentary sense of awkward indignation at having been eavesdropped.

Still, the day had progressed in completely routine fashion with the playmates resuming again their mutual exploration of each other's strange vocabulary and with the boy noticing at least half a dozen of the by now unmistakable warm water moments when it felt as if something was tracing around the edges of his mind, looking for a way in. During all of this, Billy's mother noticed her oddly brilliant boy changing in ways that for once, grabbed her attention and held it, making her both thankful for his burst of independence and curious about what was so interesting about that particular patch of ordinary grass at that particular spot at the edge of the trees.

After watching intently once or twice from her kitchen sink window and seeing nothing amiss, she'd dismissed any notion of trouble and assigned it to a simple matter of her always imaginative boy, lost again in this latest chapter of his burgeoning fantasy world and childhood bliss. At least he was out of her hair. And at least there presented no cause for anything other than a few renewed conversations about what exactly was going on in Billy's expansive and expanding brain. Although, it did seem to be harder and harder to keep apples in the house these days. They were disappearing at a rate that made mother quite certain that her son was about to launch a massive growth spurt requiring new shoes and blue jeans before fall. An evening dinner table of spaghetti and buttered garlic bread and milk seemed opportunity for some catching up.

"Do anything interesting today?" she asked her son, his eyes darting up from his plate too quickly to conceal his surprise that she was talking to him.

"Not really, mother," the boy replied.

"Is your little friend still enjoying our apples or would he like an orange or a nectarine for a change?" She watched carefully to gauge his response without setting off his alarms, if there were any.

"Fragamump likes the apples just fine, mother. Eats them all in two or three bites. Core and seeds and everything." Billy twirled absently at the few remaining strands of spaghetti on his plate. His normal excitement at any acknowledgement or inclusion of his imaginary friend seemed to have been replaced with melancholy and tight-lipped secrecy.

"He likes it here. He likes it here, a lot. He wants to stay. But he says that he will be leaving soon." Billy's mother couldn't help but notice the beginnings of tears at the corners of her son's downturned eyes. She found herself touched by the level of devotion he'd invested in this figment of his imagination and wondered if it was a normal thing for a boy who seemed to have such difficulty finding and keeping friends of his own age. They never lasted. Called him a freak. And now, was he so accustomed to that sort of mistreatment and abandonment that he was acting out the same tragic scenario even in the constructed world of a playmate that lived only in his own mind, but was going to leave him just like all the others? The thought brought her closer to actual compassion for her son's unique wiring and the burden of it than she'd been in months. She placed a hand on his shoulder and pressed gently.

"Billy, your friend is yours to keep," she said. "You don't have to make him go away, or lose him or worry that he will leave you. It's perfectly normal to have imaginary friends to play with and when we do that, it's perfectly fine to keep them for as long as we want to. It's up to us if they stay or go."

"But mother, Fragamump IS real," the boy said, sweeping a forearm blotted with spaghetti sauce across one eye to wipe his tears.

"Fragamump is real and he's my friend, but he has to go away, soon," Billy said. "He has to go back. He has to go back. Because they hurt."

The way Billy spoke these last words carried forthright conviction that his mother couldn't escape or ignore. She was staring at him intently like a captured beetle on a petri dish. It gave Billy the same sensation as when Fragamump was traipsing around the outskirts of his brain looking for something he had yet to find. *But what? What did he want, anyway? What was he searching for? Or, had he found it already? Why was he leaving? Where was he going back to?*

With a more pronounced and choreographed squeeze of her son's shoulder, Billy's mother spoke again.

"Tell Fragamump that he can stay for as long as he pleases and eat all the apples that he wants. And a peanut butter and jelly sandwich for lunch. If he wants."

Billy never lifted his eyes from the Van Gogh swirls of sauce and stray noodle and salad dressing on his empty, desiccating plate.

"He can't stay, mother. He says they hurt. Says it over and over," Billy said. "He has to go back, because they ALL hurt."

Something changed. And they all hurt.

◦━◦ ◦━◦

Ten generations and seventeen days into a world fed by corn made of fruit flies and grapes made with hummingbird hearts and cucumbers made with cow spleen and hybrid strawberries spliced with hints of sea squirt and jellyfish and butterfly, the three-eyed and seven-legged great-grand-something of William Jenner III, future pioneer of genetic enhancement of foodstuffs and car tires and industrialized, evolutionized humanity, made its conclusive and final transmission from ionic travel to planetary past. With whirring ker-glunkum and per-blinkum, the evolved vocalizations of a tortured biology halted and hitched and ceased. The desperate orange and purple time traveler's last crucial message sent and received by its home time and mission control, 700 years into the future.

Target 0794 neutralized.

Copy that.

Threat eliminated.

Very good.

Mutation reversing?

Not sure. Not yet.

Pause.

Negative. Standby for new target acquisition. Agri-Tech Labs. St. Louis. Year, 1998.

Copy that.

The gaping and squenching EKG pupils of the Fragamump's once-human and mutant eyes of metastatic gold danced rapidly and then slowed and seized, measuring out with electromagnetic precision the final, dying heartbeats of the genius boy lying a few feet away. Young Billy Jenner, future Nobel scientist and predestined arbiter of an abomination of transformed species and genetically modified Earth monstrosity, strangled and harmlessly cooling in the ancient cradle of heirloom grasses and forested floor behind his childhood home.

THE DETECTIVE MAKES
THE CASE

"I knew about it the whole time," the old man said. "I knew about it all." Even lying on his deathbed, Ernest Blackstone had a flair for the dramatic and as he wiped his quivering mouth with a bedside kerchief. The generous sweep of his arm and calculated tilt of his head revealed that it would take more than a fit of tuberculosis to rob him of his affinity for stage play. Only the chill of actual death would suffice for that.

"Oh, yes, my dear!" Mr. Blackstone brought his watery gaze back to his wife's and spoke again in measured imperial tones.

"You didn't honestly believe that a man who made a life's fortune out of detail and deduction would find himself unable to divine the whereabouts and intentions of his own wife of forty years, did you?"

The coughing again. It wouldn't be long now, and the dying detective had no intention of relinquishing his soul without finishing his final performance. He had spent his entire career catching thieves, murderers and swindlers by assembling seemingly unrelated bits of information into ironclad investigative conclusions, but even more than the forensic framework, this was the part he liked the most. He enjoyed watching the eyes of the guilty as he unveiled absolute and previously unknowable proof of their misdeeds. Seeing inferior minds resolved to their criminal doom filled Blackstone with the joy so unspeakable it shook his veins like a drug. Very often, "the unveiling," as he called it, would take place with an audience of three or four other policemen and sometimes a newspaper reporter or two, if Blackstone could arrange it. The publicity made him feel like an actor on stage, strutting and flexing to complete his final bits of oratory for an adoring crowd. Those days were long behind him now but this one final chance for vindication brought them rushing back. His wife must know that he knew, and quickly.

"Dear, dear Bessie," Blackstone resumed. He took her withered hand in his own, squeezing it gently for emphasis as he spoke. Her skin felt thin and papery cool.

"These last thirty years I have withheld from you the normal affections that a husband should give to a wife. It hurt me to do it, and I know that the happiness of our home and the vitality of our very lives has ebbed away every day since." Another coughing fit, longer than the last shook the old man's brittle frame. He wiped his mouth, again and tried to catch his breath.

"Truly, it gave me no joy to make the decision that I made, but you must understand, a man has his pride, and can never fully forgive a wife who makes other arrangements behind his back." And forgive her he hadn't. How could he, with the overwhelming and vivid evidence of her transgression forever etched in his mind? As it was so often in his professional calling, the proof was inescapably solid, and that meant there could be no mitigation. The facts were the facts. On a spring day thirty years before, he had seen his beautiful Bessie on a downtown sidewalk wearing her finest Sunday dress. He was on his normal lunch break when he spotted her and instead of heading to the diner, he decided he would follow his wife and surprise her at the next corner. It was easy enough for a police officer to stay hidden in the crowd while keeping her pink flowered gingham in plain sight. After all, it was his job.

For a moment, he had felt almost guilty exerting the full force of his concealed observational skill on an unsuspecting wife, but he pushed the feeling away. If he couldn't surveil her, who could he surveil? After the first block he found he was starting to enjoy the game. He had never doubted that other men found his wife as beautiful as he did, but seeing them react to her unescorted passage on a city street in her best Sunday finery was another thing entirely. They stared. They smiled. They whistled. They turned themselves around to have another look. And if her appearance was a matter of pride for the detective, her stalwart immunity to these boorish male indiscretions only served to reinforce his admiration. No matter the adoration thrust upon her by strangers, it appeared the detective's wife paid no attention. Just as importantly, she never noticed her trailing husband and that was just the way he liked it. He had no doubt the element of surprise was still intact. He had followed her for three blocks when she stopped in front of a four-story brick building painted green. She seemed to notice something in the sparkling storefront window before opening the door to the building's staircase and heading inside. Once she was out of view, Blackstone had quickened the final steps to the building to determine what had captured his wife's attention. A jeweled trinket perhaps? A persuasive poster-board invitation to their next night at the theatre? What the detective found instead had broken his heart. There in the window, amid a passel of yellowing notices of missing dogs and advertisements for music lessons and vocational instruction was the building's office directory. A tenant listing on the third floor bore a name of eminent and disgusting familiarity. It read:

Room 306
Mnsr. Frederique Von Papilieu Fortunes Told! Futures Revealed! Seances Performed! Spirits Communed!

Detective Blackstone knew what everyone knew about Monsieur Frederique Von Papilieu. Besides being a Frenchman with an unsavory reputation for impersonating psychic abilities, Monsieur Von Papilieu was the most accomplished thief of womanly virtue in the entire city. So overwhelming were his charms to the fairer sex that it was said he could seduce a woman four states away simply by speaking her name. Five states away if the woman in question hadn't been attended to sufficiently by her own husband.

Detective Blackstone shuddered at the thought. His own Bessie was upstairs with that French scoundrel that very moment! He doubted that fortune telling and future revealing were the full extent of her curiosities. After standing for what seemed like an eternity outside the den of Monsieur Von Papilieu, Blackstone had spun on his heel and returned to work. Other men, he knew, would have marched upstairs straight away and confronted the Frenchman then and there, but Detective Ernest Blackstone had taken a different course. He decided there would be no confrontation with Msr. Papielieu, or even with his wife, for that matter. Instead, he himself would never mention it. He would watch, and wait, and see what was what. Besides, he reasoned, it would be far better for his dear Bessie to come to her senses and confess her missteps on her own volition than to bludgeon it out of her with his rapier of condemnation. Only a true and contrite rendering would fully cleanse the wound that had been inflicted in the dear detective's heart, and the motivation must be Bessie's alone.

But that rendering never came. He had waited for it alright. Waited, and hoped, and prayed and pined that his good wife gone astray would one day walk up to him and have out with the whole sordid affair. Then and only then would they reconcile, and not a day before! All the while, the wound in his heart turned to wormwood. Bitter and suffering, he could no longer offer husbandly affection at home, or a generous word in public. The pain of his betrayed trust burned in him like a fever and robbed him of all that once brought him joy, until he was brittle and hardened like burnt clay.

Still he waited. Years passed. Their children grew and left. Their hair turned gray and their backs stooped and the light went out of their eyes, bit by bit. The changes of time seemed to hasten after that fateful meeting downtown. They lived together like two shadows on the wall that never touched. She herself had wondered at the sudden change in their love so long ago, but never spoke of it. The pressures on the man of the law were great, she knew, and who was a wife to add to the burden by asking about the state of their marriage? No, that would never do. She loved him and had resolved to love him no matter how distant he became, or how difficult her deprivation. And so they had been, until this very day thirty years later, when she feared every cough and every labored breath would be his last. The old woman turned back to her husband as he began to speak again.

"Thirty years ago, I followed you, Bessie." Detective Blackstone was wagging his pointing finger for emphasis. It had been a forceful trademark during interrogations, and he knew this would be his last.

"You were downtown, and I followed your every footstep until you reached the doorway of Monsieur Von Papilieu, the fortune teller. His reputation alone leaves little doubt of your intentions or of his. I never said anything about it because I wanted to hear the truth from the same lips that went astray."

Detective Blackstone finished his presentation, content that the persuasiveness of his case would bring forth the confession he had waited so long to hear. A pained, confused look on his wife's face only confirmed his satisfaction.

He would get his confession alright. After a lifetime cornering the criminal mind, he knew the look of the captured guilty as well as he knew his own name. But then something happened that had never happened in any interrogation room in his career. His wife began to laugh. The pain and confusion melted away from her tired face as rolls of pelting laughter streaked her cheeks with tears. It only subsided when her husband began again to cough and the reality of his rattling lungs brought her back to composure.

Finally, she spoke.

"Thirty years ago, my love, was the last happy day that passed between us. We shared our last kiss in the morning before you left for work, and that afternoon, I caught the bus downtown to surprise you for lunch. You weren't at your normal diner, so I started back for the bus stop, when I noticed your reflection in a shop window a few yards behind me. I knew what you were up to and I had half a mind to startle you with my lips, so I ducked inside the first stairwell I could find and waited inside. How come you never opened that door?"

A Sunday Out

"You and your dastardly premonitions. Can't a body enjoy a peaceful Sunday lunch without all this windy blather about bad omens and such?"

Gladys Butterworth eyes her skinny husband with a narrow, hawkish gaze. Her patent leather purse completes a swinging windup, connecting squarely with the small of the impish man's crooked back. A squelched yowl of pain escapes his frail, pinched lips. "Now, let's go inside and have a nice quiet din-din."

Without an additional word or a moan, Mr. Gladys Butterworth complies with his wife's edict, relaxing his formerly crouched posture only slightly to walk the remaining steps to the diner's front door. From the sparkling street front windows of Maggie's Red Rooster Cafe, a score of peering eyes watch the happy couple, gossiping lips and whispers in full gear. He hadn't meant to rile her so. On the fourteen mile drive from the

Butterworth acreage to Wilsonville, he had simply tried to explain his tossing, fitful sleep the night before. It was the blasted dream again. The one with the blood and the shattered windows and........ Whump!!!

"Excuse mmeeeee, Mr. Man?"

The purse again. A dreaded, patent leather wrecking ball. This time, a welting blow to the top of his right shoulder.

"Do you mind coming back to earth long enough to open the door?!!" Showering gobs of spittle are raining from her bellowing maw.

"I'm starving, here!!"

She had been on this way from the time they reached the paved road, until the familiar rooftop of their weekly Sunday restaurant came into view. The forty-foot tall, resin-cast rooster that strutted proudly along the flat tar roof of the best eatery in three states. It had taken a dozen of Wilsonville's strongest men more than a week to assemble the gigantic bird, and two days more to haul to haul him skyward, where he was fastened in place by several thick, steel cables, attached to anchor plates along the black sticky surface. A suitably massive placard hung around the bird's neck, proudly proclaiming the diner's motto: *"We don't serve no chicken scraps!"* And indeed, they didn't. For twenty years, the custom-made king of the barnyard had served as both restaurant mascot and tourist draw for an otherwise unremarkable town.

"Hellllooooooo!!!!!! Anyone in there, Mr. Man?!!"

The swinging purse struck again, landing the firmest blow so far, just below the hairline, at the nape of his henpecked, sagging neck.

"Are you having them spells again, Mr. Man??" Visible laughter now, on the eavesdropping faces. Simple country folk, bored with their potatoes au gratin were enjoying an impromptu family melodrama, free of charge. Dinner theater of the marital macabre at the Red Rooster Cafe', every Sunday, Sunday, Sunday!!! The lumbering woman's voice is saccharine now, dripping with the honeyed tones of concern.

"Guess we better get you back to Doc Grady for a check?"

Mr. Gladys ignores the amused faces as best he can and opens the door. The rusted ringing bell adds a comical exclamation to the Butterworth routine. In a hush of feigned politeness, the chittering onlookers are silent now, but still watching as the happy couple makes their way to an open booth, between the revolving florescent dessert case and the nearly brand new Wurlitzer jukebox. With obvious effort, Gladys Butterworth lowers her gargantuan frame into the creaking vinyl seat. A long squeaking belch emanates from under the table, as ample flesh contacts sticky vinyl in an obscene, screeching symphony.

Mr. Gladys waits to sit until his wife has completed her usual, unsettling routine of jostling arrangement on her side of the bench. Lines of clenching determinations stand out on her forehead as she labors to find a comfortable spot. First one way, then the other, her bulging liquid form squirms inch by inch across the seat, each movement producing an audible complaint from upholstery under siege, and muted snickers from the mashed potato eaters across the room.

"Can I lend a hand, dear?"

The question seems to hang and cower in the diner's humid, mechanically cooled air. He wishes he could suck them back into his mouth like a strand of overcooked spaghetti.

"If there's anything I can do, that is."

The eyes are answer enough, a scorching reply of squinting derision that threatened the worst kind of violence. Patent leather violence, no doubt.

"I don't need help from YOU, Mr. Man!!!" She spits the unnecessary words at her visibly trembling husband. "Not now, not EVER!!!"

His eyes lock instinctively on the floor. With schizophrenic ease, her voice reverses to a lilting falsetto, comically affectionate and disproportionately small.

"Now, sit yourself down and start hunting the menu."

Her rocking erosion into the overburdened seat is finished, but the farther reaches of her immense hydraulic geography still burble beneath the blue dress like tectonic plates. The impish man moves, but not quickly enough.

"I said sit DOWN!"

The command is met by a chorus of silent stares, and chewing jaws, stopped cold. At a window table a forgotten fork clatters to the floor from a distracted hand. Their eyes bore into him. Those horrible, staring eyes, filled equally with empathetic pity and naked disgust. With the soft compliance of a wounded sparrow, Mr. Gladys begins a slow-motion pantomime of obedience. he reaches down and into the booth with his first foot, bracing withered hands on the rocking table for support. The other foot follows limply, like a battle fatigued soldier undertaking a forced march through a minefield. He lowers his bony rump in hesitating lurches, skeletal knees and hips protesting loudly as his slight frame is suspended unnaturally in midair just above the cushion. Finally, he sits.

"Now, be a dear and open your menu."

The falsetto-love voice again.

"You know how you enjoy Maggie's delicious rhubarb pie!"

Her smile is as large and friendly as a scarecrow's as she reaches across the table to snag a lump of his sallow cheek between two strong, fat fingers. The burning pressure brings tears to his eyes.

"Maybe if he's a goody-woody, Mister Manny-wanny will get a piece after he cweans his pwatey-waity!" She twists and grinds his captive skin for emphasis with each humiliating, baby-talk syllable.

"Wouldn't that be a tweaty for my sweety? Yes, it would!!!"

Finally, her unmerciful clasp is released, leaving a stiffening welt on his right cheek. He can feel his own racing heartbeat pelting furiously beneath the reddening imprint of her fingers. *Five bruises in five minutes. She's really on a roll, today.* The thought comes and goes like a passing breeze. Mr. Gladys scans the expression of his loving wife's face and is relieved to see her thoroughly engrossed in the menu.

She can't hear inside your head, you ninny.

After twenty-eight years of marriage, mental defiance is his last refuge of expression and he often fears that even that smallest of indulgences will someday be swept away by an accidental telepathic intrusion.

I happen to hate rhubarb pie! But you wouldn't know that, would you, you disgustingly overgrown sow.

149

The words are a soothing torch inside his angry skull. He enjoys their satisfying rage like fine wine, carefully controlling his expression to avoid conveying the pleasure of the intoxicating unspoken moment.

Just once, if you'd let me order for myself, I could choose that delectable Key Lime that everyone always raves about. They you might know what kind of pie I really like.

He had admired it for years: The translucent green wonder that beckoned time and time again from inside the whirling display. A forbidden ambrosia of triangle sharp lines and mouthwatering, green-on-green contrast, topped by a snowy perfect peak of hand whipped cream. On a thousand silent Sundays, he had suffered and choked his way through a thousand slices of sour, stringy, blood-puckering, rhubarb pie, all the while feigning enjoyment to avoid the fury of his elephantine wife. How she had ever arrived at the erroneous impression that he liked rhubarb, he would never guess. It was a piece of information, now forgotten and buried in the annals of consecrated, matrimonial lore.

Why don't you just take all the rhubarb pie in the world and eat it till you choke? Kill two birds with one stone.

He imagines himself smiling at the thought, then conducts a fine-toothed mental inventory of his face to make sure this cherished secret life is still secure.

I don't know which I would miss most, "Sweety-weety." You, or that bloody, pouch-puckering dessert you gag me with every Lord's Day. Good riddance either way.

Truth be known, the practical dimensions of his wife's monumental gustatory talents placed the "Universal Rhubarb Disposal Theory" not far beyond the limits of real-life possibility. He imagines her in full gasping roar, devouring endless, red-stained handfuls of hated, rhubarb pie, her mouth a crimson cavern of gluttonous, bowel rending consumption.

That's it, sweety-weety. Don't be shy. Eat every last crumb.

Truck after truck scours the world clean of the leafy scourge before depositing the finished confections in a massive hemorrhaging pile.

Gluttonous Gladys Saves the Day!!!! Reign of the Rhubarb-Reich Declared Over!!!

Mr. Gladys bites down on his tongue to keep from smiling. The sharp pain dulls his concealed levity to a more manageable intensity, just in time to stifle an emerging grin.

That was a close one, buddy boy. You 'bout done give away the farm.

Inside his mouth, a salty pooling from his self-inflicted would extinguishes the last bits of threatening laughter inside his brain, reminding him of the recurring vision that has plagued his dreams for more than a month.

Blood. Something falling, tipping over. Shattered glass, and more blood. So much blood!

It was the sort of foggy, muted recollection that faded quickly after waking, and left him straining his mind to sort out the jumbled tangles of subconscious scenery. he had tried on several occasions to tell his wife about it. He thought the act of speaking the dream in audible words might help him reconstruct the missing pieces into a recognizable whole, perhaps containing some crucial bit of wisdom or revelation. But as with anything else he had tried to express, his attempts were met with aggressive reprisal, including his latest effort during the drive into town less than an hour ago

Five bruises in five minutes, yessirreee. That'll put a stop to those blasted premonitions. A purse swing in time saves nine....

"Yoooo-Hooooo!!!! Mister Maaaa-aaaaan!" Gluttonous Gladys rips through his thoughts with a singsong voice like a foghorn. "Quit yer daydreamin' and tell the nice lady how you want your meat."

The smoky, clattering din of the diner comes rushing back into the old man's brain with a deafening flash. A youngish waitress is standing at the table, pad and pen in hand, chewing a hardening lump of something that used to be gum between pearly, impatient teeth. She isn't their usual waitress, but her name tag says Mabel, and Mr. Gladys doesn't doubt it for a second. A quick appraisal of her shapely uniformed hips brings another thought best left concealed from walrus wife and willowy waitress, alike.

An "Able Mabel," I'd be willing to bet. "Honest-Able-Mable," born in a cabin made of logs.....

"What'll it be, bub?"

The words come out between youthful, smacking lips.

"Medium rare for ya'?"

Gluttonous Gladys has already chosen his meal, as always. Roast beef with riced potatoes and brown gravy.

The riced potatoes are easier to digest, Mr. Man. You know the mashies give you the gassies! It's the cream they use. It doesn't agree with your delicate constitution.

He has heard his wife's patronizing justifications every Sunday, forever. He knows his only remaining gourmet decision involves the handful of Fahrenheit degrees between rare and well done. His entire life, simplified to a Sunday choice between meat cooked red, pink or brown. Too late, he opens his mouth to speak.

"Oh, the looney-tooney'll just sit there all day without making a choice." Gluttonous Gladys jumps in, removing his last vestige of culinary self-determination. "Just cook it till it'll make a nice pair of shoes," Gladys says. "Bloody meat gives him the trots, poor thing."

The dewy waitress flinches visibly at this grotesquely superfluous bit of information, then scribbles the wifely prescription on waiting pad.

"Well done, it is."

Able Mabel slides a well-chewed pencil behind her right hear and makes a nimble retreat toward the kitchen. She seems visibly relieved to be walking away from the large planet of a woman and her shrinking milk-soaked moon of a husband.

Ladies and gentleman, Able Mabel has a candy caboose to match her pretty hips. Yes, indeedy.

Another concealed thought. "I can see a trip to Doc Grady is definitely in order, Mr. Man" Gluttonous Gladys is shaking her head in a pitifully dramatic display.

"Your spells are getting worse by the minute."

His wife's condescending diagnosis brings and irrepressible mental smile.

You have no idea, G.G. You have no idea!

Suddenly, Mr. G.G.'s eyes are drawn to the polished windows at the front of the diner. Outside, the hottest day of the year is giving way to an afternoon storm, gray clouds chugging steadily across the sky pulled by the strengthening gusts of a spontaneous summer squall. A tin can clutters past the windows at rocket speed, as if pulled by an invisible string. Gladys has turned now, too, her massive twisting girth testing the strength of her dress's reinforced, plus-sized seams. The swirling rustle of street debris has captured her attention, as well. Suddenly, her eyes fix on another detail beyond the sparkling panes of Maggie's famous windows. She seems to freeze for a moment as a dawning realization makes acquaintance with her lumbering, reptilian brain. The rotary windows on the Butterworth's corroded Studebaker are all the way down.

"Oh, Blatherty-Buck!!!!"

The nonsense syllables send an echoing spear through the now silent dining room. To Mr. Gladys, the almost swear words are an obvious signal of his wife's quickly ripening anger. The muscles in his throat constrict with well-trained fear.

"YOU IDIOT, IDIOT, IDIOT MAN!!!!"

Her reddening face explodes with rage, bulging veins emerging from beneath ample skin. "YOU-LEFT-THEM-DOWN????" The repeated question places the now eminent possibility of rain-soaked Studebaker upholstery squarely on the narrowest shoulders in Wilsonville. Mr. Gladys knows now, there will be no rhubarb pie. Not today. Maybe, not ever.

Sweet mother of miracles. What a loss!! What a shameful loss!

The deftly concealed thought reeks deliciously of sarcastic triumph. It tastes desperately good on his brain, the way he imagines Key Lime pie might taste, if his tongue ever had the chance.

Aaah, sweety-weety, wasn't I a goody-woody? Mister Man left the windows down on a hundred degree day? Imagine that.

The sweet sarcastic thoughts come in drowning waves, now, as the reality of his rhubarb freedom bursts free.

For shame! No pie for me! No pie for the bad, bad, boy. Big loss, you blatherty witch. Big, fat blatherty loss!!

"YOU—GO—ROLL—THEM—UP!!!!"

Gluttonous Gladdy is a hurricane now, gusting inside the diner with as much fomenting violence as the quickening thunderstorm outside the four creaking walls. Her chubby fists are pounding the table with each volcanic word, drawing the eyes of familiar strangers from one natural wonder to another, easily eclipsing the storm's power with her own overwhelming, previously private display.

"ROLL THEM UP, NOWWWWWW!!"

Splashing droplets of rain pelt the diner's windows, the first soaking volley in what is shaping into a truly legendary gully washer. Mr. Gladys realizes that not even Jesse Owens could save the Butterworth upholstery from its squishing, mildewing fate.

"NOW! NOW! NOW! NOW!"

The rocking table threatens to overturn beneath the pounding onslaught of Hurricane Gladys. The strongest gust so far. From the corner of a nervous, squinting eye, Mr. Man recognizes the cowering form of "Able Mabel," her petite, coffee-stained form folded shamelessly under an empty table, serving tray held vertically like a strategic shield against the raging, robin's egg spectacle across the room. Her willowing frame is shaking uncontrollably, as if subjected to the raucous gale outside.

Fear not, Able Mabel, the storm will blow over. Mr. Man feels an oddly protective urge sweep over him. The sight of such a beautiful creature, caught helplessly in his wife's irresistible holocaust fills him with a long-dormant resolve.

The storms always blow over, one way or another. His own familiar fear gives way to something he has never felt before, specially not when confronted by the waddling tempest known as Gladys Butterworth. A soothing certainty that defies the logic of long-suffering experience.

Key Lime pie for the soul, my man! Eat up while you can! The man once known as Earnest Butterworth savors the cooling bliss of the mental dessert. For the first time since his ill-fated wedding day nearly thirty years before, a mental smile is allowed to reach its divinely ordained destination. Neglected ligaments at the corners of his mouth tug tenuously upward, the beginnings of an unsteady, hesitating grin on the face of a beleaguered man, born again to the world.

"YOU GO NOW!!!!"

Her eyes are bulging, hypertensive saucers., but Earnest has the feeling she isn't seeing anything, or anybody in the real world. Her extended hand is pointing vaguely in the direction of the curbside Studebaker, with its rapidly flooding interior. He ignores her maniacal command.

Finally cooked your own goose, eh, Gladdy-Waddy? Blew a fuse on the main breaker panel, by the looks of things.

His burgeoning smile feels better than a hot bath. He touches the skin of his own face with a quivering hand, as if rediscovering the curving miracle lines of a long-lost expression. His fingers wipe away a hanging glob of

Gladys-goober from his left cheek. The pinch mark is still sore there, but it hurts in a different way now.

Like the puckery feeling in your cheeks when you eat something nice and sour. But not puckery-bad like rhubarb. Puckery-good, like the untasted green stuff. Key Lime pie cramps, that's what they are!

His smile has reached critical mass, now, stretching wide enough to swallow the entire florescent dessert case, whirling lights and all.

BARRRRRGGGGGGUUUURRRRRRHHHHHAA!!!!! The Gladys-monster-thing bellows from the depths of its sloshing, gargantuan mass.

That's a new one, Gladdy! You've expanded your repertoire! Go, Gladdy, Go! Blow another fuse for Daddy!

Earnest is giggling now, for a dozen reasons few in the room can imagine, much less fully enjoy. The nights of lost sleep, ears ringing from her endless, supernatural harangues. The days of irrational torture as her whining consternation filled the house, spurred on by her latest, imaginary whim.

And don't forget the blatherty rhubarb pie. Don't you dare forget that!

Cackles of breathless, impossibly genuine laughter wrack his slender frame. The reality of his pending parole from that hellish sentence of string-sour incarceration is the final straw.

Goodbye, Rhubarb Reich!!! Good riddance, and goodnight!!!

Full, walloping guffaws of laughter engulf him now, seeming to strip the years from his smallish body.

Key Lime tonics for everyone! Drink deep the Calistoga of Red Rooster rejuvenation!

For all but the happy bride and groom, life inside the diner has stopped. Every eye in the room is staring at the deformed couple, an audience held captive by the raging storm and the vaudevillian pairing of sideshow freaks at booth nineteen. The swollen, sloshing fat woman in her brutish, chemical rage, and the tiny waif of a man, lost in a private ecstasy of insane laughter across the table. Outside, the storm continues. A wind-driven river of water pours from the sky.

Suddenly, walls of the eatery seem to bow inward as the prairie typhoon's paramount gust arrives in the fullness of its destructive splendor. A series of staccato popping noises reverberate from the roof above. The ceiling appears to ripple and shudder for an instant, then settles again, as if slapped by the hand of angry, slobbering giant. Thunder, perhaps? The gunshot-loud sounds are enough to prompt brief worried glances from some in the room as the mounted lights flicker for a moment before returning to a steady blaze. Then, the eyes return, transfixed to the unmatchable pair in the corner booth, still doomed to their respective bouts of madness, oblivious to the world entire. The man in his lunatic laughter, the woman, a seething, burgundy volcano in a robin's egg dress. Slowly, the tide of manic laughter recedes from Earnest Butterworth's newly liberated face. He slows the incessant chortling to a limping idle, finally grasping and suppressing his fountain of youth behind a never yielding smile. He meets his wife's demonic gaze, pupil to pupil, and prepares to speak.

"Gladys?" His unused weakling voice fills the room like a dripping butterfly from a discarded chrysalis.

"Gladys!"

He says her name more forcefully, this time.

"Do be a dearie and run outside to the car."

Newly emboldened eyes meet hers and hold them strongly with an unbending gaze.

"I thought to suggest raising the windows when we arrived, what with the weather report and all, but I guess I neglected to say it out loud."

Wouldn't have dared, is more like it, old chum.

The words from his formerly wilted self ring true inside his brain, but that was somehow so long ago, in another world, before the mental Key Lime pie.

"Please run along and roll them up."

He finishes the casual, forceful demand with a calculating demeanor she has never seen from him before. She can feel his iron resolve, virtually begging her to defy this once impossible request.

My resolve isn't all that's stiffening, Gladdy-dear. Mercy, No!

And it was true. Apparently, his smile and laughter weren't the only things to find new life on this blessed, Sunday afternoon. The most vital parts of his long dead manhood were humming with a vigorous, tingling arousal. He welcomed the feeling like an old forgotten friend, gaining further strength from the reunion.

"Go, now, dear, while there's still a dry spot to be had."

That was a lie and they both knew it. The torrential waterspout of the past half-hour left no hope for even a square centimeter of dry upholstery, and it looked like the rain was letting up, besides. Rolling up the windows now, would be an exercise in lamebrain futility. But then, this wasn't about the windows, anymore, was it? She knew the rhetorical answer with a sickeningly terrifying conviction. How had he become so blatherty, all of a sudden? He had been such a good and pliable husband for so very long. This hardening, unpleasant change made her wish for the not so distant past, when things were much simpler, and easier to bend.

"Blathurrrbbarrrbbbuhhh."

Her gibberish protest is only a muted whimper, now, like the air escaping from a slowly deflating balloon. Beyond the freshly rinsed windows of the diner, shafts of golden sunlight are breaking through the dark and rapidly diminishing clouds. Afternoon is emerging once again, to begin the immediate task of baking the dam earth and puddling sidewalks to their previous, arid state.

"Gladys. Go, *Now.*"

He emphasizes the *now* with an insistent, yet reserved fortitude that stands in stark contrast to her own frenzied dictates of some moments prior. She doesn't know why, but she knows that she has no choice but to obey. She can feel it somewhere in her bones, like the changing weather outside.

But the rain has stopped! Rolling up the windows now makes no sense! You'll actually be keeping the seats from drying by trapping the dampness inside the closed up car!

Protests of logic cry vainly inside her brain as she rises from her well-indented nest, somehow light as a feather on obedient, zombie feet. Then, as her wrestling brain and robot limbs fight their silent battle, Mr. Earnest Butterworth drops the final, irrevocable bomb.

"Hurry along fast enough, dear and there will be a nice slab of rhubarb pie waiting for you when you get back." Had she heard him right? Did he dare offer sugary incentive for the completion of this meaningless, dictatorial task? A single glance to his eyes was confirmation enough. Reaching deep for her only recently impoverished bag of rage, the old Gladys rears up again, her face a giant bulging beet, filled to exploding hypertension with a flush of angry blood.

Blood. So much blood, and shattered glass and..... Shards of his mysterious puzzled vision return to the old man's brain, threatening to shrink him in an instant back to his normal size.

"BRRRRAAAAAARRRRRGGGGHHHHHHHHHH HHAAAA!!!!"

The towering Gladys monster explodes with regained intensity. She stands at the table's edge, a dancing obelisk of molten fury.

I'll fix you, you little blatherty man! I'll fix you good and proper!

She thinks rather than speaks the words, because part of her is still unsure what the changed little imp might do. Still, her plotting mind is fixed on a revenge that will settle the day's accounts, and then some.

Aren't the keys to OUR car in MY purse? Of course they are. And if I leave, he will have NO WAY to get home! Already, she has snatched the shiny black wrecking ball from the vinyl bench. *Roll up the windows, indeed! After the sun has come back out and dried off the day? And offer me a little pie for my trouble? Preposterous little man! I'll fix your blatherty little self! Just you watch and see!*

A murderous vision fills her face with an unfathomable joy as her trunk-like legs begin a surprisingly quick march toward the door. *On the way home, I'll turn around and come back and run you down in the road, you walking little man!!*

Blood. So much blood, and something falling over. Hadn't her blathering husband said something about some kind of gruesome premonition earlier this morning?

Chances are, you'll get your wish, after all, you spindly little spider. Just maybe, if I can aim the car straight and true, there'll be enough blood and shattered glass for the both of us. Yes, indeedy!

Mr. Man's expression remains a peaceful study in serenity as he watches her go. Not for the windows, obviously, but then today's victory was a sweet one, whether she rolled them up, or not.

A Key Lime victory for all mankind.

Finally, her trundling, blue-egg shape reaches the door, unopened since the storm's pelting arrival, and their own comical entrance moments before that. She reaches a gnarled, fatty paw to the knob, but finds the antique encasement stuck fast, seemingly trapped in its frame. With a determined shoulder, Gladys Butterworth braces a leg and pulls backward like an elephant tugging on a fallen tree. Almost at once, the door pops free and then pops wide before becoming stuck to the inside. Unmindful of the now useless obstacle, Gluttonous Gladys continues her mad dash for the waiting car. Behind her turbulent escape, only a few attentive eyes notice the reason for the door's impingement, and fewer still comprehend the mechanics of the now sagging ceiling and doorframe and the subsequent reasons for the fatal sequence of the next dozen seconds. On the now collapsing roof of the aging diner, a handful of rusted anchor plates, recently loosened by the gusting storm break completely free from their melting, tarry beds.

Deprived of the door's necessary support, the bowing roof sags further still, sending a creaking shiver from front to rear and tipping a giant, strutting creature forward from his ancient perch toward the earth below. Inside the diner come shrieks of shock and genuine fear, as a menacing shadow darkens the street. A fraction later, the screams multiply tenfold, as the building's storied windows give way in a glinting pandemonium of glass. And then they see it. Eleven tons of red, crowing mascot hurtling into view. The horrible landmark beast, his feet still firmly hinged to the roof, completes and arcing dance with gravity, plunging beak-first toward the pavement. Over and over and over, he comes. With geometric precision, forty feet of angling height turn to length, closing distance like a trip hammer on the struggling, jiggling woman, still only halfway across the empty street.

For Gladys Butterworth, the Red Rooster's timing is an unavoidable meeting with destiny. A ground wrenching impact and a crunching scream of hollow surprise happen with simultaneous horror. A fatal duet of finely-wrought juxtaposition brings a dawning certainty of an ironic demise.

From inside the freshly ventilated diner, sweating onlookers move silently to the street, gathering with dreamlike slowness in the choking muggy morass of the July day. Like travel-weary pilgrims arriving on hallowed ground, they parade in silent vigil around the final rest of the large, deflating woman, now a bloated, robin's egg oracle, cracked and fried on the steaming concrete griddle.

Two landmarks for the price of one.

The splintered shell of her blue-egg dress reveals rivulets of spilling blood, set free by the pressing weight of the crushing resin beast. Splattered crimson droplets create a polka-dot facade on the restaurant's already red-and-white storefront. Sparkling cafe' windows, once the cleanest in town, now litter the sidewalk and street like random piles of diamond leaves. *Shattered glass, and blood. So much blood.*

A painted yellow beak, in exact proportion to the red assassin's Paul Bunyan stature is buried firmly and deeply between two fatty shoulders, now stained to match its body by a careless splash of the egg-woman's ebbing arterial life. From the ruined window frame, a final shard of blood-painted glass tinkles to the ground. The sound goes unnoticed by the mob of mummified spectators, who have now turned to stare at the only person to ever truly love Mrs. Gladys Fennimore Butterworth.

All Hail! The Red Rooster-End to the Fallen Rhubarb Reich! Sieg Heil! Sieg Heil! Sieg Heil!

The quivering polyester man wipes the sweat from his glistening forehead. His smallish hands rub the salty moisture nervously into the coarse fabric of the plaid, goto-meeting outfit, chosen for him the night before, by the corpulent dictator now pinned to the ground by the world's largest rooster. He wears no expression, standing silent as the moments stretch into minutes. Inside his thrumming brain, the kaleidoscope fragments of a recurring, jigsaw dream slip fluidly into place, completing an insomniac masterpiece of brutal liberation. The once-missing pieces fit like a charm.

A moment later, amid the still standing crowd of Sunday diners, his searching eyes fix on a certain coffee-stained waitress with shapely hips.

"I think I'll have that piece of pie, now, 'Able-Mabel.'" Slowly, the faint beginnings of a smile emerge from the corners of his prim mouth, as the newest widower in Wilsonville turns to walk back inside Maggie's now open-air diner. He finds a long hidden appetite growing stronger by the second.

"And make it Key Lime, if you please."

MOLLY AND MAC

"Am I boring you? I can stop if I'm boring you. It's just that I always feel that by sharing these smallest details of our lives, no matter now mundane, it brings you and I closer, you know and I want to be close to you in that way. So much. Even if circumstance makes us impossible."

Molly Sinclair was speaking again, holding court in his heart in a way that McGregor Lewis hadn't felt in years. In every aspect, she was one of those rare impossible women that would have left even talented painters cursing their own inability to capture her true essence, but affected with a modest authenticity nearly never found in women of her caliber. She was more than a decade his junior, still damp and dewy in the fertile vibrance of her glistening newness, like a moist butterfly just emerged from a cocoon and struck by the wonder of both her wet wings and the widening vision of a still-interesting world. As a writer and venture capitalist tycoon and more importantly, as an untamed scoundrel of a man, jaded by the bruises of misspent admiration and rounding the turn into the second half of his life, McGregor Lewis knew all of this about her and was drawn equally to all of it, hoping that some of her urgency and spectacular freshness would enliven his own deepening mortality. Everything about her spoke of refreshment and unfulfilled promise. He watched her candy apple lips and pliant eyes as she spoke. She looked straight ahead, as if contemplating the windshield, or the dancing leaves beyond. She was a miracle.

"I do love you, Mac," Molly said. "I think of you all the time. Even when he's home, or I'm busy with the children, or when I'm alone at the kitchen window waiting for the cookies to brown or thinking of what to make for dinner for the next week. I think of you and want you so much that I wonder sometimes if it'll split me in two."

"I love you, forever."

She spoke the four words easily and without a trace of guile. They had been saying them to each other for a while. Every time she did, McGregor Lewis wondered how often she had spoken the phrase that day and who owned the higher tally in her mouth and her heart; he or Mr. Sinclair, Molly's husband. The thought branded him with both guilt and jealousy. He kept the uncertainty to himself to avoid wasting any of their stolen moments in the dwindling afternoon. It wasn't worth the effort. Soon enough they would part again and he would miss her terribly until their next meeting.

"I love you, Molly," McGregor said, tracing his fingertips along the softness of her left hand. "You know that I do."

The velvet of her flesh, no matter where on her body, quickened his pulse and made his breath catch in his lungs. Her power over him was complete. His fingertips stopped and recoiled slightly when they reached the metallic hardness on her ring finger. Her wedding band. His mind pushed away the intrusion with a deliberate dose of redirection that had become a familiar defense against frustrated reality. He needed her like oxygen. Far too much to allow things like reality to get in the way. But she belonged to another man. On paper, at least. Best evidence suggested Mac owned her in virtually every other way. For now.

"I will always love you."

Twenty years earlier, he had been an innocent young man lost in love with his first wife. The memory of it lingered with him now, even through the eventual failures that had doomed their love and starved their marriage of rocket fuel by middle age. They had sputtered and burned out early and now lived in separate houses in separate states with only displaced children and monthly alimony checks between them. It was a miserable tale of woe that left deep charred flesh on his unsteady bones. The winding scar tissue bound him like a mummy and made him feel like an emotional cripple trying hard to walk again. Stumbling, staggering, falling, crawling. Like a freak show specimen attempting to reanimate and make an escape. Running was still a far off dream. Molly made him want to try his damnedest. She was a ballroom dancer and an acrobat with high cheekbones and even higher rounding breasts and long shapely legs carved of ivory and the lithesome grace of an angelic apparition that filled McGregor's eyes with impossible plans and unquenchable desire. Whether sleek and straight, or done up in trademark spiral curls, her dark hair framed a luminous face of satin cheeks and large liquid-green eyes that made a middle-aged man wish for things like time machines and magic elixirs or a diviner's spell that could turn back the clock for both his heart and his fortunes. He wanted her all to himself for a lifetime. Retroactively. Instead, he owned only these few moments a week, sitting together in his automobile or hers, at the concealed edge of a tree-lined park. Autumn leaves now rustled around the tires and danced in fading green grass of summer's ending.

From their trysting place, they had watched the seasons pass from winter to spring to summer to fall, speaking deeper and more daring words as wardrobe and moments changed and changed again. Nervous pecks in slushy boots and jackets. Small stolen kisses in suits and long dresses. Passionate necking and torrid embraces in taller shoes, higher skirts and smaller shirts. Desperate groping misplaced hands behind foggy windows. Petting and climaxes and whimpers of passion in moist running tights and sweaty tank tops. Lovemaking in lowered blue jeans, embroidered white dresses, sport coats and lifted light sweaters. Or, on a few treasured occasions, completely naked and free, concealed in a mountain cabin where privacy and seclusion allowed full exploration of their desires. They had called it, "The Bat Cave," and what happened there had cemented their hearts with as much ferocity as the passion that joined their loins.

Today, she wore a plaid skirt and stockings, buckled shoes and a snug sweater top that accentuated her buxom appeal. A short, tan, corduroy jacket completed the look.

His large athletic hands had discovered her underneath secrets for another day as they kissed fervently, leaving only a few waning moments for conversation before time forced them back to their mutual routines. As always, the closing topic was her empty marriage and the impractical prospects of divorce.

"With the kids in school, you know there's just no way to make it work, right now," Molly said. "I just don't want their worlds disrupted and destroyed. They love their father and I love them. I just couldn't live with myself if they thought me responsible for destroying their family or taking away their childhood. I can't be home wrecker. Especially when it's my own home."

Her eyes were still fixed straight ahead, as if studying the choreography of the dancing leaves, or possibly envisioning them as red flaming tongues of hellfire torment reserved for those calloused souls guilty of adultery, or even of women in unhappy unions, guilty only of unintentionally falling in love with a determined, pursuing beau. And McGregor Lewis certainly qualified in that regard. He had seen Molly dancing onstage at one of the finest dinner theaters in the city. He had been on his fourth scotch and water when she had stolen the show, wearing a demure but evocatively tailored sailor's outfit and dancing to an antique song about a fellow departing for the Navy and leaving behind his best girl, maybe forever. From the opening steps, she owned the room as surely as she owned his instincts. He couldn't remember the words to the song, but her every move had pulled him more deeply into her world, until he imagined himself as the recipient of both her affections and her heartbreak and wished silently to whatever gods may be for an opportunity to experience the former, if not the latter. Both, if need be. Whatever it took.

After the show and with a head full of Molly's legs, he had bribed the maître d' to deliver a note to her dressing room, describing his admiration in urgent terms and asking for a more private audience. Somehow, she had said yes. And now they were here. Again and again. Perched precariously between lips and hips and lies and double lives and walking a tightrope without a net or a web. Any simpleton could see it was bound to end badly. Neither could bring themselves to care enough to quit. He wanted very much to marry her, but she was still living through her own first shipwreck and none too eager to trade one vessel for another without a break in the storm, or positive knowledge that what awaited was safe harbor and not another dash against the rocks. And so he waited. Loved and lusted and longed for and pined. And waited for her to make a move that might make him feel less like a guilty pleasure or a lonely afterthought to her weekly pantomime. He wondered if she ever would and the uncertainty of it was constant reminder of his own inability to draw her more permanently to him. He imagined that if he were ten years younger, with a longer shelf life and a younger man's vigor that her indecision and trepidation would have long ago departed. As it was, her repeated expressions of conflicted conscience and moral compunction felt more like a simple matter of buyer's remorse and second guessing. He cursed himself for her lack of certitude, deeply wishing that a younger version of himself might have encountered this incomparable woman at a different stage in life and proven himself irresistible in all the ways that he found her mesmerizing and impossible to relinquish. She owned him, stem to stern and relished in the knowing.

"Molly, you know what I want for us and for you," McGregor said. "I want to give us both a chance to feel as happy all the time as we feel when we're here together. Kissing and laughing and touching. I need to dream of that and hope for that for as long as I can, because I can't do anything else. You are in my very soul."

He looked at her again. "God was having His very best day when He made you, Duchess."

When he spoke like this, despite his advantage in age, he had the feeling of a forlorn schoolboy, telling the girl in the second desk that he would marry her, someday. His romantic vulnerability to her made him feel foolish and weak, but he couldn't bear the thought of not speaking his mind and having this moment be the very last opportunity to make his case. What if it were his last? On the radio, Don Henley sang of barstools and familiar strangers and the finite number of seasons given to anyone hoping to find lasting love in unlucky surroundings. Worthless evenings and worn out hearts.

"I can wait as long as you need, my darling," McGregor said. "It's not like I have other plans."

Not anymore. Maybe there wasn't time.

There are few powers as magnetic and unavoidable as a young man's need of his first serious woman. Smart women at that age don't suffer insecurity, because they know that so long as their underthings are easily removed and they feed the beast within their man, a young husband has nearly no choice other than to adore her and remain within arm's reach, or closer. McGregor had known instantly Molly's ability to reawaken those dormant places and longings within him in a way that helped him recapture a remembrance of himself in that younger time of electric youth.

For that power alone, he stood in amazed wonderment at her charms and dreamt of having her become the resident Calistoga of his miraculous rejuvenation. He nicknamed her "Duchess," after the ingénue mistress in a favorite Scorcese movie and imagined the two of them living out similarly grandiose dreams of flash and fairytales and fiendish, unending eruptions of physical delight. The last of that list seemed effortless and guaranteed. It happened already. The happy-ending fairytale tied up with a bow was still mired in doubt.

"Baby, you know I wish we could be together right now, for good. For always," Molly said. She preened her baby-fine chestnut locks behind an ear and tilted her head coyly and sensually so that her face was at the perfect angle for kissing. This time, the kissing would wait. Her eyes were urgent and expressive.

"It's like I said, though. Now just doesn't work because of school. And who knows what winter will bring. I just don't like the thought of throwing everything into turmoil during the wintertime. And God knows I won't be getting divorced during the Holidays. Who would do that to their children? Ruin Christmas for the rest of their lives? Ugggh."

As impeccable as her logic was, it was another stab to his ego. Every delay impressed within him the growing knowledge of a ticking clock and the growing unlikelihood of any kind of future between them. If it hadn't happened in the white-hot rush of their summer passion, why now, when the predictability of their meeting and repetitively conclusive conversation threatened to slip below the threshold of inherent risk? She spoke frequently from the start of her natural fears for discovery and what would happen if her husband were uncover her compromising activities. She mused from the woman's perspective about things like custody arrangements and the impact of disclosed infidelity of alimony, car payments, wardrobe budgets and the need for her to get a job. She had grown accustomed to a life of relative ease and comfort and it was clear that anything that disrupted that luxury in her future situation would not be looked upon favorably. It wasn't worth the risk. *He* wasn't worth the risk. Molly had never articulated anything even approaching that kind of negatory, but combined with what he supposed was his own guilt of their arrangement and her clear misgivings about making a decisive break, the message weighed upon McGregor like a mason's stone, threatening to crush him to bits. He felt himself shrinking under the burden, retracting into himself. Still, he couldn't bear to let go of her. Still, his hardbitten pride and self-awareness prevented begging her departure from her husband, or outright purchase of her future with him as his latest long-term investment. A single realization held him in check. She must choose freely to love him, or he would let her walk away. A Waterloo of the heart.

"You know, I grew up in a home with parents who were unhappy together," McGregor said. It was an angle he'd hinted before. This time, he gave more detail.

"Listening to them argue every day made me feel like I was a prisoner of war. At first, I wanted them to stay together, no matter what. It was familiar. It felt safe having them stay together because it was all that me, my brother and sister knew."

Now he was the one staring straight ahead, as if retracing childhood memories in the piles of accumulated leaves in the park grass. He could feel her eyes trained on his profile. She was listening. Don Henley, the lonesomest eagle, had hit a crescendo now, singing about getting up the liquid courage to cross a barroom and bare his soul to a woman hard-bitten by the pain of betrayal and bad endings. *Give me a chance, give me a chance, to show you how...*

"The three of us used to talk about it, you know. My brother and sis and me," Mac continued. "We used to talk about what we wished could happen with mom and dad. At first, we just wished they would love each other the same way they loved us. Then we just wished they would stop fighting. But somewhere along the way, we grew up enough that we knew that wasn't going to ever happen. Then, we wished that they would go their separate ways, just so all of us could have peace."

McGregor's eyes threatened to brim over. "By the time they made their break, we didn't wish for much of anything at all."

He swallowed hard and looked at her hand next to his on the console. The wedding band still taunting him from its appointed place.

"It happened way too late." His own parents had finally divorced the winter before he left for college. Too late to make much difference for

anyone but the lawyers and accountants. Finished with the story, if not the pain of memory, McGregor had put his hand on hers and looked out the window again.

"I cannot tell you what to choose, or what the right thing to do is," he said.

175

"Children define their world with mom's Saturday morning pancakes and dad's tickle fights and Friday movie nights with pizza and all the familiar things that make a family. They count on Christmas hot chocolate and Easter baskets the same way that you and I might hope for kisses under the mistletoe or spooning after a stiff drink or a tasty roll in the hay with someone sexy. Or, vice versa."

Molly laughed slightly at this. It was a subtle turn of phrase that made McGregor fascinating and interesting in a way men her own age had never been. Maybe it wasn't his age at all. Maybe it was just him. His use of words and innate sophistication had always been an aphrodisiac that she couldn't ignore. His face might have passed for handsome but his soul was deep and sexy in a way that made her want to study and know every corner, still curious as to what might be lurking beneath. He turned his face toward hers and looked into her eyes.

"But there will come a day when they know all of that familiarity has been fake and that it's been tainted by more than just the natural struggles of couples who live silently in desperation wishing for someone else to sweep them off of their feet."

He reached out once more and gently caught the curve of her downy chin between his thumb and forefinger, lifting her eyes exactly even with his own.

"Kids can smell a phony a mile away," he said. "And every moment of their lives, we're either teaching them to live that phoniness for some ill-begotten concept of the greater good of everyone else, or we're teaching them never to settle for anything less than something real, and tangible and impossible to ignore and escape."

"Do you want them to learn to make the same bargains that you've made and end up exactly where you sit in twenty years?"

He released her chin and turned his eyes again to the distance, as if waiting for confirmation from the universe that his words had struck home in a way they never had. He needed them to. He didn't know how much longer either of them could handle the risk. Or wear the shame. Where he had once been so certain of his standing, despite her assurances, he now feared that the vast space of her heart previously reserved only for him might now be contained in a couple of dusty shoeboxes in a corner closet. It gnawed at his mind like a sliver of glass in an open cut. He bled silently.

Across the park in the distance, a small pod of children too young for school were playing in the piled leaves while their mothers watched. They frolicked and bounced like brightly colored fishing bobbers bouncing on the waves. In their hoodies and windbreakers, they looked like tiny crayons spilling from an overturned Crayola box and rolling across the green of a billiards table. In the silence, McGregor turned to see her watching the gathering gaggle attentively. Her eyes had changed. As the silence stretched out between them, he recognized her no longer as an intoxicated lover overcome by the animalistic pangs of unfulfilled desire, but as a mother concerned only for the safety of her children and the security of routine. The battle had resumed within her and the mere reminder of her own role had overcome his mountain of words with a single glance. The children danced and frolicked. The autumn wind pressed in through the window seals and nudged the car gently with whistling gasps. Leaves swirled and pirouetted in the currents like a beautiful dancer, "on point," in front of the final audience of a long night, encore be damned. To McGregor Lewis, the moment carried the feeling of being forced through a narrowing passageway from which there would be neither return, nor retreat.

"Perhaps next spring will be a good time to get things rolling and make a change," Molly said finally, as if only to fill the air with something other than lost moments and pounding hearts.

Her voice seemed a shell of itself. The words, mere fulfillment of a script that wasn't her own.

"The school year will be over and the weather won't interfere as much if we have to move. Maybe spring will be the right time."

After soaking in the meaning, McGregor Lewis pressed the brake pedal and turned the key in the ignition of his expensive car, preparing for the long but short drive back to the place where her own SUV was parked.

"Maybe in the spring," he echoed, knowing better. "Something to look forward to, after the holidays and all."

The tiny dancer danced again, leaving as she always did the everlasting hope of sweetness and grace in her wake as the two rode silently forward into afternoon sunshine.

Soon she would be gone again, with only her lingering perfume as reminder she had been there at all. "Yes," she said. "Maybe in the spring will be the right time." Maybe in the spring.

HUMANITY

"My dear naive boy," Professor McCronyn intoned to the captive colleague with whom he shared the badly painted park bench.

"The outmoded conventions of violence and warfare are soon to pass into the enveloping mists of history, and you can carve that in whatever igneous mineral you please."

The dramatic oratory paused while the venerable scholar struck a match and rekindled the vanilla Cavendish in his briarwood pipe. The belch of smoke mingled with the smell of drying autumn leaves that were scattered, rustling and shiny amidst the last lawn clippings of the season.

"They are no more than symptoms of a human sickness that will be eradicated as simply as polio or consumption."

The younger man's gaze contained a concoction of bemusement and contempt. He had suffered the arrogant railings of the esteemed Doctor McCronyn first as a student, and now as a fellow professor. Not to imply that his elder

179

and tenured colleague would ever consider him an equal intellect, mind you. As far as McCronyn was concerned, the good Lord above had never created his equal in that regard, with the possible exception of Sir Isaac Newton, and only then on the very day the latter had discovered gravity. A bump on the head by that apple more than likely dislodged enough brain matter to give McCronyn the clear advantage ever after. As Human Sciences Department head, McCronyn's superlative confidence in his own understanding of the human soul was rivaled only by his conviction of mankind's inevitable evolution into a more peaceful and rational race. He was thoroughly convinced that the Big War, just concluded on the continent across the sea, was indisputable proof of his theory.

"There is no room for equivocation on this point, my boy," McCronyn continued.

"We have, stated simply, stared into the very face of the bloodiest violence imaginable, only to find it completely devoid of any discernible return. It is a simple matter of wasted resources and ruined lives."

McCronyn chewed the stem of his pipe and stared wistful across the campus commons inner square. The younger man knew the look. It meant the old goat was once again lost in the self-indulgent intoxication of his thoughts and wouldn't stop until the whole steaming load was deposited in the ears of anyone near enough to listen. The experienced knew with painful clarity that getting up to leave mid-sermon was not allowed. For an audacious student guilty of such an offense, the academic penalty would be punitive and swift. For a colleague in the same department, a similar action would mean at best, an abrupt end to career advancement, and at worst, added to the former, a volley of rumor and innuendo in the faculty lounge that would lead additionally to Christmas party snubbery and social ruin. Edgar Marsh, McCronyn's arch enemy on matters historical, once said that the old Scot never saw people, only audience members. On this unlucky occasion, it was the young professor's turn to bear the burden. He had not positioned himself as McCronyn's department head successor only to lose rank by offending the old man's ego. At least not today.

"I would make the largest possible wager on this certainty," McCronyn went on. "There is not the slightest chance that any difference between race, or religion, or people, will ever again erupt into war. What more evidence is needed of the folly of bloodshed than tens of millions dead, millions more maimed and wounded and scarred. Such a lesson will not fade quickly from the brightest minds among us, and that remembrance will ensure that even on a level man to man, violent resolution to conflict will become the ultimate contradiction in terms."

McCronyn was hitting his stride now, caressing the gnarled bulb of his pipe with a thumb and twisting at his gray mustache with the fingers of his other hand. The younger man had yet to speak a word.

"It is our responsibility to set the new example," McCronyn said. "After all, if the more learned among us cannot be called upon to be the standard bearers for the new civility, we can hardly blame the poor, unwashed, undernourished and unschooled to do the job. I would no more strike a man in anger with my hand than cut off my own arm. Words are weapons enough for this new age."

Finally, McCronyn's locomotive of thought seemed to have found a station. The old man stopped speaking long enough to repack his failing pipe. His younger colleague saw the opening and moved quickly to speak before it passed him by.

"Did you read the morning paper, McCronyn?" The young man reached inside a valise and produced a crinkled copy of the day's rag, complete with a coffee ring from his morning breakfast cup.

"With all due respect, there are headlines enough in this single edition to disprove your utopian vision with but a glance, and that's not even counting the police blotter or the court docket."

True enough, the front page trumpeted a decidedly horrible story in forty point type. A banner so tall it barely left room for an inch of copy above the fold. There was a killer on the prowl, the story said. Presumably a man, the assailant in question had an affection for blood spilled by fine cutlery and had claimed his sixth victim in as many weeks, overnight. The latest body had previously belonged to an aging local businessman, out for an evening stroll.

"He was stabbed more than a dozen times," the young professor related, remembering and disseminating this detail with the same dignified ease that had earned him a handful of sheepskins in the same time his average contemporaries finished their first.

"Detectives say they can tell the quality of the blade he used by the smoothness of the lacerations and the depth of the cuts in their flesh. Rumor is he fully decapitated his first three victims and kept the heads from two."

The fledgling professor seemed anesthetized to the grisly elements he was relating. He passed the folded newspaper to McCronyn who produced a pair of pince-nez reading spectacles from his vest pocket and placed them on the bridge of his craggy nose. He inspected the paper's front page, as if checking up on the young man's rendition of the facts.

"No one would dare question, your fervor, McCronyn," the young man continued, "but you can't possibly ignore the absolute randomness of nature."

"How do you mean?" McCronyn frowned his question to the young man on his right. There was an inescapably derisive tone to the question, as if the mere asking further disqualified the the asker from serious intellectual consideration. The young man ignored this and went on.

"The only prediction about human cruelty that can possibly hold up is this. That every once in a while, a combination of sadism, narcissism, egocentricity and violence will bring us beyond rationale to a place where only reciprocal violence can solve the question." The young man was looking straight ahead as he spoke, deliberately avoiding the probing gaze of his contemptuous colleague.

"Maniacs like our stabber, and egomaniacal monsters like Hitler have no use for elegant reasoning or polite discourse," the young man continued. "Your fancy words may be the ultimate weapon in the professor's lounge, but in the real world of insanity and rage, only violence is understood."

McCronyn let out a small hush of air as if someone had struck him solid in the ribs. The morning paper was resting on his knees, but the pages were trembling with his legs as a current of tension ran through him. He was silent a moment before gathering himself for a spattered reply.

"I beg your pardon, young master Phelps, but citing isolated instances of insanity as proof for the unchanging shortcomings of the human spirit is unpardonably ignorant. Stopping Hitler was a matter of having the right people do the reasoning."

Phelps knew the extent of McCronyn's arrogance but this newest assertion was too much. He looked stunned by the revelation.

"Do you mean to say that you could have talked Hitler out of his visions of global domination and saved the Jews from the ovens? Please tell me that's not what you are implying!"

"I'll do you one better, my good professor Phelps," McCronyn responded, "Not only could timely intervention by the proper mind have prevented the disaster of the great war, but I believe if I were face to face with our stabber, as you call him, I could in five minutes time fully convince him of the error of his ways and have him turn himself in straightaway."

With that, the older academician rose from the bench and stalked rapidly away, carrying the borrowed newspaper under one arm. From his direction, Phelps noted McCronyn wasn't even bothering with a stop at his office before heading off campus and home. The old man was angry and his day was finished.

McCronyn had walked the same path to and from the university for thirty years. His commitment to this daily ritual was as legendary as his academic stature and argumentative nature. He prided himself at covering the sixteen block distance every day with only a single steps difference either way. It was a quirk of counting the steps that made the walk a form of self-imposed psychotherapy that he had grown to require. His salary had grown tremendously over the years. Tremendously enough for Doctor and Mrs. McCronyn to afford any house in the nicest neighborhoods in the city, but they never moved. The professor needed his daily walks to and from the campus to fine tune his mind for the day's lectures. He used the return trip to clear his mind of the academic clutter in preparation for an evening with his dear wife. Even now, walking home, he could feel the steps working their familiar magic. His anger was draining away. Perhaps he had been a bit rash with young Mr. Phelps. The boy had a bright mind, after all, and had often sought guidance from McCronyn in molding his lectures and formulating curriculum for his courses. In some ways, Phelps might have been considered a McCronyn protege, if not by McCronyn himself. No one in three decades had yet merited such consideration, and McCronyn was not about to begin with a young man who believed mankind was doomed to a repetitive pattern of maniacal ambition that only violence would solve.

"Future department head, perhaps," McCronyn spoke out loud as he walked, "tenured department head, most likely, but McCronyn heir-apparent? Hardly!"

His solitary conversation found him four blocks from his ivy covered home with the sun finishing it's slow descent behind the skyline of buildings and trees. A cool breeze rattled piles of drying leaves, still reddish and golden on the ground. The old man's mood was fully restored. He always loved these last few blocks before home. It was here that he often slowed his pace to enjoy the fine collection of well- groomed lawns and healthy trees along the sidewalk. His eyes were drawn to the ordered rows of flowers that bordered front porches and neatly trimmed shrubbery that framed planter boxes along front walkways. It was all the medicine he needed. Two more blocks and he would be home.

"Actually, I'd rather not be your heir-apparent."

McCronyn was startled to a stop by the voice from behind. He turned to see professor Phelps a few feet away. How long had he been following him? Couldn't wait to finish the argument, eh?

Phelps spoke again, closing the few steps between them. "There was a time when I wanted nothing more than your approval," Phelps said. "I longed to have you recognize my brilliance as in a league with your own. I hoped that you would see a younger version of yourself when you looked at me, but you never did."

McCronyn started to speak, but the younger man didn't give him the chance.

"I don't need or want any of that from you anymore, professor," Phelps continued, unsnapping his valise and rummaging inside, "but there is something you have that I am determined to take." With terrible speed, Phelps hand reemerged from the leather case with a glint of steel that was unmistakable and deadly. A moment later, it was over. McCronyn's body slumped limply to the pavement. In the deepening darkness after sundown, it looked like a mounded pile of autumn leaves.

THE COW WRESTLERS

I f impertinence and an utter lack of self-effacement were counted virtues, Silas Mackey would have been an indisputably saintly man, with heaven on the way. As it was, those qualities in abundance did nothing but tighten fists and raise color at the local tavern he frequented, providing impromptu entertainment in the form of brawls and spilled, sloshing beer. He stood five feet, six inches, but talked as if he were a foot taller. Two feet taller if he'd had more than two rounds of draught, which was normally the case by eight o'clock on any given evening. Tonight he was already on round number four and his ruddy face was glazed with the sweat of an overworked and ailing heart. Still, his gritty voice and clenching bellows of frothing laughter captured the mood of a rowdy crowd as he regaled them with a story some had only heard a dozen times.

"There she was, mates," Silas intoned, gesturing with his mug.

"The biggest heifer in the county. Covered with mud and with rabid devil's fire in her eyes. She looked at me and I looked at her, and that was that. There was goin'ta be a reckonin.'"

"It's not nice to talk about yer' best girl thataways, Silas!"

The crowd roared with drunken overeager laughter. The rhetorical bovine comparison had come from Edwin McQuain, the local shopkeeper. He had heard the heifer story himself two dozen times and was more than willing to make Silas Mackey the butt of any joke before hearing it again. The two men had punched themselves silly in stumbling, awkward fisticuffs New Year's Eve two years ago. Both claimed to have emerged victorious from the tilt and neither had any use for reports to the contrary, or for each other, ever after. McQuain believed himself the rightful practitioner of the barroom story, and was loathe to allow his rival another moment in the spotlight. He stood to speak.

"Yeah, yeah, Silas. She charged ye' and ye' wrestled her to the peat and tied her haunches with a willow switch."

Edwin drawled the words in a hackneyed sing-song of boredom and indifference. He wasn't finished.

"After besting the beasty, you turned her into three pairs of boots and a dozen roasts for Sabbath dinner," Edwin spat.

More laughter.

"More likely, she died on the spot from tuberculosis because you didn't feed her or bring her out of the rain." They were rolling now. Straining with the laughter of the drink that aches the ribs and wets the cheeks. The interrupted story had turned to the kind of roasting a drunken crowd loves the very best. And there in the middle, Silas Mackey's red face grew redder still, roiling with a growing rage. He hated Edwin McQuain to the soles of his feet, and was hating him more deeply by the moment.

"Tis a wonder you've kept a herd at all, Mackey," McQuain continued.

"But then, the beef we've been broasting round here lately has tasted more like mutton on a bad day, so maybe that's proof your animals made it to market after all. Any steak you have to shave on the platter must have come from a Mackey cow, I always say, eh?"

They were cackling now. Unfettered squalls of loathing, rumpus guffaws.

Silas Mackey's defeat was public and complete.

Edwin McQuain took his seat to a full pint and the congratulatory claps on the back from friends and strangers alike.

Nearly forgotten in the hubbub, Silas Mackey made a stomping, stumbling path to the door and disappeared into the night.

◖․․ ․․◗

The next morning, they could scarcely believe their eyes. Standing in the early street with bleary eyes and clanging heads, the onlookers gathered amid the sprinkled and shattered remains of storefront windows. McQuain's Mercantile, Dry Goods and Apothecary was now an open air market, complete with curtains that fluttered and snagged against a sash rimmed with a toothy border of broken glass. The store's namesake stood mouth agape on the boardwalk in front of his establishment, holding an idle broom and wiping his brow. His wife was the only one who moved, busy and cross with a bristle broom and a dustpan, clearing the boards of huddled shards of crystalline tears. To anyone on hand for McQuain's illustrious performance at the pub the night before, the culprit was clear. Silas Mackey had taken his revenge.

⊂══◦ ◦══⊃

A day later on the Mackey farm there came a bellow of anger and surprise. Silas and his wife stood with hands clamped on the top fence rail of their prized sheep pen and surveyed the carnage. Four ewes and their lambs lay crumpled and lifeless in the muck, their cold and glassy eyes fixed without sight on the great beyond. Luxurious wool coats, annually clipped and immortalized in a gross of sweaters and scarves were now sodden and moldering in the foggy morning air. Mrs. Silas Mackey didn't dare to speak, or even to breathe. She felt the fence rail tremble with her husband's fermenting rage. He finally muscled a handful of words from between gritted teeth.

"If Edwin McQuain wants a war, it's a war he will get."

⊂══◦ ◦══⊃

Within the hour, the two angry men had made their way to each other, nearly colliding in the fog as they drove the town road in opposite directions, finally meeting on the village outskirts just past St. Ignatius Cathedral. They exited their conveyances and walked toward one another, feet crunching in the moist gravel. Silas Mackey carried a heavy stone. McQuain held a shop hammer and a blade from his store. Mackey too had a knife from his butcher closet concealed in the boot top of his right leg. It was a deadly serious business, to be sure. As their distance closed, neither man said a word. There was nothing to be said. And then it began. Grasping and clutching. Spitting and scraping. Grunts and glints of metal and the thudding blows of eager violence. They rolled one way and then the other, locked together in a sweating, struggling ball of hate and fury. Dabs of sheep's lint and lamb's blood on Mackey's jacket were joined by flecks of crushed stone from the road surface. McQuains' shopkeeper's apron soon gained a fresher crimson color as the contest deepened with their wounds. The blood of two men mingled in painted splotches on the roadway, tracing the path of their conflict until it ebbed and slowed and finally fell wheezing, silent. Weapons clattered uselessly to the ground.

⊙═◦ ◦═⊙

In the parlor of a quaint country farmhouse, a porcelain tea service stood full and steaming surrounded by a calico spread of scones and quince jelly. The melding aromas of chamomile and chocolate wafted aimlessly through the room shared by two graying and portly figures, dainty with their tea and smiling chatter.

"It was a lovely touch with those windows, dear, if I do say so, myself. Just right to set off the powder keg." The widow of Edwin McQuain sipped primly at her teacup, her eyes a mirthful retreat of satisfied wishes.

"But I must admit that was no trouble at all, compared with what you must have endured, dispatching those horrid animals. So much blood and mucking about."

Across the table, the widow of Silas Mackey lowered her own cup to the saucer and gazed back at her afternoon guest.

"It was a bit messier than usual, dear, but a pittance paid for the prize won." They sipped again and shared a wink and a smile before the farmer's widow spoke again. "Now how about a nice slice of mutton pie?"

SOAP BUBBLES

"Maybe I'm the lightning." Semi-reclined in the row of brightly colored plastic bench-chairs inside the Tub n' Suds laundromat, Tabitha Kenzie fidgeted with an empty fabric softener ball and stared vacantly across the room. Karrie was shifting a load of blue jeans and t-shirts from washer to dryer. The kerplunk of quarters punctuated the perpetual magnetic hum of robotic tumbling cylinders filled with cottons, polyesters and faded towels. The room smelled of detergent and mildew, but mostly of antique cigarette smoke left by customers whose only affordable amusement was self-administered nicotine and cancer by the pack. They were the only people there. Tabitha shifted her feet aimlessly back and forth across the gritty tile floor.

"You know.....I mean....what if all the things I blame on circumstance or other people, or just the 'luck of the draw,' really come straight back to me and something I did or didn't do?"

Her father had often told her that she had a habit of thinking thoughts that were too big for her head. Tabitha imagined that she was having one of those moments right then, although she had never credited her father with having the intuition or sensitivity of intellect to make such an assessment. At least she had hoped as much. She hoped he was wrong. Besides, he was too busy being gone to notice her. In his absence, her mother had done an admirable job of continuing the tradition of squelched notions and bud-nipped expectations until Tabitha turned nineteen and moved out. Now, she and Karrie shared a one-bedroom apartment on the street next to the grain elevator. Night and day, the monotone rush and roar of the grain dryers seemed to strum the little apartment like a horsehair bow drawn endlessly across a violin string. The harmonic drone lodged itself permanently between Tabitha's temples and made her teeth ache. Even the din of the Laundromat was a peaceful retreat.

"You know, they say lightning never strikes the same place twice," Tabitha picked up again, watching for some recognition that Karrie was listening, or had even heard her speak.

"But with me, it seems like the same old bolt of lightning keeps hitting me over and over, and no matter what I change or how I try to dodge, it's still there, following me and leaving its mark."

Karrie had shifted the last load from wash to dry and was arranging bottles of detergent and softener in their already stacked laundry baskets. She definitely wasn't listening. Tabitha had decided it didn't matter.

"So, what are the chances that all these horrible and painfully empty things keep happening, and each one is random and just out of the blue, like….wham, and then another one and something different and it just happens over and over your whole life? What are the chances?"

Tabitha sometimes fought to dilute her way of speaking so she didn't sound so pretentious and overwrought. People usually just called it, "talking funny," but Tabitha knew what that meant. She'd come to believe, that by and large, people don't like things that are different or unusual because it makes them wonder endlessly about how many other things there might be that don't fit neatly into the tidy boxes of the universe. They didn't want to be measured against anything that might remind them of the potential for inferiority. Her vocabulary, among other things, certainly fit the bill. Now and then, when the wrong word popped out of her mouth, Tabitha would watch as people flinched and stared, the way she imagined someone at a burger joint might react to a plate of Hijiki salad and eel rumake. *Where did that come from? What's a fifty-dollar word like that doing in a two-dollar head like yours?* She could read it in their eyes. Boyfriends especially. Girls with her clothes and pedigree weren't supposed to have thoughts at all, much less about anything deep or interesting. It was one of the money-luxuries reserved for people with nice clothes and cars and places to work and live that don't continually reverberate with the sound of freight trains and grain kernels drying for storage. In her daydreams, Tabitha imagined places where people didn't look askance at uncommon words and where anyone could sit around and talk about their observations and philosophies of life, even if they had dirt under their fingernails or a tear in their trousers. She wondered if college courtyards and university libraries might qualify. Surely in places like that, one could indulge in the proclivities of the mind without having to worry about whether your date would get up and leave the restaurant without paying for the chicken fried steak you hadn't even finished. *Or the park, or the movies...or the bed. They're always leaving you somewhere, aren't they? Leaving you and your busy mouth behind. You and all your scary words and crazy thought jumbles.* Was that her father's voice? Her mother's? Her own? Maybe all three.

Tabitha came-to to find a warm cotton sock in each hand. One striped. One covered with hearts and half moons. *They weren't a pair.* She and Karrie were standing over a basket of whites, still radiating the static and heat of the dryer and smelling of Bounce. Tabitha fished deeper in the basket to find mates, hoping the law of laundry averages and the land of missing socks hadn't claimed another victory. She couldn't afford new socks, right now. Not for awhile. After this month, maybe not ever. As they folded, Tabitha continued her monologue as if Karrie had been listening to not just her words, but her thoughts as well.

"I mean, what are the chances? Really."

She had mated both pairs and moved on to another, watching Karrie's lithe fingers dangling and arranging a white t-shirt with three holes in the neckline. It was the shirt Tabitha liked to wear on lazy Sundays when there wasn't any laundry to do.

"I'm the constant in every situation. I'm the one thing that doesn't change from one thing to the next. Anything bad that happens, it's me it happens to. Anything that goes wrong, it's me in the middle."

"Maybe, *I'm* the lightning."

Karrie didn't look up. Still folding, and well enough within earshot that Tabitha knew she had to be hearing every word.

"Anyway, I'm not sure which is more comforting; knowing and believing that it's me that's the root cause of everything that falls apart, or believing that there's something else going on...something more random that just swoops down and does its worst and then flies away, you know? They're both frightening. One means I'm defective, somehow. That some innate deficiency dooms me to go over the same mistakes until I've messed up every possible avenue in the same way. That everything I do will end in disappointment, regardless of what I do. And the other..."

"The other means that God is cruel."

The basket was almost empty as the piles of looped and squared and squeezed fabric grew higher and higher on the countertop. Then they would move the stacks back into the basket for the trip home. In the baskets dirty, then out dirty and back in clean, then out clean and back in again, folded. Tabitha had often thought about the absurdity of folding clothes. It amused her. The idea of trying to create neatness and uniformity out of a tumbled ball of chaos that obviously yearned to be free and spill haphazardly back to its naturally irrepressible state. Two minutes in the drawer at home and the futility of an hour's labor was obvious. Something to do with the "second law of thermodynamics," Tabitha remembered. *From order to chaos, dust to dust. Entropy is the natural state of being for the universe. Just check my sock drawer, Einstein.*

Truth was, she hated laundry day for the same reason she hated the infernal mill. She imagined swirling particles of soap and mouse droppings, wafting in and around her in a dancing pirouette of contamination and decay. She had often envisioned the horrid interior of the grain elevator, with its creaking, belching vibrations, spewing and spouting fetid clouds of steam and grain dust. She could feel the concoction collecting on her skin and polluting her cells. Sometimes, to purge the image from her mind for sleep, she would close her eyes and imagine the droning hulk as nothing more sinister than the world's largest string orchestra, tuning for performance. *They are only violins. A lullaby for sleep.* Unfortunately, she had yet to create a similar diversion for days at the Laundromat. She couldn't fool herself past the smell.

Across the basket, Karrie still hadn't spoken or smiled. Tabitha knew they would quarrel later about how little she had helped with the laundry, or about how unskilled she was at the various folding techniques and organizational zeitgeist necessary to complete the task. Towels this way. Jeans that way. Twice crosswise, then over in thirds. Washcloths over once and then over again. It was the same way they quarreled about dishes in the sink or how to arrange plates and cups and bowls in their tiny cupboard space. Karrie's mother had taught her exactly how it all should go, and why.

Tabitha's mother had never cared, and had certainly never put on a seminar in the proper art of towel folding or dishwashing or cupboard arranging. *Or in the proper art of anything else, for that matter.* Call it the third law of thermodynamics. Different mothers make different daughters whose differences alternately delight and annoy one another forever after. It had been mostly annoyance lately. Their quarrels had grown steadily more frequent, until Tabitha worried that Karrie would pack up and move out. Besides the friendship, Tabitha knew she couldn't find another place to live until she found another job, and recent developments promised to make that even more complicated. Her employment record read like a tour guide to the city's fast food industry, and she had just been eliminated from the final stop. She had burned seven batches of french fries and spilled drinks into the driver's seats of three customers in a single day. The former because she couldn't lean out the window of the drive-thru far enough to be graceful, and the latter because, as she tried to tell the manager, the buzzer-timer on the fryer was the exact same pitch and frequency as the hum of the grain mill. She simply couldn't hear it go off.

At that, he had given her an odd look that said he was less than sympathetic to whatever noises might permeate wherever it was that her apartment was located, and promptly relieved her of the grease covered green apron and visor that served as the franchise uniform. *No more free dinner, five nights a week. No more pilfering the discard pile for burgers that had been under the heat lamp too long.* No more rent money. Karrie had been less than pleased with the news of her latest termination, especially when she had to foot the entire bill for that month's housing. They had yelled at each other for an hour, then fallen asleep exhausted after crying and hugging and making things better over a half-bottle of Boone's Farm.

In the end, Karrie promised to stay, Tabitha promised to get another job and everything was fine. Almost. The next morning, Tabitha had felt badly about the wine, but it had been too soon to say anything, and refusing would have only raised questions she didn't want to answer. Not yet. Hopefully there had been no damage. It was complicated territory she was into now, and she didn't know what to say, or how and when to say it. *Strange problem for the girl with the fifty-dollar words. You've never been at a loss before.* True enough, but this latest curve-ball was a tad more complex than even random, mumbling rants on the origins and motivations of human existence.

Give me a good old epistemological analysis any day. Metaphysical hypothesis? No problem. Anything but this. Anything but this. Somehow, the laundry was finished and it was time to load the baskets back into the car. Through the smudgy, steam clouded window Tabitha could see Karrie struggling to hold the first basket while turning the key in the rusted hatchback. Four more loads were waiting, poised on the counter like children in bassinets. Tabitha knew she should carry them out, but thought better of it. It was the lifting. Her stomach hadn't felt right since her last day of work, since the last time she had successfully delivered a biggie-Coke into the waiting hands of a moron who evidently believed that four feet from the pickup window was a perfectly acceptable distance. *Remember! The customer is always right! Always. It's your own fault, anyway, genius. One word to the manager about anything and you wouldn't have had to work the window, at all. Even the*

company knows basic biology. Who knows what kind of mess
you made in there. And all because you didn't want anybody to
find out. In case you haven't noticed, it's not the kind of secret
that would keep forever.

And it wouldn't. In her ears, the sound of the grain
mill grew louder as the tiny car made the final turn for
home. Tabitha looked around to find her seatbelt fastened
and every basket in its place. Maybe tonight she would tell
her. Maybe they would put the laundry away together and
sit close over their T.V. dinners and then they would talk
in bed before turning out the light. She imagined how it
would be to lay her head on Karrie's chest and have out
with the whole thing, and have none of it really matter to
either of them. They would fall asleep and dream of violins.

DROWNING MAN

Felix Peabody was a man choking on saltwater. He walked every step along the main street sidewalk sucking greedily and loudly at the humid August air. Hurried and sweating, his labored respiration gave him the look and sound of a man who believes every breath might be his last. Limping rapidly but weakly on a right leg left cudgeled by a tour in the Big War, Felix was late for a lunch appointment at the Eat-a-Bite Café. He was meeting a man who he hoped would be able to offer a solution to his problem. A problem named Lenora Peabody.

They had been married in the Spring of '46, and every year since, the man known as Felix Peabody had watched himself dwindle and fade in the full length mirror of their cramped and dingy bedroom. Before the war and his return to Lenora, Felix had been an athlete of better than middling report, snaring touchdown passes and errant baseballs with equal aplomb. He had savored the small town notoriety that accompanied those exploits and hoped silently that they might be enough to overcome a nagging feeling that everyone found him more than a little strange. He was never quite sure what it was that affected people that way, but he could see it in their eyes. They always smiled and congratulated him after the big plays in the big games, but he could tell somehow that they sensed it too. He was different somehow. Somewhere down deep, something wasn't right. He knew it, they knew it and that was that. It wasn't the sort of thing polite people would draw attention to, but then, those were the sort of things that made the best gossip, weren't they?

He wondered if that was why he had settled for Lenora to begin with. She had never seemed to care about the thing that everyone felt but never mentioned. If she had, it had never seemed enough to put her off. In the years to come, it was a quality that bothered her husband more and more. Once Lenora Peabody had an idea fixed in her head, heaven help anyone who offered dissent. Felix had stopped doing anything resembling *that* long before their first anniversary. He thought of it as a matter of efficiency. After a while, it just wasn't worth the fight to throw a fuss, and so he didn't. Thirty years later, he was a man on a sidewalk who couldn't breathe and couldn't walk and couldn't catch his breath, much less a touchdown pass. And it was time he did something about it, and so he was. The man he was meeting for lunch came highly recommended by another man who would know about such things. It was a delicate matter after all. It wasn't every day that someone had the guts to do that sort of thing, even if they thought about it all the time. Some people would live every day of their lives wishing for exactly that moment, but never actually go through with the deed. *Not you, though, champ. Nosirreee. No one can ever say you don't have the guts. You are a man's man, pally.*

"And don't you forget it, *pally.*"

Talking out loud to his own, inner voice was nothing new. Truth be told, the one man dialog was the only genuinely mutual discussion to be found in the Peabody household. *If a man can't pay attention to himself, who will, right, pally?*

Felix's inner voice sounded smooth and tough like Dean Martin. The way Felix wished he could be, or could have been in another life. Felix stopped for a moment, still three blocks from the café. The effort of talking to himself had taxed his lungs too much to keep walking, and he needed a rest. He braced his right arm against the warm brick corner of a barbershop and tried to slow his gasping to a mild wheeze. His legs felt rubbery beneath him, like leftover polenta stored in the icebox and served again, moist and wiggling on the plate. He needed a drink of water and a handkerchief, but had neither. Sweat was turning his white starched shirt transparent with grayish spots in the beating sun. He fished a silver pocket watch from his pants and snapped open the lid. He needed to make better time. *This is one appointment you don't want to miss, pally.* He had missed plenty of appointments in recent months. So many, in fact that his commission as a carpet salesman had been reduced. He still had ten years until retirement, and if his sales figures didn't drop, his salary for the coming year would be only half the year before. *Took a little off the top and sides, didn't they pally?*

Pinned your ears back pretty good, is what they did. And all because that blasted Lenora can't have the car back when she's supposed to. Dumb bitch. The Dean Martin voice again. Stating the obvious.

The Peabody's were a one-car family, out of necessity. That meant that Lenora would take the car early in the morning to have coffee with her gaggle of middle-aged girlfriends and come back to the house about the time Felix needed to leave for work. For a dozen odd years, that was the plan anyway. But for the last three months, Lenora's ability to watch the clock appeared to have taken a decided turn for the worse. One day out of three she would walk in the door with a sack of leftover donuts, an hour or more after Felix was supposed to be at work. Without a word, Felix would pick up his briefcase of carpet samples and his bologna bag lunch and totter to the waiting car. If he was lucky, and the traffic was light, he could make it in by ten. It was the best he could do, but it hadn't been good enough. Just because Lenora was oblivious to the time, didn't mean his clients were too. Even though he had called to reschedule, several had complained to his supervisor about the inconvenience, and more than one had cancelled their accounts. The dock in pay was a foregone conclusion. The company wanted him out, and the sooner the better. *And kiss that pension goodbye, pally. That's the game now. If you can't make it another three years, you won't even get a percentage of the payout. And that's exactly what they hope will happen. Cheap help's the best help, don't you know, pally? Top salesman for twenty years, or not, cheap's the name of the game.*

Sometimes the Dean Martin voice could be as annoying as his wife. Almost. But then, the truth had a way of doing that to a guy. Especially when there wasn't a damn thing you could do to change it.

Oh, but there is, isn't there, pally? That's what you're doing for lunch today. And that's why you better get your rear end in gear. Step it up, pally! What are you, anyway? A limp-noodled cracker?

"Shut your mouth, Dean-O," Felix snapped to himself. "I'm about to show you what a real man does when things need fixing around here. You just watch, *pally*." Felix did his best to quicken his lumbering pace, and felt his chest tighten like a band of iron. He supposed the cigarette habit he had developed in the early months of his marriage wasn't helping him make it to the Eat-a-Bite on time. He had quit the things more than a year ago, but his lungs apparently never got the message. There was no question the damage done would eventually require his final curtain on this spinning ball. Anyone within earshot of his respiratory concert would guess the same. No doubt about it, the lungs are an unforgiving audience. Tick them off too bad and they just get up and walk off the job. *Just like someone should have done when there was still some walkin' left to do, pally, on two accounts. Talk about shutting the barn door after the horses run away? What are you planning to do with all your free time anyway? Plan your own funeral?* Felix chuckled at that as his feet touched off the final block before the Eat-a-Bite.

"Not mine, pally. Not yet."

No question he had waited a long time to make his move. Two years into the grand experiment known as the Peabody marriage should have been more than enough to sail the ship. They had both known it sooner than that, but two years was when things really started to go. She was pregnant by then, and so it seemed the deal was set. How she had gotten that way was anybody's guess. Their own physical union was more of an obligated reflex by then and he had always wondered how the sporadic opportunities for conception had found the mark. *Maybe the baby wasn't yours. Maybe those trips to the donut shop took a little detour now and then, pally? Ever think of that?*

"Rhetorical again, Dean-O, you putz." Of course he had wondered. But like the thing that everyone felt about him and no one ever said, it was one of those things that went politely by the boards. Nobody tested for paternity back then anyway. It would have been scandalously impolite and embarrassing to boot. As it turned out, Lenora miscarried in her fourth month anyway, and that was the end of that. For both husband and wife, the loss of that child seemed nature's ultimate confirmation of their invalid union. Some things worked out the way they should. Happy couples had babies. Unhappy couples didn't. They had never given fate the opportunity again. One answer was enough. *The baby wasn't the only thing that died in that marriage, eh Felix? Oh sure, you're still upright and walking around, but then, there are other ways to die, aren't there.* Other ways indeed. And some things die harder than others. *Took a while for that one to shut down, didn't it pally. Yeah, you know what I'm talking about. The urge for the skirts? The itch that won't go away. Any real man will tell you that's the last thing to go. Not without some concerted effort, anyway.*

Felix had stopped answering the voice in his head, but the truth was the truth. Lenora had never been one to let things get too out of hand in the boudoir, and never too frequently, God forbid. He had pretty much abandoned the idea of connubial bliss somewhere around their second night together, and things had dropped off considerably since then. But marital celibacy was never quite enough for Lenora. She made it abundantly clear that she wouldn't be happy until every trace of masculine instinct had been permanently and irrevocably erased. *Caught you glancing at a nice pair of legs? One month of incessant nagging. Found your skin magazine under the bathroom sink? One month of incessant nagging. What did she expect you to do, anyway? Go without for the rest of your life? Like that could happen. If putting out was too much for her to handle, she could have at least been a little understanding about what a guy needs to do.*

What a guy needs to do. Felix Peabody found himself standing in front of the Eat-a-Bite Café, just a few feet from the glass door. Slowly but surely, his addled brain brought him back to the moment as he remembered the all-important purpose for being where he was. *You've got an appointment with your future, my man. Walk through this door, find a table, and your life changes for good. One little conversation and POOF! No more Lenora. No more late for appointment mornings with your boss riding your you-know-what until you croak. No more second guessing your every public head turn, and angled glance, worried she might catch you in the act of dreaming. It all goes away, just like that.*

"Don't forget about the money, Dean-O. Don't forget about that."

Some years ago, Felix had taken out a sizable policy against his wife's mortality after the two of them had seen a heart touching infomercial on the television. Hosted by Wilford Brimley or Gregory Peck or somebody like that.

The thing had been sappy as all get out, but it had made it seem perfectly essential to have insurance documents that would compensate each partner if one or the other checked out unexpectedly. Something about making the emotional shock more bearable; taking the strain out of adjusting to a new life without the heart and soul connection between two people in love for a lifetime. Felix had found the whole thing completely foreign and awkward, given the reality at home, but the Wilford Brimley plea had come during one of the many times he and Lenora had tried to make a legitimate effort at civility. He thought that purchasing a double indemnity policy might be a nice gesture to help rebuild some kind of equity in their arrangement. *Might even be enough to jumpstart the rocking horse, if you know what I mean.* As it happened, the unlikely detour to attempted happiness had ended before the paperwork arrived in the mail. He had gone through with the subscription anyway, just to avoid the financial penalty and all around hassle of cancellation. He put half a million dollars on each of their heads, and forgot about the whole thing, until a few months ago. If the plan he was about to hatch went the way he hoped it would, a nice chunk of change would make an impromptu retirement without Lenora be that much sweeter.

He could imagine what that kind of money might make possible in his golden years. Maybe a nice beach vacation to a tropical locale where the native wahines don't wear much more than a birthday suit. *Who knows. You might even be able to make up for some lost time on the horny pony. Never too old to dream, eh, Felix? Speaking of which, think you can stay out of your head long enough to get this thing done right? Snap out of it, genius. You're not sitting on that beach just yet.* Felix mustered the awareness to obey the Dean Martin edict and came to. He was still standing in front of the restaurant, his hand now poised just inches from the door handle. He pulled it open and walked inside. Across the expanse of checkerboard floor tiles and silver-legged table sets, he saw his man. He recognized his contact from the picture given to him by his reference. The man who would know about such things had told him that this man was as close to a sure thing as could be found for small town money, and that was a bargain. Felix had cashed in a few savings bonds for the down payment and had the stash in his right front pocket. Big bills, small wad. Felix made his way to the table and sat down.

"Mr. Peabody, right?" the large man inquired.

"Glad you made it. Thought when you were late that you might have gotten cold feet." The dishes on the table told Felix he had missed the salad and the main course and was just in time for dessert. A half-eaten slice of blueberry pie on an otherwise pristine white saucer confirmed the thought.

"No such luck, mister," Felix replied. "I'm here for the long haul."

"Cold feet are for weddings and school pranks. What you're going to do is give me my life back."

The large man laughed at this and took a sip of coffee. He seemed perfectly comfortable with the topic of conversation. Felix could imagine him with a similar look on his face as he strangled the last bit of life from his latest victim. There was no doubt this guy was a pro.

"I've taken the liberty of ordering you a glass of iced tea," the large man said, motioning to a tall and sweaty glass on his side of the table.

"I ordered it when I saw you standing outside the door, there. You looked parched and I thought the timing would work out about right." The man slid the beverage into place across from Felix. An accompanying pitcher showed there was more where that came from.

"Hope you like sugar. They only serve it one way, in this joint. Sweet and sweeter."

Felix had never been one to turn down a cool drink on a hot day and he had been thirsty for blocks. Without a word, he picked up the glass and drank long and deep. It returned to the table a little less than a third full. Felix wiped his mouth with his right hand and his forehead with a napkin held in the left. He sighed and settled more easily into his chair. It was time to get down to business.

"You have no idea how relieved I was to get your call," Felix said. "This kind of thing really wears on a man. I'd thought about it for months, maybe years. But really being here, talking to you is something else. I'm glad I'm finally doing this."

The large man was staring into the tabletop. He had yet to make eye contact with Felix and didn't appear about to. He picked up his fork and made for the remainder of the blueberry pie.

"There are some situations that demand more creative solutions to a problem, Mr. Peabody. Divorces are messy. You got your property and custody issues and two lawyers with egos. It's bound that both people are gonna leave a lot of blood on the floor."

Felix nodded and smiled a small smile. How true that was. He had considered filing a divorce probably a hundred dozen times but had always hung himself up on the issue of alimony. Cutting his middle class salesman's salary in half held no real attraction, especially not with the inescapable lawyer's fees and the cost of moving. A new town at the most and a new house at the very least. Going back to tuna casserole and mac and cheese seemed too steep a price to pay. Felix grabbed for the last of the iced tea and finished it in two good sized gulps. He put the glass back on the table and sighed again. He could feel a calm and cooling sensation in his stomach spreading to the rest of his tired, aging body. The tea was sure hitting the spot.

"So how does this whole thing go down?" Felix asked. "I mean, there are a lot of ways to kill a person, but how do you know which way is the best way to get it done without getting caught?"

The large man shifted in his seat. His look told Felix it wasn't the first time he had heard the question.

"Detection is never an issue, Mr. Peabody. If it's a bullet, I use untraceable firearms. If it's an explosive, I build it myself with materials I buy from a discreet source. I dust the mechanism for prints and the explosion takes care of the rest. If it's a hand to hand, I could make it look like someone had fallen down a flight of stairs, or had a heart attack, or drowned in the bathtub. There is always a way." The large man had finished his pie and now seemed anxious to conclude the transaction to come. Talking to such a forceful and calculating figure gave Felix a sense of power and belonging he couldn't remember ever feeling before, but it also left him wishing his life had been less mundane. He hung on the assassin's every word.

"Tell you what, Mr. Peabody, I'm going to refill your iced tea glass, and by the time I put down the pitcher, I want your down payment under my pie plate. Sound fair?"

With that, the large man reached for the pitcher while Felix reached in his pocket. Ten crisp one-thousand-dollar bills found their way under the blue streaked saucer just as the last chips of ice tumbled and splashed into the tall glass.

With the pitcher back on the table, the large man quickly swept up the bills and tucked them into his coat pocket. His eyes scanned nearby tables to see if anyone had noticed history's most expensive iced-tea-refill. No one had. His easy manner returned.

"As I was saying, Mr. Peabody, the options really depend on what the customer wants." The large man was clearly enjoying the conversation, Felix thought. *This guy flat out loves his work, and he doesn't miss a trick. Poor Lenora doesn't stand a chance. Such tragedy.*

"There is a always a variable component of suffering that can be worked into the job," the large man continued.

"Say we're talking about someone who has really done the customer in a bad way. In that case, a little torture is not out of the question. I once took a job for a man whose wife had taken up with both his brother and his father, and then lost his life's fortune in a gambling scheme his own kin had talked her into."

The large man recounted the history while working a slivering toothpick in and out of a gap between two back teeth. He inspected the splinter for signs of his progress and then went on.

"I strung her out on a bare springs metal mattress without a stitch of clothing on and then attached two electrodes to the frame. If I hadn't double gagged her, you might have heard her squealing clear across the Mississippi. Sometimes the thought of that kind of suffering before death is worth as much as the kill itself. Those jobs cost extra."

Felix nodded again, but more slowly this time. He was feeling more relaxed by the minute. Everything was falling into place. He reached for his second glass of iced tea, but suddenly found his arm had a difficult time reaching the target. His fingers only grasped the glass after significant struggle and then succeeded in delivering a sloshing mouthful that soaked the front of his shirt. His difficulty with the glass went unnoticed by the large man. His oratory continued.

"But, Mr. Peabody. There are times when a completely different method is called for."

Felix found himself struggling to stay upright in his chair. The muscles in his back and neck and arms felt simultaneously more alive and more asleep than they ever had. The visage of the large man across the table now swam before him. The room dimmed and tilted. He grabbed the sides of the table to steady himself.

"Sometimes, Mr. Peabody, a customer asks for an extra special job with a result that will so perfectly mimic a natural death that no autopsy and no investigation are ever called for.'

The large man extended both hands to Felix and covered the older man's fingers with his own.

"Imagine an older gentleman with a history of heart problems who takes a long walk downtown on a summer day."

Felix could feel his extremities beginning to tense and spasm. His body was paralyzed by a spreading familiar pain in his arms and chest. Under the tightening grasp of the large man's hands, the sensation of pressure against the table surface began to tingle and fade as the killer for hire spoke again.

"Believe it or not, with just the right concoction added to any drink, I could trigger a heart attack that would be at once, perfectly fatal, and yet, a perfectly logical explanation of death. No one would suspect any kind of foul play, and the customer would get exactly the outcome they wished for. Say, half a million dollars cash, and no more spouse?"

Felix knew he was no longer capable of speaking, and was very close to losing consciousness. Still, the dagger sharp spasms in his chest told him that his heart was going through a final, deadly dance. It would be over soon. His graying vision of the room began to dim to black. He felt his body slumping toward the floor. With his last seconds of cogent thought, he could hear the large man's voice one last time.

"Mrs. Peabody sends her regards.'

THE FORTRESS

"Build for us a stone wall, lest we perish!" "We must have a wall!"

The sweating peasant band had burst into the chambers of the royal manor, wheezing and flushed from their run across far off forest and field.

"Make it strong against our enemies who would do us harm."

"We beg of you to save us, sire!"

The lord of the village and surrounding lands looked up from his breakfast of tea and wolf biscuits, indignant at this interruption on such a bright, tranquil morning.

"You are forgetting yourselves," the lord said. "We have no enemies. We are a peaceful people in a peaceful land. What is the purpose of a wall against a foe that doesn't exist?"

"But sire, they *might,*" said one.

"We have heard talk of inventions of sharp metal and heavy wood, and strings stretched tight over saplings to launch tiny daggers through the air," said another.

"We have heard that these inventions are used in great clashes of men, called battles that leave hearts pierced and flesh torn and bleeding on the grass."

"We must have a wall!" The lord stared deeply into their frightened eyes as they slipped and jostled on the polished tile floor. "You realize it will be a great expense. Your taxes will be raised to pay for this wall."

"Raise them, your excellence," one shot back.

The lord spoke again. "I will require fathers and sons from your families to work long days and nights building this wall."

"We offer them, gladly," said another.

"It will take many years to build. Longer than your lives or the lives of your children, with no rest until the end of your days."

"It will be our calling," said the last.

Unable to dissuade them, the lord summoned his chief magistrate to the room.

"Send an immediate edict," the lord said, "that all able-bodied men are to begin work on a heavy stone wall that will surround our lands on every side. They must begin at once. And double their taxes to pay for it."

With that, the work was underway. Great masses of men marched in lines and glistening heaps, gathering, carrying and shaping and stacking, until the wall surrounded the village to the height of a small child.

"Higher! Higher!" the people shouted. And so they built higher, toiling and straining, their lives wrung from them like the very sweat from their sinews. Now the wall was the height of a large man and several feet thick on a side.

"Higher, still!"

"Thicker, still!!!"

"The work must go on! Think of our enemies!"

From inside the manor house, the lord watched and waited, taxing and commanding as his people demanded. He watched as the dark stone wall grew as tall as the trees, and then higher still, casting dark shadows on green grass until it withered and died, blocking sight of golden planted fields beyond and distant painted meadows of flowers and breeze. In their hearts, the workers rejoiced to see these faraway visions of uncertain beauty disappear behind the stones. *How vulnerable they had been! How silly they had lived, to allow their children to run far and free in the fresh and growing places out there! What evil might have befallen them?*

Still, the work went on. Still, the cries of danger and fear, driving the wasted masses to their labor until they lay spent and fallen beneath the giant stone edifice they had craved and breathed to life. Inside the wall, sullen sons and grandsons labored now at their fathers' mantle, their hands slower and less frenzied at their work, the passion gone from their eyes. Quiet rumblings of discontent could be heard from mouths hungry for bread and rest and life and sunlight.

Why are we here?

Where are the enemies that we feared?

Years passed, and still the wall grew, choking clouds and sky until a swirling, shrinking circle of blue and white was all that remained.

And then, they were done.

Bending brittle necks to the sky, they stood as one, the stretched and broken remnants of men, marveling at the strength and might of the omnipotent wall surrounding them, too thick to be crushed and breached, too high to be scaled.

They were safe! They were sound! No enemy would dare come against them. No enemy. *No enemy.*

As they put down their hods and trowels and stonecutters with aching hands, the decrepit ranks of workers selected a younger man who could still walk to carry word to the manor house, to tell the lord of their victorious, glorious completion. How proud he would be! How grateful and masterful in his newly built fortress of safety! They had a new lord, now. Long gone was the man they had entreated to begin their ancient quest for peace and tranquility in stone. The new leader was the grandson of that man, made smug and serene by the wealth of youth. He had carried on the taxes of his father long after they were needed, stocking his treasury with the sweat and tears of his peasants.

"We have reserved for you a great honor, lord," said the worker, now arrived at the manor. "Our work is complete, and all that remains is for you to lock and secure the front gate of our mighty wall that will forever protect us against any enemy that wishes us harm. Here is the key."

With that, the young man and his courtesans made their way to the gate, past buzzing throngs of men made proud by their giant wall that blocked the sun. Without a word, the young ruler and his entourage of stolen wealth filed past the crowds and under and through the front archway, with its massive, impenetrable door of wood and iron, until, standing in the final, oval evidence of a world beyond, he shut the door. And locked it. The jangle of keys came too late to warn the huddled supplicants of what was to happen.

They were safe. At last.

A Father's Wisdom

"Much of life is misery, my son. The simple pleasures are sometimes all we have to keep us warm."

In the stinking, one-room tenement, Nehemiah Jenkins pours his third glass of whiskey since his son's arrival scarcely twenty minutes before. The bottle clanks more noticeably this time, threatening to shatter its slender neck against the unforgiving mass of blackened tin clutched preciously in the old man's aged, trembling hand. He offers words, but not his eyes.

"A younger man can afford to dream," the elder Jenkins continues. "A man of your age can still dream the dreams of youth, as I once did. There is still hope for you, if not for me."

With long rasping swallows, the older Jenkins sips greedily from the ancient cup. His thin cracked lips press frantically against the metal so as not to misplace a single drop. Frail stooping shoulders curve inward and down, as if to shelter the tin treasure box from some unseen thief. The bottle clanks again. Full to the top. Across the dusty, moldering table, the face of a younger man watches his father's private romance with the drink, silently listening to the words he remembers from nights not so quiet as this.

"I had grand dreams once, my son. Good dreams. Dreams of good work with good pay. Money to give you and your mother a better life, God rest her soul."

Another swallow. The old man's eyes seem to dampen as the elixir finds its way to his center, filling the special void left empty by sadness, hunger and loss. Sweet, heavenly drink. Healer, counselor, friend. His eyes fix on the solitary candle that serves as both light and heat for the tiny room. Flickering shadows dance between and around the two threadbare figures, illuminating an endless expanse of cracked plaster walls, covered by years of filth, grime and decay. In the dim, orange light, the ghosts of ruined manhood take their places at the table. Familiar guests returning to bask in the glory of their triumph. The father continues.

"Beasts like us aren't destined for easy lives."

Another clank.

"With fifty dollars in my pocket, I could have done well for us." Swallow. "Plenty of food. Fine, new dresses for your mother. Shoes for your feet. How I dreamed of giving you a better life."

Swallow.

The old man's eyes are glistening now; his empty stare still captured by the candle flame. Fifty dollars indeed!

"With more money, you could have stayed in school past your thirteenth year. Maybe even college. An education to take you far away from here, with a businessman's job, a nice house."

The younger man nods silently at this. What a thought! To travel beyond the spoiled confines of this neighborhood! He had never left the Bronx until he was nineteen, and then, only by train, in the middle of the night, on a ticket paid for by someone else. And college! How his fortunes might have changed. How very different his life would be.

"I failed us, my son." The bottle clanks again. "I failed you."

The wounds of unfulfilled promise press visibly against the father's cracked and wrinkled brow. Long faded ambitions scream inside his memory, stirred to a boil by the robbing demon still untamed for all this time. In his younger years, the father was the strongest man in the neighborhood, drunk or sober. On summer evenings, after long, sweaty days at the factory, there was stickball with his son and the other boys on the block. The older Jenkins would drop his lunch pail on the tenement stoop and take a few swings before the call of the bottle became too insistent to ignore. Up and up and up the ball would fly! Three blocks at a crack and never a miss. Shouting and whooping, a dozen bare feet would race to catch the bouncing missile, the special laughter of boys in full worship, echoing up to the open windows. A glittering tenement stadium at sunset, with Jenkins the hero at the plate.

"Strong as a bull and twice as fast, boys," he would shout with a smile, watching their desperate retrieval before climbing the stairs to his wife, and more importantly, his waiting drink. Later each night, there would be other shouts and swings and other, less happy reasons to run.

"We never had a chance."

The old man's words bring the son back from far away memory. The bottle is half empty now, poured with both hands instead of one, to the waiting tin cup on the table. Shoulders hunched farther now and less steady in the creaking chair.

"With a little luck, I might have found a different job."

Not even when he was very drunk did his speech become anything less than perfect. No slurs; not even now in his old age.

"A respectable job with a salary that would have made all the difference for us."

The father continues, still pouring slowly.

"I could have learned to be an accountant."

Swallow.

"I was always good with figgers, everyone said so, but it takes much more school for a job like that." "You should have gone to university, son. More school, more money. A lot more money than at the factory."

Swallow.

"Even a little more money would have been nice."

Without a word, the younger man listens to his father, contemplating the hard, grinding life only the poorest of the poor can truly understand. Cold nights without heat. Long days without food. And always, always, long bitter trips to the store, with an ache in his belly and his father's change clenched tightly in a cramping sweaty fist. Fourteen blocks, one way, no matter the weather. No coat.

No shoes. Past other children at the candy case, carrying his rumbling stomach beyond the delicious smells of the sandwich counter. To the dreaded familiar shelf, in the only aisle that matters. The Jenkins' Aisle. Third aisle, second shelf, tall bottle. His father was good with figures, alright. He knew the price of whiskey, plus tax, to the single penny, and never a mite left over. A deadly serious errand in a brown paper bag.

"With a new suit, that man in the department store woulda' hired me, I know it." "Nice bookkeeper's job with a good salary. And money to pay for the sickness."

The son is pouring now, as the last of the whiskey trickles from its glass cocoon. Amber metamorphosis at two bucks a bottle. The tin cup on the table does its final duty for dad and country.

"Your mother could have gotten well, with insurance to pay for a good doctor."

Now the tears come in earnest. Watery saucers finally spill over, at the only topic ever responsible for bringing a tear of any kind from the old man's eyes. The woman he had loved, and hated and hurt, with the same hands that sent a worn out stickball into orbit on those ancient summer evenings. For thirty-four years, she'd had taken his best and worst and found the former in tragically short supply. *Three blocks at a crack and never a miss.* Mercifully, a disease they couldn't afford had taken her to a place where his fists and voice couldn't reach. Tuberculosis to some, divine shivering rescue for anyone subjected to the cacophonous alcoholic fury of Nehemiah Jenkins, the drunk. Still, for all the pain his own misguided love had brought, he mourned her passing with undying intensity, the same infernal nature that had replaced her affection with fear and trembling, and had driven her heart into hiding soon after they were wed.

"She was a good woman, son." Swallow. "The best there ever could be."

No argument there. The boy had watched his mother endure a plight worse than death with a grace and quiet dignity deserving of immediate canonization upon her departure for places celestial and bright. Never once had she raised her voice or her hand in retaliation, or even defense. Restraint bestowed by religious fervor, perhaps but more likely, self-preservation, understanding the escalation such an action might have prompted. The boy and his mother had shared a bond forged deep and strong in the fires of a mutual blast furnace. The man whose anger and abuse they shared and longed to escape.

"I wanted a better life for you." The old man paused at this. Still staring into the waxy firmament of the candle's welcoming blaze.

"I wanted to give you so much. Keep you from making my mistakes, and ending up in this same God forsaken place."

The son, grown younger in the face somehow, maintains his silent but attentive gaze. He recognizes the words as those of a broken and dejected father, indulging not in self-pity, but in the genuine mourning of good intentions held prisoner by self-loathing, agony and rage. The younger Jenkins eyes are wet now too, overwhelmed by the memories of a young boy, helplessly blistered by his father's anger, and yet unwilling to fully forsake the hero who could blister a baseball just as well.

And so they sit. Two dirty men in shabby coats, together but alone, on opposite ends of a churning ritual of pain. One lost to regret, the other wishing that time could somehow be bent and stretched to bandage the wasted years in the wisdom and tolerance only the most detestable mistakes can bestow.

"You deserved a better life than this, son. Better than the life my father gave to me. You could have been so much more."

The two tear streaked faces glisten with candle flame as the last of the whiskey runs dry. The old man takes a final, hissing sip from the dregs, sucking mostly air from the gritty tin cup. He taps it back to the table and leans forward, placing his wavering gray head in the crook of two folded arms. Slowly and silent, the son watches his father drift off to sleep. As the candle burns down to the nub, he glances around the room one last time, remembering the filthy walls and the desperate life they held inside all those years before. The sorrow and laughter. The shouts, both happy and sad. The stove, unused in the ten years since his mother's death where meals, delicious but few, were prepared. The window down to the street, box seats free of charge, perfect for watching the exploits of the finest slugger there never was. *Three blocks at a crack and never a miss.* So much struggle! So many wasted dreams!

Slowly, the son rises from his seat, grasping the empty whiskey bottle from the table. He pinches the candle's waning wick between finger and thumb, sending a wisp of smoke into the suddenly darkened room. Groping blindly to his father's chair, he places a seeking hand on the old man's withered shoulder. "Happy birthday, pop." Suddenly the younger man knows there can be no answer. In that single touch, a cooling stillness, more profound than the deepest slumber, is communicated. He understands his father's journey to places far beyond this fitful life of bondage and broken dreams.

In the darkness, he makes his way to the familiar door, unbuttoning his shabby coat as he walks the three flights to the street below. Out on the sidewalk, the younger Jenkins steps briskly, breathing in the smells of the crisp New York night. A bum leans against the tenement wall, smoking a cigarette, ten steps from the building's front door.

"'Bout time, bub. A guy could freeze to death out here without his coat."

Jenkins approaches the man, releasing the battered shell's final button with dexterous fingers.

"I'm sorry sir. Took longer than I expected."

The full length rag now removed, the glare of the sodium street lamps reveals a broad shouldered young man wearing a tailored silk suit, befitting any Wall Street robber-baron, or London aristocrat.

"How much do I owe you for the chill?" Jenkins asks, handing the man a neatly folded version of the borrowed trench.

"I'd call it even-steven for a swig of what used to be in that bottle you're holding." Jenkins recognizes the famished look in the man's eyes.

"Empty, yes." Jenkins replies. "How does ten dollars and a ride to an excellent restaurant sound?"

"It'll work in a pinch, mister." Visibly dejected by the loss of his first choice, the man reluctantly concedes the second offer. "But, beg your pardon. Where do you hope to get this ride you mention? You may dress like a fancy million, but I don't see no wheels on them shoes."

Just then, a stylish limousine of copious length and obvious expense rounds the corner at the end of the block. "Right there we are, my good man," Jenkins says, moving into the street to meet the car.

"Jeepers, buddy!" the man says, flabbergasted by the shiny machine. "You play for the Brooklyn Bombers, or somethin'?"

Smiling gently, and saying nothing of the man's sports ignorance, Jenkins opens the rear door of the limousine, gesturing the tattered wayfarer inside.

"We have company for dinner, Haywood. Please make him feel at home." "Yes of course, Master Jenkins," the chauffeur replies, "Chez Luis, I presume?"

"Nah, Haywood, we'll get this man some real food," Jenkins says. "I'm guessing he's more of a meat and potatoes kind of guy."

"Of course, he is, Mr. Jenkins," Haywood replies. "... and we'll be off, just as soon as you get in." The car's owner detects a note of concern in his faithful driver's voice. "This neighborhood leaves me feeling less than optimistic for our safety."

"Hold those horses, Haywood," Jenkins says, still standing beside the idling auto's open door, rolling the empty whiskey bottle from hand to hand. "There's one more thing I need to do."

Stepping to the front of the car, the man who played stickball on this very street, tightens his grip on the last empty bottle of his father's wasted, enslaved life. *Third aisle, second shelf, tall bottle, never a penny more.* He looks down to find a familiar chink in the pavement with his right toe, the hand hewn mark that served as the pitcher's mound for those summer evening games, so long ago. *The glittering tenement stadium at sunset, with the hero Jenkins at the plate.* Then with a practiced motion as famous as his smile, Jenkins winds up and lets fly. Inside the waiting car comes a donning gasp of recognition as two astounded fans get a free glimpse of the right arm considered far and wide to be the heart and soul of the New York Yankees. A full five seconds and three blocks later, a tinkling explosion under a street lamp as the bottle returns to earth in a tinseled shower of broken glass redemption. *Three blocks at a crack and never a miss.* Finally, after savoring the whirling flight and sound of the now ruined bottle, the man paid in gold bouillon for fanning batters from Baltimore to San Francisco turns back to stare one last time at the terrible darkened window, four floors above the pavement.

"Strong as a bull and twice as fast, Pop, just like you."

With that, Bobby "Jumping Bean" Jenkins flexes comfortably into the upholstered interior of his warm limousine and disappears into the gentle night.

THE ARTIST

The artist had lost his vigor, and for days and weeks, his second-story studio flat rang out with the ranting fits of a once-great mind consumed by the loss of genius.

"MISERABLE!!!" he bellowed.

"INSOLENT WORM!!!"

The cowering, crouching miscreant flung himself violently around the room, tumbling easels and tossing canisters of paint and bristle-brush in a manic hurricane of excruciating rage. Neighbors shouted and complained as he pounded fists against paint-stained walls and against the brickwork of his own skull with equal bluster. The pugilist's endeavor left his gnarled fists clenched and grimy with his own blood and his brain ringing with the blows.

And then there was calm. After exhausting himself with the frenetic choreography of gnashing, suicidal boiling, he would sit, sobbing and heaving in a creaking chair, awaiting the next arrival of foment. *Waiting for the tub to run over, again.* Inside his mind, he had become a bronze cauldron in a dimly lit antechamber that served as a catch basin for a tinkling waterfall torture of discontent. Eyes fixed in a dull stare, the artist gave himself completely to the image in his mind, watching the water level steadily slosh and rise until it reached the rim of the basin and cascaded to the floor below. Streaming thoughts of torment and self-hatred paced themselves perfectly to the predatory progress of the watery basin, filling the artist's mind with the miserable knowledge of his decline. Scattered around him in the indiscriminate jostlings of his ruined studio were the canvassed evidence of previous inspiration, now utterly beyond his reach. Dozens of portraitures of his best work, alive with color and vibrant in their texture and divine skill stared back at him like the mocking audience of a fool. Outlined in tinted grease and muslin, the timeline of his decayed sovereignty of the palette lay before him, screaming in his ears with a thousand shrill voices. Women in wide-brimmed hats, mocking and staring. Men in stove pipes and coats with tails, smiling smugly at his decadent demise. Knowing glances of loss and decay.

Couldn't paint if you wanted to.

Couldn't paint well enough to whitewash a fence.

Lost your moxie! Lost your gift!

You old poseur! Imposter!

Ram the brush in your eyes and end it all!!!

This last thought tempted him, mightily. How he longed to the feel the piercing end of a tapered handle find its mark, plunging him eternally into the welcoming, comforting darkness of impossible rest. Blindness would be his cure. Oh, how he'd imagined it! In that enveloping landscape of blackness there would be no need of paint, or canvass, or need of inspiration. The world of color and shade, shadow and nuance would forever be beyond his reach, and so, as far as his artistic ambition and lost potential were concerned, there would be no more conflict. It would all be over. The question would be settled. The burden, gone. He'd approached it before. More than once, he'd held his stoutest, maple-shafted fan brush in quivering hand, mere inches from his right eye, conjuring the courage to make the thrust. For more than an hour he'd stared at the conical invader without motion, willing himself to carry out the act, but without avail. His arm would not, could not move. The same thought held fast his hand each and every time. He had two eyes. To complete the treatise would require two separate motions of violence, when even the first required a volition he was so far, unable to muster. What if, after depriving himself of his right eye, he found himself unable, or unwilling to resolve the second go? The thought terrified him even more thoroughly than the fitful reality of fully sighted existence. He would be a one-eyed former artist forever cursed with the millstone of damaged sight, compounded by the visible testimony to his lack of resolve. Walking the streets of the marketplace, he could imagine the stares and jeers.

"Poked his own eye out, he did, crazy fool!"

"Just the right one though, because he wasn't enough man to finish the job." Wasn't man enough. And wasn't that the root of it all? He knew that it was, for, as self-ascribed genius,

Hamilton Pershing had proudly intoned to two dozen of his sycophantic protégé's over the years of his tyrannical reign, "an artist paints with his privates. Nothing more, nothing less." Now faced with the dimming light of his virtuoso abilities, Pershing could feel a commensurate weakening in that other area of masculine endeavor. The bold audacity that once possessed his every artistic compulsion seemed to have withered, in direct contraction to the absence of his most instinctive impulse. Freud would have understood. Ego, after all, was the driving inspiration for any endeavor requiring the courage to believe that a man had something rare and worthy to be shared with the world. Pershing knew that even a single brush stroke required the intrinsic belief that someone, somewhere would someday pause to peruse, and consider the artist's motivation and incomprehensible skill.

Look at the subtle upstroke, there!

What a sublime demonstration of palette!

Such a divine richness of texture!

How could he.....?

Why did he.....?

In the encroaching darkness of another wasted day, even the simple imaginings of audience pleasure were a curse to the artist's mind. It was the tearing edge of brilliance that mere observers could never suspect, believe or comprehend. The same photographic precision of detail that endowed Pershing's brush now supplied an awareness of self-decline too vivid to be pushed away, too sharp to be swallowed. Would moments of private brilliance, or of appreciative onlookers ever be his, again? What would life be without the knowledge that he could add and subtract from the universe bits of beauty and light so rare that newspapers wrote of his exploits? How could he endure the offensive minutiae of mundane life without the elixir of genius that had secured his reputation? On and on, the parade of sanguine introspection invaded his thoughts, pressing him ever closer to the precipice of madness and utter desolation. His wishes for death and self-destruction doubled and tripled, and doubled again, until he found himself wishing for the envisioned metaphor of cliff and chasm to become real, that he might throw himself into the waiting arms of dark oblivion with a single step. The blinding paintbrush beckoned. Blessed sacrament of peace.

I'll do it on Sunday, he thought, sealing a self-promise to settle the question, once and for all.

If inspiration proves beyond my reach, and cannot be retrieved even by a fatal deadline, Sunday will be my rescue. Forever, rescue. Forever, darkness. Forever, sleep. Four more days.

His plans set, the artist felt a sudden easing of anxious mélange that had afflicted him for weeks. His chest softened. His neck lengthened and straightened. His head ceased the throbbing roar that had sounded like the approaching march of a demon army, both day and night during the darkest moments of his torment.

Four more days.

In the sudden ebbing of his misery, Pershing felt his eyelids droop and flutter closed, carrying him far away into lands of long shadows, and soft dreams. In the chair next to his open window, the artist bowed his head and slept. The tub had run over, again.

⊂═•⊱ ⊰•═⊃

Hamilton Pershing awoke in the bowels of hell. The orange glow of licking flame surrounded him. His mouth and lungs convulsed with choking clouds of thick smoke. The room was on fire! A smoldering timber from the quickly blackening ceiling crashed to the floor, sending a shower of crackling sparks against the glistening row of the artist's best works. The canvas quickly caught flame, smoldering in growing orange circles that devoured flowers and faces and reflective pools of pristine waterfront reflection with mindless hunger. His life's devotion was melting away.

"NOOOOOOOOOOOO!!!!!" His futile shout came out through parched lips, driven by lungs that were rapidly losing their ability to take in air. One by one, the hours and days and weeks of his life's labor succumbed to the embers, twisting and dancing in their frames like oil-soaked marionettes. Siennas and crimsons and yellow ochres and midnight blues lit like fireworks on a summer's night, rushing up and away in quick succession. A woman in a white dress and wide-brimmed hat burned alive, never making a move to retreat as she stared gaily out across a passel of sailboats on a glassy smooth cove. A man in top hat and tails became a human torch, smiling suavely at a young girl on his right arm as his face bubbled and boiled and disappeared into the flames. Masterpieces of rare distinction, and abandoned pieces of bitter frustration lit and blazed with equal ferocity. The flames paid no respect to legacy or lore. Each canvass was a new morsel for an insatiable, consumptive beast.

"Nooo." The artist was beside himself now, dancing among the devil tongues like a crazed native in a voodoo trance, alive with the bitter rage of his self-immolation and loss. He no longer had the breath to scream. One by one, the captured moments of his genius gave way to the fire, turning to oozing piles of greasy tinder, as if they had never existed. As if *he* had never existed. The hours of sweat and toil and joy and tears that had filled his days with the indulgent wine of self-worship wafted upward in billowing acrid smoke. His life was burning. His paintings were going away, and he would follow. What use had any of it been? What real value had anything he had ever done? He and his vanity were kindling on the fire of the universe, and fodder for a cosmic match. Eyes stung by smoke and pinched tightly by the advancing heat produced tears of humble surrender. The artist knew himself as the helpless worm that he was, and found peace in the revelation. His pride, vanity and arrogance burned as brightly as the oiled canvass, set ablaze by an angry god. Somewhere in the prison of flame, he was a man reborn.

Taking his eyes from the now consumed pilings of his collected vanity, the artist looked at the open window across the room and the promise of escape. He wanted to live. Whether he ever touched a brush to canvass again, or drew the praise of the multitude, or found himself the magnet for a procession of autograph-seeking sycophants, he wanted to live. He wanted to breathe. Shrouded now by curtains of flickering flame, the open window beckoned, and safety beyond. Then, as he took his first step toward waiting exodus, he heard it. From beyond the door of his blazing flat, a plaintiff wail so small, so pitiful, it could barely be heard above the blaze. Someone in the hallway? Still? Someone left behind? Who but a neurotic old man bent on self-destruction would have stayed so long? In the rushing din of his building's fiery demise, the artist had been vaguely aware of the shouts and footsteps as people above and below fled for their lives. The natural instincts of human preservation had emptied the building in moments, leaving the artist alone to contemplate the pyre of his artistic exploits and his resigned, impending fate. Or so he had thought. The wail came again, jolting the artist with its helpless, terrified tone. It was a child, boy or girl he could not be certain, of an age where cries of joy or fear sound remarkably similar, regardless of sex. Age, perhaps three or four. Trapped and alone.

Trapped.

A third wail, louder this time sent his feet to action. With determined gait and disregard for the wall of fire surrounding him, the artist made for the hallway door. He crossed the room in an instant, holding his lips tight and ignoring the scalding blast furnace that lapped his paint-stained pants and smock. His hair curled and singed, falling to the floor in smoking clumps. His skin puckered and blackened where the heat did its worst. And then he was at the door, grasping the poker-hot doorknob in a seared palm and pulling with all his might. Another wail. Louder and closer. The hallway was a vision from hades, filled floor to ceiling with the roiling cloud and ringed with pockets of fire that advanced like a horde or torch-bearing mongrels. Would the floor hold him? Would he crash down and through to be roasted amid the coals of the collapsing hulk? As the fire's self-generated rush of wind pushed through the smoke, there was a sudden retreat of the cloud that revealed all.

An urchin, perhaps three years of age was crouched and clinging to an island of floor untouched by fire, covering her face with her hands. She rocked and wailed against the hallway's far wall, unable to move a step. With a quickness that banished any notion of age, the old man ran for her, plunging headlong and uncaring through partitions of fire that burned into his bones. In a final, desperate thrash he reached her, lifting her in his arms and throwing her slackening body over his left shoulder. She seemed barely aware of the surrounding hell, or of the angelic messenger sent to spare her life. Her nightshirt hung in ashen ribbons around her. With his last remaining burst of life, the old man turned back toward his apartment door and the open window that was waiting beyond. Could he save them both? Would his roasted limbs bear up with no luxury of breath?

Like a banshee moving across a foggy moor, the man felt himself floating, gliding, lifted and carried on legs he could no longer feel. Were they even his own? Was he even still alive? Through flame, and over weakened planks spending their strength as fuel to the raging beast, the old man raced on and on. He was alive with fire now, and still he ran. His skin bubbled and crackled like the oiled canvasses of his ruined paintings. Through his door and across the blazing room he went, leaping the now blazing timber that had fallen and ignited his painted, treasure-trove, reaching the window in what seemed a dream he could not escape. The open window. Through the blazing gateway to safety he could see the faces of the gathering crowd, one story below. Their voices pierced the veil of the fire-dream, bringing the old man back from somewhere beyond to the swift urgency of the moment. He felt himself thrusting the girl forward, out and down. His hands emptied of their burden as she fell free. Free to breathe. Free to live. Free to go on.

"Toss her down!"

"Let us catch her!"

"Oh, my god, he's saved her!"

"Thank god! He's saved her!"

"He's saved her!"

"She'll be alright."

"Now, jump! Jump down!"

"Save yourself, man!"

"Save yourself!"

"He's burning!"

"He's burning alive!"

"Jump, man! While there's still time!"

But there was no time. There was only heat. And smoke. And flame. And peace. And a thrashing artist's final blinking retreat into the vast stillness of the universe beyond, a masterpiece, at last.

THEY LIED

"But why do they do it?'
"Do what?"
"You said everyone does."
"Yes, everyone."
"But why."
"Because they must. *We* must."
"We? You mean you do it, too?"
"Of course! Why should I be any different?"
"I just thought…" "
Yes, of course you would. You do it too, you know."
"I do not."
"Of course you do. There's no shame in it."
"But it's lying."
"Yes. I suppose it is."
"And that doesn't bother you?"
"It would bother a heck of a lot more if we didn't."
"How can you say that? Of all the…"

"It's like this. Say a rather homely chap was to happen upon you on the street corner. He smells terrible, and…"

"What does he smell like?"

"Good gosh. Why?"

"I'm trying to picture it."

"Fine. The homely chap smells of bangers and mash and three-day old whiskey."

"I should think he'd smell worse if the bangers and mash were three days older than the whiskey."

"Murgatroyd! Fine! The bangers and mash are three days older than the whiskey. May I go on with the analogy?"

"Of course. I'm just suggesting."

"Fine."

"So, go on."

"Right. So, as I was saying,"

"Which part?"

"What?"

"Which part are you taking up again, the part about the homely chap?"

"If you'd only let me speak, I'd be getting to that."

"I'm sorry."

"It's alright. But yes, that's the part." "
Alright, go on."

"Very good. Now, this homely chap comes up to you on the street, smelling of bangers and mash and three day old whiskey…"

"I thought we decided to age the bangers and mash and not the whiskey. For the smell, remember?"

"Stop interrupting me!"

"But we decided."

"Yes! Yes! So we did. I had only forgotten. Now, may I go on?"

"Of course. I'm sorry."

"You keep saying that, but I'm doubting it's true."

"I'm sorry. I just want to understand exactly what it is that you're saying."

"Fine."

"You're cross with me."

"Not any more than can't be helped."

"What does that mean?"

"What do you mean? I was merely expressing the triviality of your offense. It was nothing."

"I see. Finish your little story then."

"You're doing it again."

"Doing what?"

"You're doing it. You interrupt, express remorse and avoid any understanding of what I'm trying to say..."

"But I didn't mean to..."

"Oh, rubbish. You know precisely what you're doing."

"You're making something out of nothing."

"I think not. You even went so far as to call my illustration, a little story. It's very patronizing when you do that."

"I meant nothing by it. It's not a large story, is it?"

"No I suppose not."

"It's a brief story, true?"

"Yes, yes, I see your point."

"So stop your whining about it and finish, will you? And don't be cross. I hate it when you are cross with me."

"I'm not cross."

"You were."

"For a moment. I'm over it. Let's continue."

"Very well."

"So the homely, smelly chap comes up to you on the street."

"Yes."

"And you're immediately struck with a sense of superiority."

"I'm what?"

"You automatically assign yourself as the superior in the interaction."

"I suppose…"

"There's no supposing about it. You're a professional woman. Finely dressed, neatly groomed and on your way to an important job that pays you more than this man could ever imagine."

"Yes, I suppose all that would be true."

"But what do you say to him?"

"What do you mean?"

"Do you tell him any of that?"

"You mean about my innate superiority?"

"Yes, of course. What else would I be referring to? That's annoying."

"Forget it. I just wanted to be sure."

"So?"

"Of course not. I'd never say any of that. What's your point?"

"That's precisely my point. Everyone hides the truth, every day, with everyone else they encounter."

"What makes you assume that everyone goes around automatically putting everyone they meet on the rungs of some ladder of perceived importance? The whole idea is disgusting."

"You just admitted that you would feel all of that. Homeless man or not, don't we all do that?"

"Alright, point taken."

"My point is that everyone does that, and lies about it."

"Everyone?"

"Everyone."

"And?"

"It's an ancient instinctual behavior."

"Oh, here it comes."

"Humans are pack animals. We instinctually realize that lying to each other; concealing certain truths is crucial to maintaining connection."

"You're enjoying this, aren't you. Is there some truth you're concealing from me, right now?"

"You'd love to know that, wouldn't you?"

"I think any wife would."

"I'm concealing nothing. I only hinted otherwise to add intrigue."

"It's a fine way of doing it."

"Deepest apologies, lovely. I meant no harm. Now, may go on with my postulate?"

"I know you will."

"What do you mean by all that? I thought you enjoyed our little interludes of philosophy and whatnot."

"Maybe I lied."

"Maybe you…oh for heaven's sake. You're a cheeky one tonight, aren't you?"

"Go on, dear."

"Go on with what?"

"Get on with it, dear."

"Alright, then. As I was saying, humans are pack animals. We've adapted over the millennia to behave in ways that maintain order and harmony within our social order."

"And lying helps us do that?"

"Of course."

"And everyone does it?"

"Everyone."

"Even you."

"And you."

"I don't."

"You do."

"I don't."

"You have."

"I wouldn't."

"You did."

"What do you mean, 'I did?' When did I?"

"Do you remember the night of the Ergotzke's dinner party?"

"Vaguely. I remember I had one glass of sherry too many."

"Just one?"

"Hey! I don't remember you complaining on the drive home."

"Just ribbing, darling. No complaint."

"What do my drinking habits have to do with lying?"

"Nothing, darling. I wasn't finished."

"I see."

"Do you remember Mrs. Ergotzke's chocolate soufflé'?"

"Of course. It was dreadful. Soupy, undercooked and quite bitter."

"That's right."

"But what of it?"

"But that's not what you told her."

"It's not what I…"

"You told her it was the best soufflé you'd ever tasted."

"I didn't."

"You did."

"I did?"

"To the very word. And you ate every bite."

"Well, I suppose it's because she's your boss's wife."

"Exactly."

"I suppose I didn't want to offend her."

"Precisely. And why not?"

"Oh, enough. You don't have to treat it like an inquisition at Scotland Yard. I see your point."

"The maintenance of social advantage, pure and simple."

"Alright, the advantage in that case is clear. But what about the homeless chap? Why shouldn't I simply tell him exactly what I feel. He has no power to help me."

"Because."

"That's not an answer."

"Of course it isn't, but the reason is very plain."

"Your reason is, I'm sure. The truth is a different matter."

"Such honesty, when it happens, is considered rude and gauche. That, and simple convenience, I suppose."

"Convenience?"

"It's easier to simply walk by in your cocoon of understood superiority than to make any acknowledgement at all, genuine or otherwise."

"Maybe I just don't want to inhale any more of the bangers and mash and whiskey aroma you so deliberately described."

"Perhaps."

"Well, it's my motivation were talking about. Why theorize about it when I could simply tell you why I'd behave a certain way?"

"Because you wouldn't."

"I would."

"You didn't."

"I will."

"Alright, duly noted."

"I wouldn't say anything to the chap out of kindness."

"Kindness? Wouldn't kindness speak to the chap and perhaps offer him some food or other assistance? Some compassionate acknowledgement of his plight?"

"But if he smelt of bangers and mash, hadn't he a full belly, already?"

"That's not to say his next meal wouldn't be in doubt. What about that?"

"But he smelt, too of whiskey. Isn't that where a given pound would be spent, anyway?"

"Perhaps, but I only meant that silence and kindness aren't the same thing."

"Would politeness suffice?"

"Better, I suppose."

"Good then. I'm so glad to arrive at a word that passes your approval, darling. Such relief."

"Am I doing it, again?"

"Just a touch."

A FINE CATCH

Harold Merrill was forever waist deep in water but never wet. Ten yards from the shoreline in one of the endless small lakes of his fisherman's life, he whipped the tip of his rod through the evening air and spooled a splashed spinner bait into the green murk about twenty yards away. It was a good metaphor for his life in some ways, Harold had often thought. Surrounded and immersed in what had passed for the average existence of an almost retired auto supply store owner with two grown children and a silent wife, but guarded or deprived from anything that might resemble the actual experience of it in the same way his insulated chest waders kept him dry and isolated from the secret wetness of remote lakes where he fished, these days as much for solitude as for whatever hapless fish might prove easily fooled. In the water, but not of it. An interloper with an agenda. Peace and quiet and beer and crickets in a place where Marjorie had no interest in following and no reason to quibble with the time spent.

Fishermen were just philosophers with restless hands, his grandfather had told him when he was a boy. *Funny Chinese proverb, Harry boy. Chinese said it's good for a man to marry, because if he marries well, he will be happy and the world can always do with more happiness. And if he marries poorly, he will become a philosopher and the world can always do with more philosophers.* And sometimes, or maybe, most times, Harold knew a man's hobbies were as much a matter of philosophical self-defense as actual interest. As time passed it was a distinction that disappeared, even as the truth of his grandfather's words had unfolded over a lifetime, leaving him to understand the socially acceptable therapy of filaments and sinker weights and brightly colored canisters of stinky glitter paste that now passed for the latest and greatest ways to convince fish to commit suicide. Night crawlers and minnows and rotten liver had given way to newfangled Play-dough mixed with anchovies at eight dollars a can. World had gone crazy, Harold knew. In all the ways that mattered most.

Another cast sent his spinner looping toward his left and back against a portion of grassy bank underneath the sagging arm of a blue-gray Russian Olive tree overhanging the water. The splash and sink took only a second as Harold began the slow reeling and jerking retrieval of the neon-green and yellow fringed contraption with the silver propeller spoons and large white eyes. He was chasing largemouth in the waning days of another summer as tufts of cotton descended on the water to the accompaniment of singing cicadas and the plastic applause of the cottonwood gallery of one of his favorite retreats. The lake had a gently sloping muddy bottom and hardly any large rocks to trip his predictable footing as he walked slow motion in search of bass willing to justify his time.

Ker-blooop. Another cast, this time just nicking through the Russian Olive overhang, tempting a snag but missing the branches by mere inches with meticulous precision and parting the leaves harmlessly on the way to the water. Harold hated wasted time of snagged lures and broken lines or of pulling mossy clumps from a fouled spinner that found pond bottom in the wrong place. The hassle of it interrupted the purpose of it all and reminded him of the encroaching irritability and lacking patience that defined the general grumpiness of his later years. Not all empty nests were created equally or happily, in the same way that not all marriages or golden anniversaries were equally golden. About the same time that fishing bait had started looking like jars of neon war paint for an evening at Studio 54, Harold had learned the truth of what middle aged men in a world of chemical enhancement and reclaimed vitality had been learning, or likely already knew, even before little blue pills and yellow pills and television commercials with sexy women promised a second chance at the perpetual excitement of adolescence. Wives came in exactly two varieties: Those thankful for their husband's extended return to youthful vigor by any means necessary and those utterly annoyed that their peace and quiet and earned retirement from marital duties had been rudely interrupted by uninvited pharmaceutical intrusion. A hard truth, indeed. An inaugural and still full bottle of Viagra tablets stood testimony in the Merrill medicine cabinet to which category Marjorie had vehemently joined. There would be no second honeymoon for the Merrill household, no matter how many footballs Brett Favre threw through tire swings or how many his-and-her bathtubs were situated on sunset hillsides to show that the moment was just right. Theirs had been a brief and one-sided discussion on the matter shortly after a particular trip to the pharmacy had yielded the promised results to a less than receptive audience of one.

To Harold, the whole experience gave the faint feeling of having a death sentence overturned on a technicality, only to have the warden misplace the paperwork and throw the switch anyway out of spiteful routine. Commutation, denied. As his coffee shop buddies reveled and beamed and shared stories of their unexpected and youthful return to marital bliss, Harold had come home from the store one day to retrieve a set of toolbox keys and had overheard his lecturing wife proudly informing her Thursday morning ladies group of her bemoaned cancellation of the Viagra experiment. In full and shameless detail. Including Harold's defeated exile to the living room recliner until the offending hydraulics had a chance to subside, untouched and unused.

"Can you imagine the nerve?" The indignant, offended tone.

In total, the ordeal had left him feeling robbed and alone and had signaled the final dying in his heart of whatever had passed for the cordial consideration of the long-negotiated rapprochement of the Merrill marriage. The cruel emptiness of it gnawed at him, but he kept it to himself and made his peace the best he could. And went fishing. A lot. Most days. For a time, he had pondered the possibility of an affair, more out of vengeance and vindictive protest than out of any real prospect or desire to be unfaithful, but had dismissed the idea as admitted completion of Marjorie's triumph in the matter. Giving in to that impulse would mean that she had gotten the better of him in a way that would bother him more and longer than the coldness of her rejection or the grief of his longings for physical release. And if it had ever become known, his children would never forgive. And that was that. No other reason was needed.

Another cast. Another trolling retrieval at the slow, methodical, predictable pace. Not a nibble or a strike. No matter. Harold smiled faintly as he remembered his oldest daughter's wedding and more than that, their private conversations in the days leading up to the happy nuptials. Chelsea had chosen a good man who was finishing up a law degree and was clearly going places where she would be well looked after and happily blessed. And they were in love. He remembered standing with her on the back deck after a dinner of barbecue and watching her far off gaze as she assured her father of the soundness of her decision and the life that would follow.

"Daddy, not all loves are created equally," she had said. She was a philosopher like her father, fisherman or not.

"Sad truth of it is, there are some people you could spend a lifetime with and wonder what the boredom and drudgery of it was all about. And there are others, or maybe just one in all the world who can touch your heart so deeply in a moment that your heart will swear you've been loving them for a universe of lifetimes." Her lustrous eyes sparkled as she spoke, her face a perfect study in the truth of her words.

"That's how it is for Jack and me, Daddy. And even if all that had ever transpired between us was limited to one single moment, or any of the thousands of moments of our time together, the beauty of it would be enough to last me a lifetime."

Harold recalled her taking his hand earnestly as she pleaded her case and the peace and calm that he had felt, realizing that his little girl had been given the greatest of gifts and that she was happy.

"Daddy, there are times with Jack when the things he says, or the way we kiss, or the way he looks at me takes my breath away and makes me feel like I'll live forever no matter what and at the same time, makes me not even care if I died at that very moment because I would die happy knowing that I've been loved and touched and known by my one special person in a way that's more perfect than I ever dreamed. He's my match, Daddy."

Seven years in, their happiness seemed undimmed and untarnished. Harold counted it as thankful evidence of the law of averages and grateful proof that marital unhappiness didn't have to be a hereditary curse. His son Eric had married too and was doing fine in both work and love. The knowledge of happy children was Balm of Gilead for a father's soul.

With the sun now fully concealed by the horizon, Harold knew he was down to his final dozen or so casts of the day. He began trudging-careful footsteps back toward the shoreline and his waiting truck, casting and reeling as he went, working the shallows, probing the spots where he knew submerged logs or large rocks gave bottom cover where fish prefer to live. No luck. Ten yards from shore, he reached for steps with always-cautious feet, making sure of solid form before planting his weight. He'd entered a patch where he knew the angled drop-off from the bank was a bit steeper and the cold water was lapping now just below his sternum, pushing the safe limits of his chest waders as he worked his way back to the shore. His seeking right foot found what felt like a flat rock momentarily and then slipped and slipped again and then found nothing. His left foot and then both feet plunged into open space, sinking vainly for purchase in the moss of the lake bottom, flailing to find and regain stride. And still nothing. As his head went under, green water gushed into Harold's waders, filling them like a bucket under a waterfall and pulling him down and down and down. His right hand released his fishing rod as he began paddling frantically while trying to slip the shoulder straps and escape the sucking cocoon of heavy rubber skin and weighted boots. Still he sank. No bottom to be found.

Stepped in a damn big hole, or off the edge of the drop-off, genius.

Harold's fleeting rush of recrimination gave way to sheer panic as the last gasp of topside air faded and tightened and soured in his aching lungs. Still he fought to free the concrete load of the flooded waders sealed firmly to his struggling legs and thrashed with frantic arms as he strained upward toward the vague glinting circle of blurred daylight above his head. The circle was shrinking and Harold knew he was sinking fast. Going up was impossible.

Swim sideways, you fool. Use the bottom. Walk it. Claw it if you have to. If your breath holds out you might just make it. One chance.

As a teen, Harold's mind flashed with a memory of an incident with his best childhood friend in his 14th summer. The two had nearly drowned trying to cross a rushing patch of dirty river at flood stage, losing their footing and being swept along in the swirling current in what they both later recounted as an almost certain case of death by stupidity. For whatever reason, after struggling to exhaustion trying to swim against the flow, they had both discovered that if they swam with the current, they could easily navigate to the other side. Giving themselves up to the power of the river, they swam stroke for stroke to the opposite bank, traveling more than half a mile downstream from where they started, but blessedly alive and no worse for wear. They talked on the walk back upstream about how difficult it had been to overcome their instinct for resistance and to swim with the rushing current, no matter where it took them. If they had struggled against it for even a moment longer, both knew they would have been too fatigued to reach the other side, no matter what they did. Fighting their fears of being swept away and going with the flow had been their salvation.

Go with the flow.

An eerie calm descended over Harold's mind as his feet finally touched the lake's bottom depth with six feet of water above his head. Maybe eight. He turned quickly in what he only hoped was the direction for shore. His lungs were empty of oxygen. His diaphragm was a dancing spasm of hypoxic autonomic shock. Still, his feet began to move. One step and three, and five and eight. Like a scrambling sprint on an inclined treadmill, or maybe like an astronaut on the surface of the moon, Harold fought against the weighted wall of water, hauling his hundred pound waders and leaden body in a desperate dash. He was actively fighting the impulse to breathe, his lungs spasming and threatening to force open his starving mouth in search of oxygen. How long had he been under?

A minute? Two? Longer?

The threat now was unconsciousness. If he could stay upright and awake...

⌫⋅ ⋅⌦

After parking his pickup and stowing his Plano tackle box in the appointed slot under his garage workbench, Harold Merrill opened the door from the garage into the kitchen, a vision of sopping clothes and soaked hair. Marjorie froze in the midst of a half-loaded dishwasher and surveyed her husband, head to toe.

"Well, don't just stand there and drip on my clean tile floors, Harold Merrill. Get a towel!" Marjorie said. "Of all the ungrateful—do you have any idea how hard I work to keep this house and kitchen clean for you and you walk in here like you just went skinny-dipping with your favorite floozy and give me an hour's worth of mopping?"

Stifling an urge for rejoinder, as Harold crossed toward the hall linen closet, he had the distinct sensation of a fourteen-year-old senior citizen, out of breath and out of strength, swimming downstream.

"Free to Speak"

FREEDOM OF SPEECH: "THE CRUCIBLE OF VERBAL DISSENT WHICH BRINGS FORTH THE SHINING GOLD OF LIBERTY,"

POLAND, 1942 A.D.

Heinig Pulagski was cold, always cold. Standing in perfect alignment with a handful of shivering, terrified human beings, he dared not look to the right or the left, focusing his eyes in an unseeing gaze at the dingy stone wall on the opposite side of the narrow cobbled street.

"Get up, you

"*Juden*scum! Get up!" The Nazi commandant was yelling again, gobs of unfettered spittle flying from his gaping mouth that was set in a ruddy bulging face with demon

258

eyes. The squadron of German soldiers overseeing a forced march of Heinig's peasant work detail had been brought to an abrupt halt when a teenage girl had collapsed in tears, unable to move another step. Her outburst was a virtual death sentence, they all knew, but strangely, the bellowing cartoon of a man who could order a bullet for her fate had become so preoccupied with his echoing oratory, he had yet to give the command.

Quiet, girl, hush your whimpers and get up, if you know what's good for you. Get up! Heinig pleaded inside his mind for an improbable end to this episode and a resumption of their march back to the enforced living quarters, a few blocks away. His fingers, hands and feet throbbed mercilessly with the encroaching fire of frostbite. He longed for an end to this day. *Please, God, let her life be spared, and let us all get moving again to get warm.* She was a girl of fifteen or sixteen, Heinig thought, and pretty, her tear-streaked face grimy with soot from the grisly assignment that had occupied their afternoon. Heinig and the others had been forced to help relocate a pile of dead bodies that the Germans had been unsuccessful in burning completely and had decided to move instead to a mass grave that had been dug one-hundred yards away.

Can't even cremate a body properly you hideous, brutal German pig-dogs! Not enough kerosene on a cold winter's day? Masters of the World, indeed! Heinig had allowed his hidden contempt and brief amusement to distract him from the horrors of the scene that seemed something straight out of the caverns of hell. Charred human remains lay in interlaced and stiffened poses, their clothing and outer coverings reduced to delicate, ashen layers that fluttered like tissue paper in the winter breeze. Thankfully, Heinig had been handed a shovel and ordered to help deepen the trench where his burned countrymen would be given their final, reprehensible resting place. From the looks of the crying girl's clothing, there could be no doubt she had been among those charged with the worst of the task, grasping and tugging and dragging at the sotted piles, pulling the pitifully disfigured victims to the edge of the pit where they were stacked like cord-wood before being given a final shove into the abyss. After a day's labor on the edge of sanity, the poor girl had finally cracked, and would likely pay with her life.

"Shut up, you worthless Polish slime! Your life is nothing to me! You are nothing! Your country is nothing! You and your miserable lot belong to the Fuhrer, Herr Hitler! You belong to him! Your bodies belong to him!" The commandant was still at it, whirling his arms and roaring insult in some protracted, futile appeal to make the girl be quiet, as if it were a battle of wills to be won or lost in a Blitzkrieg of words, rather than tanks and planes and trucks filled with swollen Nazi soldiers in their shining black boots.

"Leave her alone, you fat, Nazi pig." Heinig only realized he had spoken the words when he heard them with his own ears. His frozen cheeks tingled with adrenaline, as he realized he had come suddenly to a place from which there would likely be no return. Heinig's resolve strengthened with the rush of the moment, as he realized too, that he no longer cared whether the words he had just spoken would cost him his life. In a miraculous burst of rejuvenation, he felt the defiance roil and charge inside him, filling his heart and mind with a sense of purpose long left dormant by the suppressed rage of imposed silence. There was no need to be silent now.

"Yes, I'm talking to you, you pathetic excuse of a man," Heinig said, directing his words and his eyes to the pudgy commandant, who seemed frozen with disbelief at the boldness of the younger man.

"Stop yelling at her and give her a moment to pull herself together, you slobbering goon." The German had stopped his maniacal rant against the girl, who still whimpered and shivered at his feet like a newborn lamb. Heinig wasn't finished.

"What fate do you believe awaits you when this mortal life is finished, you impossible fool?" Though he was fluent in the language of the Reich, Heinig spoke the words in his native Polish, knowing full well that most of the German officers given assignment for the occupation of his country either knew the language, or had learned enough to converse effectively. The look on the commandant's face left no illusions of a language barrier. Suddenly, one of the squadron soldiers sprang to action, moving toward Heinig with rifle butt raised, delivering a crunching blow to the side of Heinig's skull. A lightning bolt of pain sent Heinig crumpling to the pavement, a trickle of blood beginning above his left eye.

"Leave him alone!" The commandant screamed the order just as the soldier had raised his weapon for a second blow.

"Don't touch him again, you, sluggard," the commandant continued.

"Leave him alone and leave him to me!" The rotund, toddling man gathered himself as best he could, pulling his attention entirely from the young girl at his feet who had finally ceased her crying. She was now staring squarely at Heinig with a look of gratitude and admiration in her clear blue eyes that he knew would be an angelic memory for the rest of his life, however long or short it might be. Heinig had the full attention of the commandant, too, who now approached the young Pol with a mixture of shock and fury on his ruddy face, smoothing his officer's cape that had become a disheveled mess in his whirling display against the crying girl. It was a rumpling attempt at dignified elegance that fell pitifully short, and inspired Heinig's final, decisive act of richly calculated defiance.

"It will take more than a smart crease in your disgusting uniform to make you again into a man, you bowl of snot," Heinig said, relishing this long draught on the fine wine of brave expression.

"Besides, I don't believe there's dress inspection in hell, you soulless Nazi creature from Sheol!"

Heinig never heard the first shot. A tendril of curling smoke from the protruding barrel of the commandant's Walther pistol and a burning slash through his chest were the only evidence of what had happened. The shots that followed turned the narrow street into a roaring cacophony of rifle flashes, German curses and thick clouds of stinking sulfur.

At the end of it all, Heinig lay shattered and bleeding in cooling repose on the gritty cobbled street. The urge and ability for movement and breath were entirely gone. In his last dimming flicker of earthly thought, Heinig's eyes captured a vision that filled him with peaceful warmth and carried him far beyond the pain of his dying body and frozen fingers. It was a picture of a soot-stained, tear-streaked girl, now standing, strong and resolute, in a column of ragged men and women, ready again to march for home.

"FREE TO WORSHIP"

FREEDOM OF RELIGION:
"THE FREEDOM UPON WHICH ALL OTHERS
DEPEND."
BOHEMIA, 1422 A.D.

In frantic steaming gasps, the young boy's breath tore from his lungs with pelting fury as he ran, his feet pounding a staccato rhythm on the hardscrabble path through a dense thicket of gnarled branches and twisted trunks. Behind him, the band of pursuing soldiers jostled and trundled in their holy armor, their torches casting a broad and undulating dance of firelight and shadow on the canopy of trees ahead. Their angry shouts and the strain of the chase echoed in the boy's head, forcing him onward with a pace that threatened to burst his heart in his chest. Dressed in tattered leggings and tunic and draped with

264

his father's horseman's cape, the boy knifed through the stinging chill of the night air with an urgency befitting a cargo of gold coin, or rare treasure, for indeed, it was treasure he was carrying, wrapped tightly in muslin cloth and bound with cord, tucked beneath his right arm as he ran: a prize worth more than all the glittered, gilded finery of a king's ransom; a prize that would mean a heretic's death if he were captured.

As he ducked and dodged through the patchwork maze of grasping, scratching snarl, his mind flooded with the horrible images of moments before. The ambush quickness of the soldiers' arrival at his home. His mother's shriek of terror and surprise. His father's hurried instructions and desperate scramble to find the copied sheaf of scriptures, bound in calfskin and wrapped in a skein of muslin that his mother had cut and stitched with great care just for the purpose.

"Run far and fast, my son," his father had said, handing over the family treasure with glistening eyes, knowing fully the fate of the blade that awaited him after the soldiers' search. The ache in Nicolas's lungs now doubled and tripled as he imagined his strong and handsome father struggling against the band of helmeted soldiers. His father was a rough man, hardened and tightened by the labors of a plowman in fields that were not his own, but Nicolas knew that his odds against the cruel steel carried by the bitter messengers of God's wrath would require either mercy, or miracle to survive, and he expected neither. Owning a Bible, or any portion of the Lord's book was a sin more grave than consorting with familiar spirits, or outright witchcraft, and carried punishment to match. Death by scalding. It was a method chosen specifically to intone the eternal torment that the King's churchmen said would certainly be visited on anyone guilty of such loathsome conduct. Who could possibly consider themselves worthy to hold the words of the Savior in soiled, lowly, common hands, much less to claim ownership over them in written form? It was heresy indeed.

"There he is!" a soldier shouted, waving torchlight in Nicolas's direction as the pursuers corrected course and began again to narrow the gap. "Upon him, and with all haste!" The sound of the rumbling, clanking band of men filled Nicolas's head with the din of angry mutters and indignant rage. Such mercenaries were paid handsomely to enforce the edicts of the church—far more than the pittance of a normal henchman's humble pay. Even in the gauzy haze of his oxygen starved mind, Nicolas had no doubt that these men would take great pleasure in killing him, whether paid or not for their trouble. It was not a supposition he hoped to answer. *Faster! I must run faster!* Nicolas urged himself on, remembering the gravity of his father's charge and the man he would likely never meet again in this earthly life. *Protect the book, son. We must protect the book!* In what sort of monstrous world should a man be faced with likely, or certain death, simply for hoping to commune more closely and sweetly with his Heavenly Father? Could there ever be a place where people rich and poor, commoners and royalty alike, might be allowed to openly believe, worship and profess their deepest stirrings of faith without fear of retribution or punishment? Nicolas and his family had often talked of such a dream, no matter how fanciful or far away it might have seemed.

"Someday, my son, perhaps good men will realize the cruelty that exists in the power they wield over the soul of another," Nicolas's father had said. "What sweet music that will bring, should we ever be truly free to sing and praise our Lord apart from the watchful eyes and sharpened lances of the King's church." In what sort of monstrous world should a man be faced with likely, or certain death, simply for hoping to commune more closely and sweetly with his Heavenly Father? Could there ever be a place where people rich and poor, commoners and royalty alike, might be allowed to openly believe, worship and profess their deepest stirrings of faith without fear of retribution or punishment? Nicolas and his family had often talked of such a dream, no matter how fanciful or far away it might have seemed.

"Someday, my son, perhaps good men will realize the cruelty that exists in the power they wield over the soul of another," Nicolas's father had said. "What sweet music that will bring, should we ever be truly free to sing and praise our Lord apart from the watchful eyes and sharpened lances of the King's church."

THE UNICORN AND
THE BOY

(With help from my lovely daughters, Ashleigh and Alexia)

I n a green and flowered mountain, there lived a purple, polka-dotted unicorn. His nighttime shelter was a cave that was very dark and cold. On sunny days, he would rise early and leave the dank confines of the cave for the gentle meadow, where he would stretch and frolic in the morning air. With his tummy rumbling for a mountain breakfast, the unicorn would feast on the mountain grasses and tender blossoms of the meadow, and wash it down with the crisp and bubbly water from the gurgling stream, nearby.

After a juicy repast and a morning tussle with a pack of bearded goats, the unicorn would sometimes run and hide, fearing the hunters who came to search for him, high above their valley town. And they had reason to hunt, for it was believed that the glittering single horn upon the unicorn's head held a magic so deep and true that a single touch could turn pebbles into diamonds and stones into gold. Hungering for the horn's power that could make any man the richest on earth, the men would search and search as dawn turned to midday and midday turned to dusk, leaving them tired, hungry and empty handed for their journey home. So long had they hunted that their discouragement had turned to anger, bitterness and jealousy, as the quest for the magic horn consumed their every thought. Men turned against one another, believing that each in their own devious way was plotting a new advantage to find the horned beast that had so long eluded them. But none so far had caught more than a glimpse of the lithesome creature that they all craved to catch. Little did they know that the unicorn had a quest of his own. The unicorn wanted a friend. After winters and summers high on his mountain, the unicorn was tired of being alone. He played with the goats, but could not speak to them, because he could not understand their constant baaaaa-ing and blea-ea-ea-ting. And the goats could not understand him, either. They just stared at him, chewing large clumps of juicy grass as the mountain wind played in their bushy beards.

Then one day after a long time of hoping and waiting, the unicorn saw something he had never seen before. he smelled it before he saw it, as he often did whenever hunters came trimp-tramping up the rocky path to his home. But this was no hunter. He carried no knife, and no spear. No bow and arrow. He carried no torch to burn the grass to mark his path. Around his neck he wore a weathered satchel containing a small lunch of sausage and cheese. He was a man-child from the village, but very different from the men who seemed forever intent on finding the unicorn and depriving him of his magic horn. Even from across the meadow, the unicorn could tell there was no greed in this man-child. He seemed content to tumble and dance in the tall flowers and whirl in the playful fragrant breezes of the mountainside.

"He is a kind and gentle boy," the unicorn said to himself as he watched. "Perhaps he will be my friend."

Carefully and quietly, the monster slowly emerged from his hiding spot in the trees and walked toward the gentle man-child. He took small steps at first and then larger and larger, until the unicorn was galloping across the meadow in long and happy strides. The boy had stopped his playing, now and was standing very still, watching the unicorn walk toward him. Closer and closer and closer the beast came, until they were standing just a few feet apart. For a long time, the man-child and the unicorn stood as they were, staring and blinking at each other in the warm summer sunshine. Neither dared to breathe. With a closer view, the unicorn saw that he had been right. the man-child's face was a good and kind face. His eyes were peaceful and pure, with no hint of anger or fear, and not even a glimmer of the greed and lust for riches that he had seen so often before in the hunters who had made their chase. This was a boy of compassion and loyalty. The unicorn knew it to be true. Then, after a long while of standing and staring and wondering, the man-child opened his mouth and spoke.

270

"You're......you're real?"

The boy struggled with the words, never daring to take his eyes from the magnificent creature before him for fear it might evaporate like a vision in a dream. The unicorn laughed a rich and sonorous laugh that filled the meadow and seemed to make the colors deepen and change.

"Yes," the animal replied.

"I'm as real as you are. As real as the rocks and trees and flowers and the birds that sing songs in this very meadow every sunrise."

"I've heard many stories about you," the man-child said, still staring with eyes wide.

"The men in the village talk endlessly about you, and the magic they say you possess. The magic to turn pebbles into diamonds and....."

"......And stones into gold." The unicorn interrupted, finishing the boy's thought with what he knew to be the very real and very troublesome legend of his powers. After the words, the unicorn hung his head sadly. Was he wrong about this boy? Perhaps the man-child had come searching like all the others to steal the horn for himself and with it, the power to command all the riches of the ages. Just then, it was the boy's turn to laugh.

"Hahahahahahahah—hahahaha!" He chortled.

"Such silly stories men will tell.," the boy giggled.

"As if the horn from an animal's brow could contain magic. Silly, indeed."

Slowly, the unicorn lifted his head. He couldn't believe his ears. The boy didn't want his horn, after all. What's more, he didn't seem to believe in the tales told by the men in the village who brought their greedy roving bands seeking the magic horn.

"I mean, it is a bunch of nonsense, isn't it?" the boy asked.

"All that blather about gold and diamonds with a touch of your horn?"

The unicorn and the boy looked deeply into each other's eyes. It was the kind of look meant to separate honesty from falsehood. Finally the unicorn answered.

"It is as you believe it to be," he said.

"I knew it all along," the boy proclaimed. "I knew it."

The boy exhaled deeply as if relieved to be free of some piece of ignorance and burden handed to him by the elders of his village.

"Jonas the blacksmith used to spread tall tales about how any man who could capture and tame you would be the richest man in all the earth."

The boy's gaze was faraway now, dancing with memories from long ago. His voice dropped to a whisper.

"He used to say that anything that touched a unicorn's horn would turn to gold and diamonds and that the power would go on and on and never be used up."

As the boy recounted the memory, the unicorn nibbled at the tender patch of grass between them and lashed at flies with his glorious flowing tail. He listened on and on to the boy's words, understanding more deeply with each moment why the hunters had been so bothersome and persistent.

"....but I always knew it wasn't true," the boy finished, finally resting his tongue and his thoughts long enough for the unicorn to speak.

"And that my dear young lad, besides making you a very special child of man, makes you my first and only human friend."

The unicorn went on to tell the boy about the endless hunts and about days and nights spent running far ahead of the charging men whose torches blackened the grass and made it not at all fit for a unicorn to eat. And how lonely he had been for so very long, perched high in his mountain meadow, far above the valley. He left nothing out and when he had finished speaking, the two friends stood silent again, staring at one another and wondering what to do or say next.

In later days, they would both remember that it was at that precise moment that same simultaneous lightning bolt in time that the unicorn and the boy had the same irrepressible thought.

"I wonder, my young friend," the unicorn began, his eyes twinkling as brightly as his beautiful glittering horn.

"I wonder if you'd do a kindness for me." The boy's eyes were dancing too, as if he knew exactly what the unicorn wanted to say—and indeed a moment later, he realized he had.

"Consider it done," the boy said.

⊂═⋅⋅═⊃

The boy was running now, panting hard along the rocky path, down the mountainside toward his home in the town below. His pumping arms carried him forward and his fists, tightly closed with the strain of speed, carried something else altogether. In one hand, he held a simply stone.

In the other, seven strands of what looked like horsehair, plucked from the bow of a violin. But it was of no color ever seen on any horse, either before or since. A deep majestic purple with silver polka dots, exactly the color of the unicorn's flowing tail.

When he reached the town, the boy flew through the streets crying out at the top of his voice. He called people from windows and doorways, from the open market and the corner pub. he ran on and on, through streets and alleys, calling children with gilded hair and old men with sloping backs. From one end of the town to the other, his young and strong legs carried him, his pleading voice echoing over and over. "To the public square! To the public square!," he shouted.

"I bring you fantastic happenings from Magic Mountain."

The boy's cries turned heads and stilled kitchen brooms. No matter who they were or what they were doing, the people of the valley village quieted their work to listen to the shouting boy with dancing eyes. Then he said the one thing that no one in the village could possibly have dreamed.

"I have touched the unicorn! I have touched the unicorn! I have touched the unicorn!"

Within a handful of minutes, every able-bodied man, woman and child in Valley Village was standing in the central square to hear the news.

The men in the crowd were pained by the revelation deepest of all. In the few moments it had taken the boy to recount his day's adventure, those who had devoted their lives and livelihoods to searching for the forbidden treasure began to cry and wail. They boy before them had seen the unicorn, alright. They all agreed, there was no doubt of that. The long strands of hair from the unicorn tail were proof beyond any argument or reason. But it was what he held in his other hand that brought the most tears on the day. He had seen it with his own eyes, the boy said. He had placed the rock in his hand and at the unicorn's instruction, stood tall and straight and true as the animal lowered his silver horn and touched the stone with graceful flourish.

"And I watched as any of you," the boy said, holding his closed fist high to the crowd, "with quivering limbs and nervous eyes I watched and waited to see if all the splendor of the legend would come to pass." At this, every person, young and old pressed in ever closer to the boy and waited for the words he was about to speak.

"And....and......"

The boy was taking obvious relish in the moment now, the only time his voice had ever mattered to more than his handful of his friends, much less the entire village. And just when he knew he had them in the palm of his hand, he spoke the fateful words that would shatter a myth older than anyone could remember.

"He touched the stone......and........and......nothing happened."

A shocked gasp rose from the crowd like smoke from a waning fire. They began to mill and murmur and then to sob and shout as the boy unfolded his fingers to reveal a slightly oblong, slightly speckled and completely ordinary rock from his sweaty fist. The vision doubled and then tripled the outcry of the onlookers as they struggled to relinquish beliefs and dreams intertwined with the pulse of an ancient magic they had been so certain could change their fate.

"Impossible!" one shouted.

"He's a liar," said another.

"He wants to keep all the gold for himself," said yet another, as it seemed for a moment that the mobbing throng would tear the boy limb from limb. And they might have done just that if Jonas the Blacksmith hadn't set his broad shoulders in an arcing course that brought a massive wooden mallet into violent collision with the brass gong at the center of the square. The reverberating tension grabbed and held the air and shook it like a sapling clasped by a giant fist. When the sound died away, Jonas addressed the crowd of ringing ears.

"You are all forgetting yourselves," the giant of a man said. "Have we ever known this boy to lie, or bear false witness of any kind to any of us?"

Jonas swept his arm in an accusing fashion, motioning his disgust at the most pitiful of the mourners, still dabbing streaks and tears from their frowning faces.

"He is an honest boy who speaks the truth," he continued.

"And his humble face is testimony enough that he has spoken the truth, this very moment. Now let him alone and get on with your business."

One by one, people in the crowd took their leave and began the sullen trudge toward home or work, or wherever they had been when the wailing boy with the unicorn's tail had summoned them with his terrible, powerful news.

Finally, only Jonas and the boy remained. The big man reached out and ruffled the boy's golden hair with a coarsened hand and smiled his widest smile.

"They don't know it yet, my lad," Jonas said.

"But you've given them back, er....I mean you've given us back the light in our eyes and added new purpose to our years." The blacksmith shifted his weight, as if to shrug off the lifted burden of the wasted time and tears. "None of us will ever hunt the unicorn again. I'll see to that."

And with that, he turned and left his young friend standing all alone in the dusky village square, thinking of all that had just happened. The boy remembered, as he tucked the ordinary rock into his ordinary pocket and set off for home, that it hadn't been the townsfolk he had most wanted to set free.

❦

The next morning, the boy could barely breathe. Leaving his cottage without even a breakfast or a goodbye, he was running again, this time up the rocky steep path that led to the peaceful meadow with its velvet grass and knee-high flowers. He was going to see his friend. Over toppled boulders and gravely stonefalls, the boy scrambled and skittered. He hopped rotten logs and rivulets of snowmelt from high on the peak above. His lungs burned in his chest and his legs ached, but the boy didn't dare stop. He had good news to bring the unicorn and his heart would not allow even a second's delay to catch his breath. *How happy he will be. How happy to know that this mountain, his mountain, is his and his alone, with no hunters to try and steal his horn.*

The thought added strength to the boy's stride and speed to his steps. Moments later, he rounded the final bend before reaching the meadow where he had first met the beast with the silver horn that had taught him all about the secret beauty of his mountain home.

And then he saw him. Standing regally on a jutting outcropping of chiseled stone, the unicorn's mane and tail tasseled and tossed in the morning breeze. The boy's crunching steps had already alerted the unicorn to the man-child's approach, but still he stood his ground and waited for the boy to climb up to him. And he wouldn't have long to wait he noticed. The boy was running with astonishing speed, somehow stronger and older and more grown up just in the overnight since they'd first met. A moment later, they stood side by side as the boy pelted out his first words between gasping, gulping breaths.

"It—was—all—very—simple—really," the boy said, recounting his wondrous triumph in the village square and the power of that single stone.

"I told them everything that I'd seen and all about the things you'd told me and showed me and even about the test you asked me to perform that proved there's no magic that can turn a stone to gold."

The boy's cheeks were flushed now with the excitement of the retelling and he showed no signs of slowing down.

"I told them that all their stories were rubbish because I'd seen it with my own eyes and then I pulled the stone out of my pocket like this and I......."

The boy's voice caught in his throat. He stood as if caught like a bug in a bucket of honey, his eyes fixed on the stone held high in his right hand. A stone that now reflected a blinding shaft of the morning sun in the dancing flashes of yellow fire. The stone had turned to gold.

"What say you now, you son of man?" the unicorn intoned, laughing deeply as he stepped closer to the awestruck boy.

"Do you still doubt the power of the magic in my silver horn?"

"But it was j-j-j-just a stone," the boy stammered.

"It was just a stone and you touched it and yesterday it remained unchanged. I showed the villagers. It was just a stone. I told them your magic wasn't real." "You told them what you knew to be true," the unicorn said. "And you told me that it was as I believed," the boy shot back, still unsure what had happened and why.

"That's what you said."

"And it was true, my young friend," the unicorn gently explained.

"After a touch of my horn, the magic is only made real with the rising of the sun on the second day. I would say the transformation was made complete somewhere along your racing steps to the meadow this morning and not a minute before."

The unicorn sidled up next to the boy, letting him feel the safety of his strength. "You must have felt it suddenly grow heavier in your pocket." The boy smiled at this, but did not speak, still lost in the wonder and mystery of a power too beautiful to be understood. He could feel the unicorn's warm breath on his skin as the majestic creature spoke again. "What you hold in your pocket is yours to keep," the unicorn said.

"And for your trouble in restoring the peace of my mountain home, all the stones that your eye can see will be yours as diamonds and gold."

The boy's eyes were brimming over now. He imagined himself made rich by a single act of kindness that he had dared to extend to this long suffering and magical beast. The boy thought to himself: *Imagine the villagers when they find out that I'm the master of the unicorn's wealth. Imagine how jealous they will feel when they discover I've mastered the magic they've longed to attain for so long. Imagine.....*

The boy stopped. In his mind's eye, images of his endless fortune were eclipsed by those of endless streams of hunters and treasure seekers, once again and ever after, flooding the meadow with their smoking torches and sharpened steel, seeking with renewed vigor to conquer the source of his wealth. It was all he needed to see. With that, the boy leaned back and then forward and whipping his arm in a blur of motion, sent the golden stone flying far and high and far again. It disappeared over a rise in the meadow and made an echoing crack against the distant tree at the forest's edge, safely hidden from anyone who might come searching for a magic unicorn with the power to make all the riches of the world.

With a gentle sweep of his foreleg, the unicorn lifted the boy onto the smooth purple ocean of his strong back and started for the meadow below. As they began a laughing game of hide and seek high above the world, the boy and the unicorn once again shared the same thought at precisely the same moment, a thought that bathed them both in the warmth of the morning sun: The knowledge that the kindness of a true friend is a far greater treasure than all the gold in a unicorn's magic horn.

ABOUT THE AUTHOR

Shad Olson is an Emmy-winning television journalist, author, political satirist and radio host living in Rapid City, South Dakota. He began writing as a boy on the Nebraska plains, where the beauty of rural life left plenty of open spaces to be filled by an adventurous mind. Reruns of old radio shows instilled a lifelong love for the artistry of storytelling and the power of vivid wordplay to create richly painted scenes in minds of readers and listeners.

His journalistic work has won countless awards in both radio and television, including Emmy Awards, Edward R. Murrow Awards and numerous acknowledgments from the Associated Press for news excellence. His fiction, non-fiction and poetry have appeared in newspapers and magazines across the nation. This is his first collected work of short fiction.